THE BODY IN THE CHAMBER

Shadow Cutpurses Thrillers
Book Three

Adele Jordan

SAPERE
BOOKS

THE BODY IN
THE CHAMBER

Published by Sapere Books.

24 Trafalgar Road, Ilkley, LS29 8HH

saperebooks.com

ISBN: 978-0-85495-613-5

ACKNOWLEDGEMENTS

I wish to thank the whole team at Sapere Books for publishing this book, including Amy, Caoimhe, Natalie and Matilda. If it had not been for their diligent work and their devotion to the written word, I would not have had the opportunity to finally write some stories in my own name.

I'd also like to thank the Sapere team of other writers, including C. V. Chauhan, Michael Fowler and Ros Rendle. Together, the team often share ideas and once a year we have a writing retreat together. These fellow writers in particular have helped to inspire this story, and I am grateful for the kind feedback they offer.

CHAPTER 1

"Have you not heard? The news has shaken everyone. The palace is in uproar."

Gwynnie Wightham ignored the two whispering clerks. Pulling the coif tighter about her ears to cover her light brown hair, she lifted a tray of freshly baked manchet bread and walked confidently down the corridor as if she belonged there.

She wore a pale blue woollen gown, a little finer than the old and faded dresses she used to wear before she had come to Greenwich Palace. Though still made of cheap material, it was warming to have a gown that wasn't patchworked. The white apron around her short frame ensured that if anyone glanced her way, all they would see was a maid delivering bread to the lawyers' rooms. Shifting the tray to one shoulder, she reached for the handle of Elric Tombstone's door. It would not budge.

Cursing inwardly, Gwynnie glanced around. The two clerks were now at the end of the corridor, but she caught a scrap of what they said.

"It was murder."

"And he escaped?"

They were so absorbed in their conversation that they hadn't spared her a second glance.

Gwynnie waited until they had disappeared from sight before turning back to face Tombstone's door. Elric was her employer now. He paid her well enough, and besides, they had an understanding. She would be his shadow in the palace — using her skills of thievery and ability to disappear into the shadows to unearth information for his benefit — and in return he would not go hunting for her mother, Emlyn.

Together, she and Emlyn had been known as the Shadow Cutpurses, the infamous jewellery thieves that the ballad sheets liked to talk so much about. Her mother, however, had another accusation levelled at her — that of murder. With Tombstone's employer, Master Neville Pascal, Magistrate for the City of London, vowing to see Emlyn hang for her crime, Gwynnie had made a deal. She would work as an informant for Elric, and he would keep their secret.

Turning her attention back to the door, she tried the handle again. It still would not move.

Gwynnie hurried to place her tray down on a stone windowsill. It was late afternoon and darkness fell swiftly at this time of year, making the shadows from the torches on the stone walls dance. Glancing over her shoulder to ensure no one was around, she reached into the sleeve of her gown and lifted out a thin metal rod that was kept in place with two threaded hooks inside her sleeve.

She had used this implement many times in the past to open doors and windows that were locked tight. It had been some time since she had needed it, but today she was quite determined to access the room of her employer. She pressed the short rod into the lock of the door and turned it sharply. Nothing happened. Gritting her teeth, Gwynnie twisted the rod back and forth, but the lock refused to yield.

Suddenly, she heard voices approaching. Gwynnie twisted the rod a little more frantically.

"In the name of the God above," she muttered in frustration as the voices grew nearer.

Retrieving the rod from the lock, Gwynnie pushed it into the gap between the door and its frame. It only took a little wiggling this time and the lock popped back into place.

"I am telling you we'll have to shut down the palace. Close every gate. Put every guard on alert." The voice was loud and commanding. Gwynnie looked up as she slipped the rod back into her sleeve. She knew that voice. She had heard it countless times since arriving at Greenwich Palace. It was Thomas Cromwell, Lord Privy Seal to King Henry, and where Cromwell went, so too did Pascal and Tombstone.

Gwynnie pushed against the door and slipped inside, hastening to close it behind her so that it was nearly shut. Pressing her face close to the gap, she listened intently as Cromwell and his men passed.

"Sir," one man said querulously, "you must understand that we cannot shut down the palace now, when so many are on their way. People are arriving for the Yuletide celebrations —"

"And do you wish them to become victims of murder? I said, shut it down. Close the gates. Give the order." Cromwell marched on, his short yet rather rotund form filling the passage.

Gwynnie's eyes flicked from one man to the next. There was no sign of Tombstone or Pascal. It meant she had a few more minutes alone in this room at least. It could be just enough time to discover the secrets she knew Tombstone kept about her and her mother.

Closing the door with a soft click, she turned to face the room.

The moon afforded a soft silverish light through the solitary window, though in the darkness Gwynnie could barely make out the desk, let alone the scrolls and leather-bound books that she knew would be stacked neatly on the surface.

Moving gingerly forward, Gwynnie reached for a tinder box and struck a taper. In the soft orange glow of the flame, she set to work, searching through the loose leaves on the desk. Finding nothing relating to the Shadow Cutpurses, she moved on, looking through the scrolls instead. Whenever she heard footsteps passing the door, she halted, listening, waiting to see if she would be disturbed. Fortunately, no one came.

Gwynnie knew that Tombstone had collected an entire dossier about the Shadow Cutpurses. A few months ago, he had shown her a ballad sheet entitled *The Shadow Cutpurses at large in London's streets*. Yet the sheet had been dated 1516. Gwynnie had been just seven years old at the time, long before she would make her first steal and she and her mother would earn that same title.

Tombstone had suggested that two others must have adopted the name before Gwynnie and her mother did, but if that was the case, why did Emlyn never tell Gwynnie?

"Who are they? Who were the first Shadow Cutpurses?" Gwynnie whispered aloud as she turned her back on the desk and faced the shelves behind. She spied the shelf where she had seen the papers relating to her mother. It was far above her head height, and Gwynnie was forced to climb. She grabbed the kirtle of her gown and tucked it into a belt around her waist, freeing up her boots. Careful to scrape any dirt off on Tombstone's rug first, she stepped up onto the lower shelf and reached with her hands to climb higher.

Outside the window, Gwynnie could hear a flurry of activity. Alarmed voices yelled at guards, demanding that every window be shut, as well as the gates. The church bell was rung, its melodic chimes sounding eerie in the darkness.

Gwynnie didn't have time to wonder what had caused so much panic. This was the first opportunity she'd had in months to search Tombstone's chamber, and she was not going to squander it. If she could just spy what was inside the dossier, then maybe she would know something of the secrets her mother had been keeping.

As she reached the top shelf, she stretched out a hand, only to find it empty.

"He's emptied the shelf," she murmured aloud.

Footsteps sounded in the corridor.

Gwynnie retracted her hand fast, wincing as she caught a splinter from the wood, and jumped down off the shelving. There was no time to leave the chamber, for the footsteps were now outside the door.

The door handle turned, and Gwynnie stepped away from the shelves, dropping down into the Savonarola chair as if she had been there for a while.

"Gwynnie?" Tombstone appeared in the doorway, his copper eyebrows shooting up.

"Good afternoon," Gwynnie said pleasantly, as she rested the heels of her boots on his desk.

"How wonderful. You have taken to breaking into my office again."

"I only did it a few times before."

"A few times?" he spluttered, stepping forward. When he saw her boots on the desk, he pushed them off then rearranged some of the papers, so that they were perfectly neat again. His grey eyes narrowed. "You have been looking through my things?"

Gwynnie affected a yawn. "I might have moved some of your papers when I sat down. I put them back." She smiled innocently, though it was a ploy that rarely worked with Tombstone. He pointed at her, prompting that confidence to slip.

"You are as innocent as an adder," he grunted, though there was a small smile on his lips.

When they had first met, nearly a year ago now, Tombstone had rarely smiled or laughed in her company. These days, he allowed himself to smile a little more. It might have had something to do with the fact that in the spring, Gwynnie had pulled him out of the Thames when he had been badly injured.

"What harm could innocent little me do?"

Her sarcasm wasn't lost on Tombstone. "Tell that to Daundelyon," he replied, then waved for her to get out of his chair.

Gwynnie huffed and stood up. She did not want to be reminded of Captain Piers Daundelyon. She had fought the privateer and Spanish spy in the spring, drawing blood in an effort to prevent him from fleeing justice. She had discovered just what she was capable of and that perhaps she was more like her mother than she had thought. Maybe bloodshed came easier than she liked to think.

"And Fitzroy," Tombstone added.

Gwynnie stiffened. When the news had reached the palace in the summer of Henry Fitzroy's death, Gwynnie hadn't known what to believe. King Henry had spread the rumour that his son was sick, though both she and Tombstone knew that the real reason Henry had sent his illegitimate son to his country house was to cover up the fact that he was a murderer. Was Fitzroy truly dead? Or was it another lie?

"I didn't hurt Fitzroy," Gwynnie murmured. "If he is dead, then it was by nature's hand."

When Queen Anne had been executed at the Tower in May that year, Gwynnie had seen Fitzroy with her own eyes. He had crept back to London to witness Anne's death, and he had not looked ill to Gwynnie that day. She brushed aside all thoughts of Fitzroy.

"Aren't you going to sit?" she asked Tombstone, pointing at the seat she had vacated.

He shook his head. "No. I just didn't want you sitting there."

"God forbid a maid should rest her feet for a minute. You know I've been working in the laundry all night and all day? My feet are killing me."

"We both know you're not just a maid, Gwynnie." Tombstone threw off his outer robes and delved a hand into his doublet, pulling out some papers.

"What are you doing?" she asked, trying to slyly prise the splinter out of her palm.

"How did you get that?"

"The kitchens," she lied, cursing that Tombstone was always so perceptive. He broke off from looking through the papers and marched over to the buffet cabinet in the corner of the room. Opening a door, he reached for a carved wooden box in which Gwynnie knew he kept some herbal remedies.

Tombstone had revealed very little about his parentage, other than that his mother had been a healer and had passed on her knowledge of medicines and herbs to her son. Of his father Tombstone had said nothing, though Gwynnie had seen a family likeness between the lawyer and his senior, Pascal, and she suspected their relationship was something much deeper. Just a few months before, when Tombstone had been injured in a fight, Pascal had run to his side as any concerned father might have done.

"There are tweezers in there." He put the box down and turned back to the papers on his desk, moving so haphazardly that he nearly tripped on the edge of the rug, an unusual occurrence for him.

"Are you going to tell me what has you in a state? Or shall I be left to guess?" Gwynnie asked as she pulled the tweezers out of the box.

"You haven't heard?" He looked up sharply from the papers, wiping a hand across his copper beard. "The whole palace is talking of it. What have you been doing?"

"I told you. I have been in the laundry." She cast a quick look at the shelves behind him, relieved that he hadn't noticed that she had nudged some of the scrolls on the lower shelves with her boots.

"Gwynnie…" Tombstone planted his palms on the desk between them. "A murderer has escaped from the gallows at Tyburn."

"Tyburn?" She raised a hand to her own throat. There had been a time when she had feared such a place. When she had been accused of murder, she had thought Tyburn would be her fate. "Who escaped?"

"They call him Connal Devlin, or Devlin the Devil, if you believe the ballad sheets." Tombstone went back to searching the papers, making his usually neat desk a complete mess.

"That name…" Gwynnie frowned; she was certain she had heard it before.

"He was talked of for weeks," Tombstone said, shaking his head in dismay as he continued to search. "Do you not remember the story? He was a soldier, stationed here in London. A brutal man. He killed six men."

"Six?" A memory resurfaced. Brynne, a fellow maid in the palace kitchens and a good friend, Irish by birth, had been heartbroken to hear of an Irish man committing murder. "I remember now," Gwynnie whispered. "It happened in the barracks here in London, didn't it?"

14

"Ah, here it is." Tombstone brandished a ballad sheet. "Here's the full story. Take a good look at that face, Gwynnie, a really good look."

Gwynnie took the scroll and peered down at the face emblazoned in ink on the parchment.

Connal Devlin's face had been turned into that of a demon. Whoever had recreated his image in the engraving ready for the printing press, had drawn Devlin with horns to complete the illusion of a devil.

She read the words printed alongside his image:

Devlin was known to be in a dispute with his superiors about good King Henry and the monarchy. He killed six men in a fit of rage and was seen running from the building afterwards, shouting vengeance on King Henry. Rosary beads were found in his room soon after.

"Rosary? He was a Catholic?" Gwynnie said. "He killed them all because of his Catholic faith? To what end? To enact some vengeance on this world?"

"Or to enact some vengeance on the king for taking the whole country away from his Catholic God." Tombstone gestured toward the parchment in her hand. "The tale is all over London. This morning, with the noose around his throat, he was heard shouting that he'd see that vengeance delivered before he died; then he tore himself free of the rope and used it to nearly strangle the gallows man to death."

"Nearly?"

"He ran away before he could finish the deed. God's blood, how can one man escape a whole hoard of guards at Tyburn?" Tombstone cursed and turned away. He searched through the shelves until he found a knife in a tiny scabbard. He latched the scabbard onto his belt.

"Indeed," Gwynnie replied with interest. "How could a trained soldier escape men who have less than half the military training that he has?"

"Your sarcasm isn't helping right now."

"I didn't come to help," Gwynnie mumbled to herself, casting another resentful glance at the shelves.

"Focus, Gwynnie." Tombstone pointed down at Devlin's face. "Remember this man. If he intends to hold true to his promise, he could break into the palace at any time and attack someone — even the king!"

"He can attack the king for all I care," Gwynnie murmured. Tombstone waved madly for her to be quiet.

They both knew how they felt about the king. Having witnessed the beheading of his second wife, Queen Anne, in the spring, neither of them liked him.

"We have talked about this," Tombstone whispered, his face pinkening as he looked at the door. "Unless you wish to join the late queen, no one can hear us say such things. Besides, this is not about the king. If this man is a devil, who knows who he may hurt to get to the king? We must be on our guard."

As he went to find another knife, Gwynnie focused on the ballad sheet.

Connal Devlin's face looked mean and angry, with a wide-set jaw, cropped beard, and large eyes that glowered out at the onlooker. Gwynnie prayed she would never meet the man in that picture.

CHAPTER 2

"Shut the gates. I said, shut the gates!" Orders were roared around the palace. "Close Donsen Tower."

Gwynnie scurried back from the edge of the river, hurrying alongside Tombstone who had just given orders for the wherrymen to cease bringing any man, woman or child across the Thames to the palace. Rain had started to fall and with the darkness, it was making it all the more difficult to see.

"They surely can't close down the whole palace?" Gwynnie wiped the parchment and tried her best to keep it dry. Already, the ink portraying Devlin's face was beginning to blur. She folded it and tucked it into the bodice of her maid's gown.

"We have to try," Tombstone muttered. "What other choice do we have? They say Devlin ran from the gallows screaming King Henry's name. He could be on his way here now, intent on harming the king."

Gwynnie shuddered at the thought.

They dived through Donsen Tower gate before it was closed by the yeomen. One of the guards passed Tombstone a burning torch, which sputtered and struggled to stay alight in the rain.

"He would be a fool to come here," Gwynnie murmured.

"What?" Tombstone said distractedly, striding across the inner courtyard.

"A man convicted of murder vows to race to the palace and kill the king? Oh yes, let's just declare it for the whole city to hear. Because that will make reaching the king easier."

Tombstone halted so suddenly that Gwynnie nearly walked into his back.

"Go on," he urged in a low voice.

"All I'm saying is that if he truly intends to carry out the deed, why make the threat so loudly that everyone will hear him?" She shrugged. "Why put the whole city on their guard? A man intent on murder would surely keep it a secret."

"It makes the kill easier." Tombstone spoke in a surprisingly dark voice. Seeing her eyes narrow, he continued, "And don't look at me like that. We both know who is the more dangerous between the two of us, don't we?"

It had rested uneasily on her shoulders these last few months, how when it came to the crucial moment, she was prepared to draw blood to see justice done. What unnerved her even more was that she knew she would make the same decision again if it came to it.

"I am my mother's daughter, after all," Gwynnie whispered to herself.

A memory crept into her mind: last January, Emlyn had stepped aside, allowing another woman to murder the man she had believed culpable for the death of her husband. Emlyn's willingness to see death done at another's hands still made Gwynnie shudder.

Tombstone walked on through the courtyards, marching past Friars' Church where voices could be heard inside, singing hymns.

"Are the king and queen in there?" Gwynnie asked, racing to catch up with him.

Tombstone nodded. "They are." Today marked the first day of the Advent fast, and the ceremony inside the church was a traditional event. "Mark my words," Tombstone continued, "the reformers will not like the fact that another Catholic tradition has returned to the palace."

As Tombstone marched on, clearly intent on checking the other gates in the palace walls, Gwynnie hesitated by the church window. Clambering onto a low stone wall, she reached up and peered in. The interior of the church was warped by the coloured glass, which added a sheen of red and gold upon the king and queen who stood at the front of the church.

The king had grown larger in his girth, his doublet struggling to fit across his waist. Beside him, Queen Jane was petite and delicate, her blonde hair tucked beneath her gable hood. Atop that hood was the distinctive emblem of the Seymour family, a phoenix rising from a tower, surrounded by roses threaded in red silk. Gwynnie could not make out her face, but she could see her small hands and thin arms.

It had not escaped the court's notice that since the king had married Queen Jane, the court had returned to more Catholic traditions. Gwynnie had even heard the palace staff whispering about such things.

Her friend Brynne spoke with relief, for she hid the wooden cross she wore around her neck beneath her wool gown. Brynne's husband Samuel, one of the palace cooks, was more cautious. He chose not to try to predict what the king would do next.

"Gwynnie?" Tombstone called.

"Yes, coming," she called as she jumped off the wall and hurried to catch up with him.

Ahead, four guards were trying to close the heavy oak gate.

"I said, close it!" a senior yeoman bellowed at the men.

One of the younger men shot him a resentful glance, clearly thinking it would be easier if the older man joined them rather than just barking orders. Tombstone must have thought the same thing. He shed his outer robe and passed it to Gwynnie to hold, then moved toward the gate to help close it.

Shuddering in the cold, Gwynnie placed the robe around her shoulders, instantly looking like a woman of greater position than she was. When Tombstone glanced her way, he laughed and shook his head when she made a show of toying with the ermine collar.

"Open the gate!" a voice boomed from outside the gate.

"Close it," the senior yeoman insisted. "We are following orders. Not another man is to enter through these gates."

Gwynnie stepped back as the rain came down harder, the drops jumping in the puddles. The men thrust their shoulders into the gates and Tombstone reached for the bolt, ready to slide it across. Suddenly a blade was thrust through the gap between the two doors. Tombstone leaped back, narrowly avoiding being cut with the sword.

Something was barged against the other side of the gate. The wooden doors opened inward, forcing the yeomen to scramble back. Tombstone scuttled away too.

The sword was pulled back as the gates opened and a cart forced its way through the gap, accompanied by the man carrying the blade. He was so tall and finely dressed that not one yeoman dared to step in his way. The cart was followed by a carriage, one so splendid that the yeomen did nothing to intercept it. They simply stood watching, slack-jawed.

"This is an outrage!" the senior yeoman shouted. He stepped forward, thrusting his pike out in front of him as if he'd be able to fight off the cart and carriage all on his own.

"Do you want to be the one to point out to him that an escaped convict is unlikely to have such a fine carriage at his disposal, or shall I?" Gwynnie said to Tombstone, finding the situation rather amusing.

"How can you jest at a time like this? That killer Devlin could be here at any moment."

"He's not about to climb down from that carriage." Gwynnie nodded at the finery. The curtains were red embroidered silk, and the woodwork was carved with a myriad of fruit, including pomegranates.

"I said, no man can enter the palace." The senior yeoman halted in front of the carriage door.

"Am I a man now?" a deep and gravelly voice asked from within the carriage.

The door was flung open so fast by the man with the sword that the yeoman was forced to scuttle back, fumbling to keep his pike aloft.

One silken green boot emerged from the carriage, quickly followed by the voluptuous black and green skirt of a very rich and heavily embroidered dress. The woman lifted her chin, the Spanish headdress set high on her head, lined with pearls arranged in fours to look like tiny crucifixes. Her face, wan and rather heavy-cheeked, with a large flat forehead, turned to look at the senior yeoman.

"Am I to be shut out of my own father's palace, sirrah?" she barked.

"Is that...?" Gwynnie whispered to Tombstone.

"It is."

Gwynnie swallowed. She hastily took off the robe and tossed it back to Tombstone, who caught it haphazardly. The movement caught Lady Mary's attention.

Daughter to King Henry, denounced as illegitimate when he had ended his marriage to her mother, Catherine of Aragon, Lady Mary had not been seen in the palace for some time. Gwynnie had heard the staff whispering about how wrong it was for her to be ousted as a bastard child, yet Mary was no child now. She stood tall, hardly appearing the outcast with her fine clothes and elaborate carriage.

Though once she had held the title of princess formally, these days it was a sin to address her as such. She was 'Lady' Mary, on the king's orders.

Lady Mary fixed her gaze on Tombstone and Gwynnie as she flicked her fingers, a silent instruction for her staff to see to her things. The senior yeoman hastily bowed then urged the other guards to return to closing the gate once again. Mary swept past him imperiously.

Disconcerted to have a woman who should have been known as a princess staring right at her, Gwynnie dropped into a low curtsy, her head bowed. Lady Mary turned her eyes from Gwynnie to Tombstone.

"What is your name, sirrah?" Her tone was a little kindlier than it had been for the yeomen, but not by much.

"Elric Tombstone." He bowed. "Lawyer. I believe your chambers have been prepared for you, Your Grace."

Mary inclined her head a little and then strode away. Behind her, her ladies fell into step.

"Well," Tombstone sighed as they watched retreating back, "perhaps she is not so like her father. I expected her to vow to flog us for trying to prevent her entry into the palace."

"Did you not notice there was something else she did not say?" Gwynnie asked.

Tombstone frowned. "What?"

"She did not ask why we were closing the palace gates in the first place." Then, "Why have I not seen her here before?"

"You must have heard the rumours." Tombstone glanced around and whispered, "King Henry has not wanted a staunch Catholic under this roof in a long time, least of all a Catholic who is also his own daughter. The Lady Mary was as good as bullied into signing a document this year which declared her illegitimate and insisted she accepted her father as the head of the Church. Any man with a grain of sanity in his head must know that what she signs might not be what is in her heart, and yet the king has welcomed her back to the palace regardless. The tides are changing, though, aren't they?"

"Gwynnie, Gwynnie! You're needed, lass."

Gwynnie put down the tray she had been holding and rushed across the kitchen. Samuel was pounding some dough before throwing it into a bowl ready to prove. At his shoulder stood Brynne, her green eyes staring vacantly down at the dough. She held a small pewter button that she repeatedly turned over in her fingers. Gwynnie could see a shamrock emblazoned on the pewter.

"What do you need?" Gwynnie asked. At this time of year, the palace kitchens weren't as sweet-smelling nor as busy as they were at feasting time. There was plenty of bread, but nothing in the way of sweetmeats and treats. Even the amount of meat had been reduced, for the Advent fast had begun.

"Could you take that up to Queen Jane's chambers, please?" Samuel asked, pointing at a tray beside him which he had covered with a cloth. "She has asked for a light dinner in her chamber…" He trailed off, looking at his wife beside him.

Brynne gave no sign of having heard him. She turned away, staring down at one of the vast stone fireplaces. Her eyes didn't even tarry on the boys turning the great spits or the maid adding logs to the fire. She just stared blankly into the flames.

"Brynne?" Gwynnie picked up the tray. "Are you well?"

"Aye," Brynne said, though she didn't look up from the flames. "I'm perfectly well."

Gwynnie turned to Samuel. His wide face wore a heavy frown as he reached for another ball of dough and kneaded that onto the wooden block counter in front of him. Brynne had not been the same since she had been hurt in the events that had taken place in the spring. Stabbed, her injury had been a foul one; it had been days before she could rise from her bed, and weeks before the pain had stopped completely. Yet she had remained distracted. Samuel's words came back to Gwynnie: *She sees things in the darkness. She fears them… Her body is recovering, even if her mind…*

"Best take the tray to the queen now, lass." Samuel's voice broke into Gwynnie's thoughts. "She'll be done at church."

Gwynnie nodded and scurried off, carrying the tray high on her shoulder. Outside in the dark courtyards, all was quiet. The rain had sent most people back to their chambers, yet there were more yeomen guards around than usual, thanks to the threat of Connal Devlin reaching the palace. Many of them stood alone in doorways, gripping their pikes rather tightly. Others marched up and down, their gloved hands gripping the collars of their uniforms to keep the rain off the backs of their necks.

As Gwynnie reached Donsen Tower, she held up the tray. A yeoman guard at the door peered out at her from beneath his felt bonnet.

"Good evening, Ricard. How are you?" she asked.

"Cold and shivering," he grunted as he unlocked the door of Donsen Tower.

"And how are you really?" Gwynnie lowered her voice as she passed him. The night that Brynne had been injured, Ricard had been stabbed too. He had recovered well, though Gwynnie had spied him clutching his abdomen more than once. Whatever he claimed, the injury had lasted.

"I'm well enough." He smiled, though it was brief. "Hurry to your task, Gwynnie. If the rumours are to be believed, no one should be wandering about the palace alone tonight."

She nodded and walked on. Inside the palace building, light shone brightly from burning torches and heavily engraved candelabra. Gwynnie hurried up the staircase and turned to face Queen Jane's chambers. They were not the same rooms that had belonged to Queen Anne. Those chambers were in the west wing and were now locked up tight. No man was allowed inside and the falcon, Anne Boleyn's symbol which had once been carved into the door, had been chiselled out so all that remained were ugly notches in the wood.

"Ah, for the queen?" a lady-in-waiting said as she opened the door. "Excellent, she is famished. Come." It was the Countess of Rutland, Eleanor Manners. Tall with a heavy overbite, she looked down at Gwynnie with a small smile that looked more like a smirk due to the set of her jaw.

Gwynnie stepped into the outer chamber of the queen's rooms. As she placed the tray down onto the table, she felt in no hurry to leave. She slowly took the cloth off the tray, drawing out the minutes she could be here as she looked around the room.

In this outer chamber were more ladies-in-waiting. Two were laying out fresh clothes for the queen, gushing over the finery of the material. There was Elizabeth Tyrwhitt, a young lady with blue eyes and light ginger hair. Beside her was Mary Zouche, a glimmer of fair hair visible beneath her high hood. The two young ladies didn't even notice Gwynnie as they ran their hands over the silver embroidered dress before them.

Across the room were two slightly older ladies. Margery Lyster was fiddling with the queen's jewellery box, with Lady Monteagle at her side. The two ladies, though they were dressed just as finely, were a little demurer in their choice of clothing.

It struck Gwynnie that another should have been in attendance in this room. Lady Rochford, since testifying against Queen Anne and her own husband, Lord Rochford, in April, had been a nearly constant presence at court. It seemed that since she had helped King Henry be rid of his last wife, she was a trusted person in the palace. The first time Gwynnie had seen Lady Rochford in attendance on Queen Jane, she had watched with disdain, knowing that Lady Rochford had conspired to cause Queen Anne's death.

Yet Gwynnie took comfort in one thing. Very little escaped Gwynnie's notice, and just as Lady Rochford hid rosary beads in her sleeves, so too did Queen Jane. It was possible that Lady Rochford would extend a kindness to Queen Jane that she had not done with the last queen.

This Christmas, though, Lady Rochford was not at court but spending Yuletide in the country with family. Relieved not to have to look the lady in the eye, Gwynnie felt a little more at ease in Jane's chambers.

Gwynnie tarried a little, gazing surreptitiously at the jewellery box the ladies fiddled with, trying to spy what jewels they would pull out, as Lady Rutland walked toward the door leading to the queen's most private chamber. As she laid a hand on the door handle, a piercing scream erupted from within.

Gwynnie froze as the scream dissolved into panicked cries.

"Your Majesty!" Lady Rutland turned the door handle, but it would not move. The lady banged on the door as the hysterical cries continued.

"Can't you open the door?" Lady Monteagle asked, running forward.

"Of course I can't!"

Together, the two ladies pulled on the door handle, but it was no good. It wouldn't budge. The two younger ladies, Elizabeth Tyrwhitt and Mary Zouche, gripped one another in their panic.

"Go and fetch help," Margery Lyster ordered them. "Find guards to break down the door. Go — now!" The two women turned and scurried from the room.

Lady Monteagle stepped back from the door, tears in her eyes as the queen's shrieks grew worse, now so piercing they made Gwynnie's ears ring.

Without thinking, Gwynnie moved toward the door and along with Lady Rutland, tried to force it open.

Gwynnie was reminded of screams from another queen's chamber. That had been the day Queen Anne had lost the child she carried. It had also been the start of her downfall, leading to her death at the Tower of London.

"It can't happen again," Lady Rutland muttered, and she flung her shoulder against the door, but it merely rattled in its frame.

"Lady Rutland, it will do no good. Step away from the door. A yeoman will break it down," Margery Lyster ordered.

As Lady Rutland stepped away, Gwynnie saw her chance. She couldn't just stand by whilst a woman screamed on the other side of the door.

"No, no!" Queen Jane was shouting now. "It cannot be happening. It cannot be!"

"What cannot be?" Lady Monteagle called out, her voice tremulous.

Gwynnie turned her back to the other three ladies and dropped the rod from the sleeve of her gown. She thrust it into the lock. Two turns and one sharp angle to the right and the lock popped back. The sound was drowned out by Jane's cries as Gwynnie thrust the rod back up her sleeve.

"There must have been a weakness in the lock," Gwynnie called to the ladies as she pulled the door open.

As one, they darted forward into the room. Gwynnie was the first in, and came to a skidding halt.

At any other time, she might have noted the grandeur of the room, the wall hangings, the fine cloths, how every surface was bedecked with some beautiful item, but not today. As Jane screamed, cowering in a corner of the chamber, she pointed a shaking hand toward the heavy tapestry-like curtains around her bed that she must have just pushed aside.

There, lying across the bottom of the bed, was a dead man.

CHAPTER 3

"He's dead, he's dead, isn't he?" Queen Jane's screeches were much louder inside her room.

Lady Rutland, Lady Monteagle and Margery Lyster ran to Jane, grasping at her outstretched hands. Margery Lyster tried to stroke Jane's hair to pacify her, though it was like pacifying a wild wolf.

Gwynnie stumbled toward the dead man at the bottom of the bed. As she reached the body, she stretched out a hand in an attempt to feel his pulse.

"He's still warm," she muttered, her voice tiny. In a flash, she was back in Henry Fitzroy's chamber eleven months ago. That night, Fitzroy had strangled to death the man who had tried to blackmail him. Gwynnie had felt for a pulse and, just like now, there had been no fluttering beneath his skin. This man was dead.

"What has happened here?" Lady Rutland demanded. She had managed to pull Queen Jane to her feet and was steering her out of the room. Lady Monteagle followed closely behind, as Margery Lyster picked up a dropped hood and cloak which had been left in a bundle on the floor.

"I ... I pulled back the curtain and there he was," Queen Jane cried, the terror palpable in her tremulous voice and shaking hands. "He must be some thief. An intruder. I thought I saw a shadow, over there." She pointed toward a window in the chamber. "Then I thought it was my imagination. Oh, what horror is this!"

"We need to get her out of here," Margery Lyster urged, helping Lady Rutland as they practically carried Queen Jane from the room.

Gwynnie looked down at the dead man. His clothes were fine. Unlike Gwynnie, he did not wear the garb of a servant. In fact, he was dressed rather well. He did not look like a thief, but then again, Gwynnie and Emlyn had often donned different garb in order to walk into a place where they should not be.

She waited until the others were out of the room then reached for the man's hands and turned them over. They were smooth, not coarse from hard labour. On one hand he wore a ring bearing a family crest of two eagles facing one another, their beaks practically intertwined and their wings pulled in demurely.

This was no poor man but an aristocrat with important heraldry.

Gwynnie stepped forward to examine his injury. There was just one wound to his stomach, but the injury was deep — deep enough to cause death.

Gwynnie gulped and turned away, reluctant to stare anymore at all the blood across his abdomen. Moving back, she looked around the room.

"Where's the knife?" she wondered aloud. There was no blade left on the bed, nor kicked away on the floor. She bent down, peering beneath the bed, but there was no glistening knife there either. Whoever had killed this man had taken the weapon with them when they left.

Standing again, Gwynnie made her way toward the window where Jane said she thought she had seen a shadow. Gwynnie had almost pressed her fingers to the glass when she saw something shining in the candlelight. She retracted her hand fast and saw that the window was ajar, from when someone must have pushed it shut behind them. Across the frame was a smattering of blood, left there by the bloodied hand that had done the deed.

"What is all this? What has happened?" Cromwell's voice sounded behind Gwynnie. She turned and dropped a curtsy as he pelted forward, halting when he saw the body. Behind him was a young footman who crossed himself, sending up a silent Catholic prayer to heaven. He was slapped on the arm by Cromwell for daring to do such a thing. "Fetch Tombstone and Pascal here at once," he ordered the boy.

As the boy left the room, Gwynnie heard Jane's cries again, though this time they were at a distance. She must have been taken from her rooms by her ladies, though it had apparently done nothing to stop her terror.

"You!" Cromwell's deep voice made Gwynnie jump. She turned to face him. "You're like a rat, aren't you? You always seem to turn up when anything ... foul happens in the palace."

"Your man pays me to be his rat," Gwynnie muttered crossly. At a quirk of her eyebrows, Cromwell looked away. His large face turned on the man laid across the bed just as Tombstone entered the room. He ran toward the bed and felt for the man's pulse, just as Gwynnie had done.

Behind him, Pascal walked in a little more slowly, striking the ground with his cane. He halted in the doorway, dabbing a handkerchief to his balding head to mop away the sweat. "What happened?" he asked.

Cromwell said nothing but flicked his fingers at Gwynnie.

"Was that an order for me to talk?" Gwynnie folded her arms.

"Gwynnie!" Tombstone barked, clearly thinking it unwise for her to test the patience of a man like Cromwell. She sighed and stood taller, choosing to address Tombstone with her tale rather than the others.

"I was delivering a tray of food to the queen when she started to scream. The ladies tried to gain entry, but couldn't get in. As two went for help, I … opened the door." She chose her words carefully. Tombstone nodded. Clearly, he didn't care that she had opened the chamber door, though the others plainly did.

"Unthinkable," Pascal muttered. "A maid picking the lock on the queen's door."

Cromwell breathed in so deeply that his shoulders appeared to broaden twofold.

"What next?" Tombstone asked, urging her on. He was now examining the wound more closely, bending his head so near that behind him, Pascal shifted uncomfortably.

"Queen Jane was in that corner, screaming." She pointed across the room. "He was as you find him now, and then there's this." She gestured behind her at the window. "The queen said she thought she saw a shadow by this window. There's blood on the frame."

Pascal peered over her shoulder at the window. "Unthinkable for any man to climb out of such a window," he mumbled to himself.

"If a woman can do it, I suppose a man could too," said Gwynnie, subtly reminding him that she had climbed out of Fitzroy's window. "Believe me, sir, if a man was desperate, he could make such a climb." She nodded at the nearby rooftop. It was a perfect ledge for any intruder to reach for and make their escape.

"Well?" Cromwell barked. "How long has he been dead, Tombstone?"

"Not long. His skin is still warm to the touch. By my estimate, he must have been killed whilst the queen was at the fasting service." Tombstone studied the man's face. "I do not know him. Do you?"

"No." Cromwell shook his head. "Then again, so many new faces have arrived in the palace these last few days that I cannot tell one from another." He stepped away from the body, clearly disgusted by it. "We need to move him, now." He didn't wait for confirmation but swept out of the room.

The moment he was gone, Gwynnie hurried toward the bed. "Look at his hands," she whispered to Tombstone in a rush. Without hesitation, he did as she said.

"True aristocrat?" he murmured with interest, clearly noting the ring on his finger, as she had done. "Trust you to notice his jewellery."

"I was trained to notice," she reminded him in an undertone. "Look at the blood on the window too." He followed her toward the glass.

"Strange," Tombstone grunted.

"What's strange?" Gwynnie asked.

"With this kind of injury, you would expect a lot of blood. Look at the man." Tombstone gestured over his shoulder. "Yet as they climbed out of this window, the killer only managed to get it on one part of the frame."

"Perhaps they only bloodied their hands in the struggle," Gwynnie offered.

"They? Not he?" Pascal cut in. He was gripping the handle of his cane rather tightly.

"What am I thinking? You're right, Pascal." Gwynnie placed her hands on her hips. "A woman is not capable of such evil, is she?"

"This is not the time for an argument," Tombstone cut in, turning to Pascal. "I'll question the guards, see who has been in and out of this tower. With the increased guard, someone must have seen something."

Gwynnie bent over the man again. Before Cromwell could move the corpse, she wanted to remember as much as possible. Any small detail could afford a hint as to who he was.

He had a handsome face. At least, it would have been handsome had it not been contorted in pain. His black hair was a strong contrast to the pallor of his skin. His nose was rather regal, his cheekbones high, and his ruff immensely stiff, for it had been starched heavily. Gwynnie shifted her gaze to his cuffs. They were a little frayed, unlike the rest of his pristine attire. It was as if someone had scuffled with him, pulling at the cuffs of his doublet.

"Find out how he got in here," Pascal muttered to Tombstone. "I shall make enquiries regarding a missing man in the guest quarters."

"Very well." Tombstone stood straight and looked at Gwynnie. "Are you done?"

Gwynnie wrinkled her nose. There was a strange scent hanging in the air.

Above the floral posies that had been left around the room, of dried thyme, sage and daisies, another scent lingered. Gwynnie had to fight the tangy smell of blood to be able to discern the man's fragrance. He had doused himself in something excessively sweet, something remarkably like honey.

"Gwynnie? What is it?" Tombstone asked.

"I was just wondering..." She paused, stepping toward the man and pulling at his ruff. "If you were going to break into the queen's most private chamber, would you wear so much fragrance?"

The sound of hurried footsteps forced Gwynnie to step back as men entered the room at Cromwell's command. He appeared behind them, and they followed his orders swiftly. Gwynnie stepped closer to Tombstone.

"Anything else you noticed, Shadow?" Tombstone asked her quietly as the men carried the body from the room on a stretcher.

"One thing," Gwynnie whispered. She told him about the cuffs as they descended the staircase of Donsen Tower and stepped out into the inner courtyard. As Pascal and Cromwell followed, she broke off to listen to their panicked conversation.

"The king will not want to be disturbed. The Pilgrimage of Grace has him in a panic," Cromwell said in a rush. Gwynnie listened with interest.

The Pilgrimage of Grace was a phrase that had been bandied around the palace much of late. As far as Gwynnie knew, there wasn't much 'grace' about it, or indeed a pilgrimage. She had heard that a force of fighters had gathered at Pontefract Castle, threatening to march on London. Depending on which rumour she believed, they numbered anywhere between ten thousand and thirty thousand men.

"The leaders of the rebellion are due to arrive in a matter of days. The king has made it clear to me that he wants nothing to distract him from this matter," growled Cromwell.

"You wish to keep the fact that a dead man was found in his wife's chamber a secret from him?" Pascal's bushy white eyebrows shot up.

"No, of course not. We'll just tell him a dead man has been found in the palace."

"If we can persuade him that we will sort it, that it need not come to his attention, then at least his irascible temper will be calmed for now," Cromwell said quickly to Pascal, encouraging the man to walk alongside him at a difficult speed. "In the meantime, you and your man investigate what has happened here. For the queen's sake."

"Of course, my lord."

"Tombstone," Gwynnie hissed, pulling on his arm as they trailed behind the others. She released him as another scream split the air. Gwynnie froze as the men carrying the body far ahead of them nearly dropped their charge. Cromwell spun around so fast that Pascal had to leap back to avoid being hit.

"I've seen him. I've seen him!" It was Lady Rutland. She came running toward them, tears on her cheeks.

"Calm yourself, dear lady," said Pascal, stepping forward and offering his hand in a kindly way. "Come, tell me what it is you have seen."

"Oh, the devil must have done it," Lady Rutland wailed. "He must have broken into the queen's chamber and killed that poor man."

"What devil?" Tombstone asked, stiffening at Gwynnie's side.

"I've just come from settling the queen into another chamber. I was on my way to collect her things when I saw him, creeping around in the shadows. One of the palace gates must be broken, for *he* is here. You have not managed to keep him out of the palace as you promised to do. He turned and fled when he saw me, disappearing into thin air."

"Who are you talking about?" Cromwell demanded impatiently.

"Connal Devlin. I speak of the murderer who has come to the palace to kill the king."

CHAPTER 4

"This cannot be happening," Tombstone muttered as they stared at the broken gate.

"Do you want me to hit you to make sure you're not dreaming?" Gwynnie asked, leaning back against one of the trees in the orchard. The tree's boughs hung overhead, like great skeletal fingers reaching out across the cloudy sky. The only light glinting off them came from the lantern Gwynnie carried and the burning torch that Tombstone now pressed closer to the gate in the palace wall.

"No, thank you," Tombstone said without humour. "There was a guard here. I ordered two men to guard this gate myself."

"It's easy to overlook." Indeed, had Gwynnie not known this gate was here, she might have missed it herself. It blended with the walls so completely, it was almost impossible to discern in the darkness. "I wonder how he found it."

"What?" Tombstone was distracted, running a finger over the splintered wood around the lock.

"How did Devlin find this gate? Do you think he's been to the palace before?"

"I have no idea. He was a soldier, though. Perhaps he had been ordered here on one occasion." Tombstone stepped back and gestured to the broken wood. "What do you think?"

Gwynnie moved forward and raised her lantern to examine the lock. The orange light bounced off the fragments. "Messily done. He's no lock-picker, that much is certain, and then there's this…" She placed her fingers around the lock, which had nearly been torn off. It seemed the intruder had prised the heavy iron plate away from the wood. "It's more than was needed. He was clearly determined to gain access."

"Hmm." Tombstone had turned grave. "The question is, can we be certain it was Devlin the Devil?"

"I'm told demons can find small corners to hide in. Perhaps it would explain how he managed to find this entrance."

"Don't talk of superstition." Tombstone shook his head impatiently.

It was an agreement they had between them, not to discuss religion or superstition. With what a person should believe at court changing by the day, it was deemed safer not to have such discussions aloud.

"Lady Rutland was panicked," Tombstone reminded her. "She could have been mistaken in her hysterics."

"I wonder if you would say such a thing if she were a man," Gwynnie muttered with arched eyebrows.

"I only meant it is dark out tonight. Anyone could have made a mistake. And any man could have broken in through this gate. We do not know it was Connal Devlin."

Gwynnie nodded. She had to admit there was every possibility that Lady Rutland had been mistaken.

"Well, what now?" Gwynnie tried to close the gate again, but it merely sat awkwardly in the frame.

"I'll order more men to guard this gate and find out what happened to the yeomen who were supposed to be watching over it. I'll ask questions in the meantime to find out just who our dead man was." Tombstone paused. "Did you recognise the heraldry on the ring?"

"The two eagles? No." Gwynnie's lantern began to dim. She lowered it to her side, making the light so feeble that Tombstone's face was in complete darkness. "Do you want me to see if I can discover it?"

"No. I want you to find Devlin."

"Find him? I thought we just agreed that we don't even know if it was him who broke in tonight —"

"Then find out if there is someone hiding in the palace who should not be here. Search every corner and let me know when you find him."

"Oh, wonderful. Send a shadow to catch a devil. And what if he kills me too?" Gwynnie asked drily.

"I would never send you to your death, Gwynnie." Tombstone's voice had deepened. Rather startled by the declaration, Gwynnie shifted her weight between her feet.

"There was a time when you might not have minded doing so. I'm a thief, aren't I?" she reminded him. "Aren't you the dutiful lawyer who will see justice served, no matter what?"

"Don't remind me of my principles." He shifted the torch in his hand, allowing her to see just how strong his scowl had become. "I do know that you don't belong on the gallows for larceny, Gwynnie."

Gwynnie smiled. "Ah, is that a declaration that you like me after all? That this last year in your service has earned me some respect?" She couldn't resist teasing him as he turned to walk away. She hurried to catch up with him, elbowing him for good measure. "Perhaps even your friendship?"

"Perhaps." He offered the smallest of smiles. "Whatever the reason, I am not asking you to do this because I intend for you to die at a devil's hand."

They came to a stop in the open gateway leading to the tiltyard.

"I ask because you are my shadow. You can move around the palace unseen. And if anyone can track a murderer without being caught, then it's you." He gestured toward her with the torch. "Now, will you do this for me?"

"Do I have a choice?" They both knew he paid her to act on his behalf, and she stayed because it meant her mother would remain safe.

"You were tempted to leave once before," Tombstone said quietly. A yeoman guard marched past, prompting Tombstone to step closer to her and lower his voice. "Are you tempted again?"

She knew what he was referring to. Months ago, a ballad sheet had reached them about a jewellery thief in Bristol who had been hurt. Gwynnie had been certain it was her mother. She had set her mind on leaving the palace, but then something had stopped her. It was the reminder that if she went, her deal with Tombstone would be void.

No matter what small friendship there was between them, Gwynnie knew that if she left, there would be nothing keeping him from going after Emlyn.

"I'm staying," Gwynnie said firmly.

"Then we have a deal." Tombstone nodded decisively as he turned to walk across the dark tiltyard. "I'll see to my tasks, and you see to yours, Gwynnie."

When Gwynnie returned to the kitchen, Samuel passed her a cup of mead. "You look exhausted, lass," he said. "You should get some sleep."

"Thank you." Gwynnie took a sip as she stifled another yawn.

"Where did you get this mead from?" Brynne asked Gwynnie as the three of them sat around the fireplace, enjoying the honey-sweet drink. The other staff had long gone to bed. Samuel had stayed up late, claiming he was watching over the latest batch of cobs cooking in the bread oven. Brynne had come to keep him company, and Gwynnie had gone back to the kitchen after searching every inch of the tiltyard and orchard, with no result.

"I found it," Gwynnie lied. "Some guard must have left it at his post and forgotten about it." She knew it was Brynne and Samuel's favourite drink. A few days before, she had lifted it from Pascal's private stores, though he had so much, he hadn't even noticed it was missing.

"Well, thank you." Samuel passed another cup of mead into Brynne's hands. He patted her on the shoulder affectionately as she leaned into his side. "Now, are you going to tell us why you're up so late?" Samuel asked, turning his focus on Gwynnie.

"No, Pa," she teased him.

"Your pa would be mad to see you up so late. You need your rest, lass."

"Well, he's not around, so it does not matter." She hadn't told Samuel and Brynne that her father was dead, much less murdered.

"And your ma?" he asked. "When she left the palace, surely she thought you would be safe here, not working yourself to the bone doing whatever it is you do for that lawyer."

Brynne flinched, causing a little of the mead to spill over the rim of her cup. She mumbled an apology and mopped the mead from her gown.

"Brynne?" Gwynnie whispered.

"She is suspicious of that lawyer," Samuel explained when Brynne showed no sign of answering her. "We've known you long enough to see you're in his service, Gwynnie. To be honest ... I don't trust him either."

"Do *you* trust him?" Brynne's sudden words made Gwynnie jump. For the first time in days, Brynne was truly paying attention to the conversation. In fact, her focus was entirely fixed on Gwynnie as she waited for an answer.

"Yes," Gwynnie murmured. "I've seen him do things I didn't think him capable of, and he ... he saved my life."

She couldn't tell them Tombstone had saved her life as part of a deal. To do so would mean confessing that she was a jewellery thief to the two closest friends she had in the palace. She couldn't lose them. They were as good as family to her now.

"Then we shall trust him too," Samuel said as he poured himself another cup of mead.

"Shall we?" Brynne gripped her cup, her green eyes widening.

"Brynne, why do you fear him so?" Gwynnie asked.

"I distrust all lawyers. All constables. It's this mess with ... the Irish soldier." She stuttered out the words. "I still cannot believe it."

"Ah, Brynne." Samuel put down the cup and she leaned toward him, one of her hands gripping his forearm. "Just because he comes from your homeland, it does not mean he is innocent." Brynne released him at once, outrage in her face.

"I still choose not to believe it," she hissed. "For all we know, Devlin is innocent, accused of something he did not do."

"He was seen running from the barracks building where those men were murdered," Samuel reminded her. "He was the only survivor from that room; he emerged covered in blood, a bloodied weapon in his hand. They say that when he broke free, he screamed of Catholic vengeance and wanting to kill the king —" He broke off as Brynne waved her hand dismissively. She fell silent, plainly refusing to say another word.

"Gwynnie," said Samuel, turning to her, "will you at least get some rest now? You have to be up to do the laundry in just a few hours."

"I will." She downed what was left of the mead, though she had little intention of doing the laundry when she woke. She would return to her search of the palace. "Goodnight," she said to Brynne and Samuel.

"Goodnight, lass."

Brynne gave no sign of having heard her. She was staring into the crackling flames once again. As Samuel shifted his focus to his wife, Gwynnie left, hurrying through the corridors to her chamber.

When she pushed the door open, she hesitated before entering. The room, barely larger than a cupboard, was cold and uninviting. She stepped forward, eyeing the small cot bed on one side where her mother used to sleep before she had run from the palace. Gwynnie lit a candle from a tinder box and sat down on her own bed, staring at the empty straw mattress opposite her.

It was moments like this when the emptiness felt oppressive. Gwynnie was truly alone, and on some nights, it was too much to bear.

"Enough," she whispered aloud. "No good comes from dwelling." She stood and shed her coif and gown, pulling on a thick woollen chemise. As she climbed into bed, she refused to give in to self-pity.

Instead, she turned her thoughts to what she had seen in the queen's chamber that evening. She thought of the dead man on the queen's bed. She thought of the rain-blurred face of Connal Devlin on the ballad sheet, and what everyone kept saying about Devlin as he fled the gallows.

Perhaps Devlin had vowed to kill the king for forcing the country to turn its back on Catholicism, but that didn't explain why Devlin would go into the queen's chamber.

"There's more to this," Gwynnie whispered to herself as she drifted off to sleep.

CHAPTER 5

"Did you hear? The whole palace is talking of it."

"Aye, it was him. Devlin the Devil. Lady Rutland saw him with her own eyes."

"He's here?"

The whispers filled the great hall as Gwynnie walked between the long tables, carrying trays of food permitted for the fast. She placed the trays down on the tables, watching as the courtiers fell upon them like starving vultures.

"It had to be him. Too much of a coincidence, isn't it? A murderer breaks into the palace and a man ends up dead," another man said with his mouth open as he chewed a large chunk of bread. "You'd have to be a devil to kill a man in the queen's own chamber."

Gwynnie walked on. Everyone seemed to be talking of what had happened the day before, but not one person was questioning why the dead man had been in the queen's room in the first place.

Under the pretence of collecting trays, she headed towards the royal table at the top of the great hall.

King Henry was absent from his place, though this was no new thing. Since the news of the Pilgrimage of Grace, he had barely been seen sharing his meals with his court. Queen Jane sat quite alone at the top table, staring down at her plate, her face as white as snow. When Lady Rutland approached her, the queen clearly pleaded with her to leave, for she swiftly departed.

Gwynnie stepped up onto the platform, collecting empty trenchers, just as another approached the queen.

"I see you are heavily guarded now, *Mother*." The word was spoken with some bitterness.

Gwynnie peered around the edge of her pale coif to see it was Lady Mary who had spoken. Without waiting for an invitation, she sat down next to Queen Jane. She gestured with her hand to the guards standing behind them, all carrying pikes and staffs.

"What an ordeal you have been through," Mary declared, though she spoke with great forbearance. "To discover a body, and in one's own bed as well —"

"Yes, it was an ordeal. A great shock." Jane's voice trembled as she reached for the cup before her. "If you have come to offer your sympathies, I thank you, but I have no need of being reminded of yesterday."

"Sympathies? Oh, yes. Of course I offer sympathies." Mary leaned forward and patted the queen's hand, though Jane quickly moved it out of her stepdaughter's reach. "Dear *Mother*," Mary went on, stressing the word once again. "I am sorry for your ordeal."

There could be no more than eight years between the two women. Jane was undoubtedly the senior, but not by much. Mary may have just seen her twentieth summer, but she had a commanding air that made her seem much older.

"Do you know who the gentleman was?" Mary asked, leaning forward.

"No. I had not seen him before," Jane answered calmly.

"Never? Wasn't there anything identifiable on his person?"

"He looked like an aristocrat, but I did not know his face." Jane took another sip from her cup. "If you have come for gossip, Mary, find another to discover it from." With a sudden regalness in her countenance, Jane lifted her chin. "I will speak of this no more."

Mary gave the smallest of smiles. For a moment, Gwynnie presumed she had been impressed by the queen's fortitude. The lady's eyes then slid away and landed on Gwynnie.

"Are you listening in on the queen's conversation?" Mary's voice was sharp.

Gwynnie bowed her head and curtsied. For a change, she thought it best not to say anything at all. She turned to walk away, but not before another scrap of their conversation reached her ears.

"Don't hold onto those here," Mary urged.

"How can I not?"

Gwynnie glanced back, seeing that Jane was gripping her rosary beads.

"Things are changing, but they are not yet altered altogether." Mary gave a small shake of her head. "I keep mine hidden." She waved her sleeve a little. "You would be wise to do the same."

Jane stuffed the beads up her sleeve. The action was performed so quickly that Gwynnie only glimpsed the amber cross before it was hidden.

She hurried out of the great hall as quickly as she could. As she stepped out into the middle courtyard, she pressed herself against the wall and took a deep breath.

The courtiers passed by, not noticing her presence at all. This was the usual way. Three men walked past her, all wearing heavy, fur-lined cloaks to ward off the cold.

"You still haven't seen him?" one asked another in a northern accent.

"No. He must have been to town. He visits the brothels —"

"Don't say that here, you fool." The eldest rubbed his brow in frustration. From the similarities in their faces, all heavy-jawed and long-nosed, Gwynnie judged them to be a father and two sons. "He must be somewhere. Percy, today you must search the taverns in the city. Owen, search the Thames banks. If he's drunk and washed up by the tide, I want to know. That daft boy. Some heir he's making." The elder man rubbed his face once again, his anger palpable.

"We'll find him, Father," the other young man declared. He was the tallest, his black hair greying at the temples, despite his younger years.

"Then do so," the man muttered sharply. "The heir to an earldom has gone missing. What sort of statement does that make when we have come to the palace for Christmas? With what's happening in Yorkshire..." He broke off, shaking his head. "That damned fool Aske, leading these rebels in his *pilgrimage*." He practically spat the word with disdain. "And he's coming here, to the palace!"

"Here?" The voice of one of the younger men became so high that it squeaked.

"He's being escorted here by the Duke of Norfolk himself for peace negotiations."

The man's words made Gwynnie stiffen. She had seen the Duke of Norfolk in the palace, though she had thought his influence had ended when he had sentenced to death his own niece in the Tower of London earlier in the year. It seemed she had been wrong. King Henry was now sending the Duke of Norfolk to do the job of a guard and escort a wanted man to the palace. "Robert Aske will end up dead for this. I'm sure of it."

"You don't know that," the young man beside him argued.

"I know it," the elder hissed. "Any man involved in this rebellion will end up dead, sooner or later. We need to be careful. Anyone associated with the rebellion..." He trailed off and stood taller. "Find him," he urged again.

Gwynnie's eyes slid to the rings on his hand. She marvelled briefly at the number of jewels there, all glinting despite the dullness of the day. There was one particular iron-coloured ring that contrasted all the others. As the man turned toward the great hall, the light fell in such a way that Gwynnie could see the shape emblazoned onto the ring.

There were two eagles, each one with its beak turned toward the other, with the wings pulled in.

"Tombstone? Tombstone!" Gwynnie hissed at his door as she knocked loudly.

"Not now, Gwynnie," his voice answered back.

"You're going to want to hear what I have to say."

"Can this wait?" he demanded.

"Very well. I'll leave you to it then." Gwynnie stepped back from the door. "Perhaps you don't want to know who the dead man is after all."

There was a sudden scrambling on the other side of the door. Gwynnie stood still, her arms folded, a victorious smile on her face as she waited for the door to open. Only, when it did, Tombstone was not alone.

His copper hair was mussed, his doublet laces rather misaligned, and the clerk behind him kept his back to the door for some time, rearranging his clothes.

Gwynnie's jaw fell open.

"Not a word," Tombstone ordered, gritting his teeth. She promptly closed her mouth and waited.

The clerk turned around, his face rather pink. He was a handsome boy, a year or two younger than Tombstone perhaps, his eyes turned demurely to the floor. He and Tombstone exchanged an uneasy glance before he left through the open door, hastening down the corridor.

"You would think there was someone chasing him," Gwynnie murmured with interest, watching him go.

Tombstone flung the door open wider, beckoning her inside. "Not a word. You promised."

"Calm your bile." She looked around the room. Tombstone and the clerk must have been in the midst of their passions, for his usually neat desk was now a mess, with papers everywhere. "It's hardly the first time I've interrupted you with one of your … dear friends."

Tombstone shut the door with a heavy thud and turned his eyes to the heavens, as if praying for patience.

"Your laces. You might want to do them again." Gwynnie waved a hand at his doublet. He smoothed his hair and unfastened the laces, tying them again. "Do you know what I wonder at?"

"What?"

"You always seem to have a new man."

Tombstone's lips parted for a moment. "Gwynnie! We're not talking about this." He sat down in the Savonarola chair, pulling on his boots.

"Why not?" Gwynnie shrugged. "You're a man who seems to love easily. Can I not remark on that to a friend?"

Tombstone sighed. For a change, he didn't deny the fact that they were friends. He just paused with his boots and stared back at her. "I don't remember saying love had anything to do with it."

"Oh." Gwynnie glanced at the door through which the clerk had not long left.

"What? You've never broken the rules, Gwynnie? Never wanted to know what such things could be like?"

Suddenly, all of Gwynnie's confidence left her. She turned and walked to one of the caquetoire chairs by the fireplace.

"Is that a no?" Tombstone asked with interest.

"I didn't come here to talk about such things." Gwynnie crossed her legs under herself in the large chair. "I came to tell you what I have just seen."

But Tombstone was now leaning forward, his manner alert. He scratched the copper beard on his chin. "You have never had a love, Gwynnie?"

"Once. A long time ago." Gwynnie fidgeted, toying with the laces of her coif. "He decided another was for him within the space of a week, though, so we hardly progressed to…" She waved a hand at him, not wishing to use any words for what she had just nearly witnessed. "Now, shall we talk of the dead man?"

Tombstone nodded. Gwynnie did not miss the look of sympathy in his eyes, so she focused on telling him what she had overheard.

"A man and two sons were talking as they went to breakfast. The father is an earl. His eldest son and heir is missing. He's sent his two sons to search the brothels and the riverbank for him. Whoever his son is, he's evidently a man with an eye for liquor and women. The father didn't sound impressed by his son's reputation."

Tombstone finished tying his boots and pulled on a large outer robe, covering up his doublet. "Is that it?"

"He wore the same ring." Gwynnie held up her hand, waving the finger where she had seen the ring. "It bore the mark of the two eagles together. You'll find the father now in the great hall."

"Trust you to notice the jewellery." Tombstone smiled. "Shall we go and find out this man's name then?"

Gwynnie leapt from the chair as Tombstone led the way out of the office. In the corridor, they came across the clerk who had just been in Tombstone's chamber. He was talking with an elder man and gave no sign of noticing their presence, apart from an intense pinkening in his cheeks.

As they left the lawyer's chambers, Gwynnie eyed Tombstone carefully.

"Are you keeping your life a secret from Pascal still?" she asked, watching as Tombstone's expression darkened.

Just a few months ago, Gwynnie had caught Tombstone in a compromising position with another man. Only that time, she had not been alone. His employer had also witnessed it — Pascal.

"I am," Tombstone spoke simply. "He may cut me out of his life completely if he thinks..." He trailed off.

"Your secret is safe," Gwynnie whispered. Whoever Pascal was to Tombstone, family or not, Tombstone clearly craved his good opinion.

As they reached the great hall, Gwynnie picked up a tray another maid had left by the entrance and, parting from Tombstone's side, she walked through the tables. She placed down trenchers of manchet bread, then hesitated beside the man with the eagle ring, clearly pointing him out to Tombstone.

As Gwynnie turned away, collecting empty flagons, Tombstone moved to the man's side.

"Excuse me, sir, may I introduce myself?" Tombstone bowed to the man in greeting. "My name is Elric Tombstone. I'm a lawyer in the employment of the magistrate of London. May I enquire as to your name?"

"The Earl of York, Nathaniel Ashdown." The man stood from the bench, though he gave no sign of even inclining his head to Tombstone to acknowledge the introduction with any degree of respect. "This is an unorthodox meeting."

"Perhaps, but there is a purpose." Tombstone brushed aside the fact that the earl wasn't content with a man so far beneath him introducing himself without someone more important present. "May I enquire as to your eldest son? Does he wear a ring such as this one?" He gestured down to the ring on the earl's finger.

Gwynnie busied herself with cleaning the earl's empty trencher away as the earl raised his hand. His fingers shook a little as he evidently began to realise this conversation could be leading nowhere good.

"He does. Have you found him?"

"He is missing?" Tombstone sought to clarify.

"He has been missing overnight, yes." The earl stared at Tombstone. "Do you know where he is?"

"If you will come with me, my lord, there is a conversation we need to have, but not in here." Tombstone nodded at the busy room around them.

The earl looked ready to argue, but then he silently nodded and walked out of the room. Tombstone hesitated.

"I meant to give this to you earlier," he whispered to Gwynnie, passing her a scrap of paper. "I found it in the streets of London yesterday. You and I both know who it may be speaking of."

Gwynnie took the paper from him, though she didn't open it at once. She waited, watching as he left the room on the Earl of York's tail. The moment they were out of sight, she placed down the tray she had been carrying and moved to a corner of the room, opening up the folded scrap.

It was a ballad sheet, smudged with dirt and rain, as if someone had discarded it in the gutter after reading it.

Connal Devlin was once more depicted in an engraving that had been block printed onto the page. Only this time, it was an image of him at the gallows. As well as the devil horns, the engraver had given him goat's hooves and a curly tail, so that he looked more beast than man.

Gwynnie scanned the words, but they told her no more than she already knew. She was about to fold up the piece of paper when her eye was caught by another article, tucked away at the bottom of the page.

The Bristol Thief is Back.

Gwynnie bolted from the great hall, holding the ballad sheet close to her chest. Only when she was standing in a corner of the middle courtyard did she dare to open it up and read it. A rhyme recounted how the notorious jewel thief had come back, seemingly from the dead, to renew their robbing in Bristol city.

The final two lines of the rhyme made Gwynnie's heartbeat quicken:

Yet the thief is only mortal, for a dagger struck them in the chest.
Is it possible that now the thief will fall to an eternal rest?

CHAPTER 6

"Don't even think about it." Tombstone sat opposite Gwynnie by the fire as she shook the pamphlet at him.

"What would you do in my position, Tombstone? If it was your mother who might have been stabbed?"

He winced and stared into the flames beside them. The sunlight had left the room, for the days were short. The only light came from the flickering fire, the orange glow falling on Tombstone's face.

Knowing he would not talk of his own family, Gwynnie waved the ballad sheet again. "She's hurt."

"If Emlyn is thieving again, then she can't be badly hurt. You know we can't trust anything reported in these ballad sheets." Tombstone nodded at the paper. "For all we know, it was just a scratch."

Gwynnie screwed up the paper into a tiny ball, not wanting to admit he was right. Some months ago a messenger from Bristol had delivered an old pamphlet about the Bristol Thief with Gwynnie's name scrawled across the top. He had also said one word: *Emlyn.* Gwynnie believed the message was from her mother and proved that Emlyn was still alive.

"This wasn't supposed to happen." Gwynnie sighed and stared into the flames.

"What wasn't?" Tombstone asked.

"She was supposed to stop stealing. That was always the plan. When we came here —" Gwynnie waved her hands around to indicate the palace — "the plan was to steal for the last time."

"Not everyone wants to be saved, Gwynnie."

Gwynnie huffed.

"Gwynnie, listen." Tombstone leaned forward. "Put business aside for a moment. Even forget that I vowed never to go searching for your mother if you worked for me."

"It's so easy to forget," she mumbled wryly.

"I don't think running off to Bristol to search for Emlyn is a good idea."

"Oh? And why is that?"

Tombstone sat back. "I do not want to see you get hurt." He held her gaze. "You may be foolish —"

"Thank you for that."

"And a thief —"

"What compliments you are paying me."

"Not to mention dishonest. You took Pascal's flagon of mead, didn't you?"

"How did you know that?"

"I saw your eyes linger on it the last time we were in his room. Next thing I know, it's missing. I know enough of your character to guess that you took it at the first opportunity."

Gwynnie stared at Tombstone as he cracked a smile.

"Gwynnie, your heart is still a good one." He turned serious, his smile fading. "And I don't think you should go racing after your mother to save her when she plainly does not wish to be saved." He leaned forward again. "I need your help here."

"You want me to help find Devlin the Devil."

"I do. I also need you here for another reason." Tombstone lowered his voice. "You saw what happened in May."

The reminder of Queen Anne's execution made Gwynnie's blood run cold.

"You heard too about Queen Catherine. What they found of her heart…"

The rumour that Queen Catherine's heart had turned black from poison had not gone away. According to the spy, Captain Daundelyon, one of Queen Catherine's maids saw it herself and was convinced she had been poisoned on the king's orders. Knowing that he had ordered the murder of his second wife, Gwynnie now realised what King Henry was capable of, and it seemed all the more possible that he had ordered the murder of his first wife too.

"And now a man has been found dead in Queen Jane's chamber. Enough scandal and danger followed the last queen. What would the king make of this? How long before whispers suggest that Queen Jane had a hand in the murder of this man? How long before someone suggests that the man was there to see the queen? Alone … in private."

Gwynnie stiffened. The last queen accused of entertaining a man alone had been executed. The thought of Queen Anne's death still haunted her, waking her in the middle of the night. Could it happen all over again? Would one wrong whisper to the king lead Queen Jane to the chopping block?

Tombstone gripped the arms of his chair. "We must protect her, Shadow."

"We can *try* to protect her." Gwynnie chewed her lip as she thought of the woman who had sat alone at breakfast that morning, hiding her rosary beads. Who knew what King Henry would do with this wife if he decided he was finished with her too? His absence from the feasting table was already causing whispers in the court.

"Then I'll make you another offer." Tombstone rubbed his brow. "Because I know what you were searching for when you broke in here yesterday."

Gwynnie sat up straight, her eyes wide.

"I had a splinter from that shelf too." Tombstone jerked his thumb in the direction of the empty shelf. "You were searching for the papers I have on the Shadow Cutpurses."

Gwynnie sighed. "Why bother denying it? You know so much, and yet you will tell me nothing…" She trailed off as he raised his hand.

"I have my reasons, though you may not agree with them, but I'll make you a new deal, Gwynnie." He reached beneath the neckline of his doublet and pulled out a solitary key. It was small and thin, the iron handle curved into a perfect 'O' shape. "Help me find Devlin, and I will give you everything I have on the Shadow Cutpurses."

Gwynnie didn't speak for a moment. She looked longingly at the key, wondering if it opened a coffer or a lockbox, and just where Tombstone had hidden that box.

"Well? What do you say?"

A memory crossed Gwynnie's mind. It was the urgent whisper her mother had once uttered as they had walked the streets of London, watching the fine ladies pass by and following any that had worn jewels.

"We do what we have to in order to get what we want in this world. Remember that."

Gwynnie nodded. "Very well, we have a deal."

Gwynnie pressed herself against the wall of the food stores, making her body as small as she could. She was short, so it wasn't difficult to hide in the space behind the crates that had been piled up in the corridor. Peering around one of these crates, she watched as two burly men retrieved a barrel of wine. One rolled it forward as the other followed behind him. Judging by the way he was singing, Gwynnie assumed she was not the only one to occasionally take something from this store that did not belong to her.

She waited until the door at the top of the stairs closed, then stepped out from her hiding place. She hadn't brought a fresh torch or lantern with her, but used what little light came from the one candelabra that was burning brightly. Tiptoeing through the stores, she tried not to make a sound as she searched every chamber.

She checked the wine room, the grain store and a chamber with a low ceiling that was saved for brandies and sweet wines. She searched every nook and crevice, but there was no sign of anyone sleeping amongst the barrels and crates. There wasn't even any sign of someone eating from the food reserves that were stored down here in case the palace became isolated in a flood again.

Gwynnie left the chamber and climbed the stairs, entering a main passage in the staff quarters above. There, she found Tombstone waiting for her, looking through some papers he had clutched in his hand.

"Well?" he whispered as she approached.

She shook her head. "Nothing. If I were hiding in the palace, that is where I would sleep." He raised an eyebrow. "Very well, my mother and I did sleep down there when we were hiding from you in January. It was either the stables or the storerooms. Everywhere else has too many curious people passing through."

"We have already searched the stables. Twice."

Gwynnie indicated the papers in Tombstone's hand. "What's this?"

"The dead man's name."

Gwynnie took the papers. The top sheet displayed the family tree of the Earl of York. Beside Nathaniel Ashdown's name was that of his wife, Laura, though she was listed as being deceased. His three sons sat beneath his own name: Percy, Owen, and the eldest, Jasper. He was listed as thirty years old.

Gwynnie turned the page. On the second sheet, Tombstone must have asked the Earl of York to write down his son's many haunts. There were a number of taverns and other establishments that Gwynnie presumed must have been brothels.

"Jasper Ashdown," she murmured aloud, thinking back to the man she had seen in Queen Jane's chamber. She saw his handsome face again, twisted in anguish, and the frayed cuffs of his doublet. She pushed the papers back toward Tombstone. "Did his father know what he was doing in Queen Jane's chamber?"

"No, but I saw this." Tombstone pointed at the name of one of the places Jasper had visited.

"A brothel?"

"That's no brothel, Gwynnie. It's a house known for gambling."

"And how do you know that?" Gwynnie raised her eyebrows. Tombstone offered the smallest of smiles before changing the subject.

"Where shall we search next?"

"The attics." Gwynnie led the way.

In the rafters of Donsen Tower, Gwynnie climbed up a ladder, tucking the skirt of her gown into her belt as she folded herself up very small in order to fit through the tight gap of the attic.

"No man could have made his way up there so easily," Tombstone called up to her.

"He'd have to be as small as me to do it," Gwynnie agreed, poking her head above the timber beams to find the attic opening up before her.

She reached down and took the candle Tombstone offered, lifting it high above her head. The yellow light fell on strips of cobwebs that hung like tapestries from the walls. Gwynnie wrinkled her nose at the smell of damp and mould in the air. The space was empty.

"Well?" Tombstone asked.

"Nothing, and these cobwebs haven't been disturbed." Gwynnie sat on one of the beams and pushed the candle along the wood, craning her head forward to be absolutely certain. She and her mother had considered this as a hiding place once, but Emlyn was so tall that climbing in and out would have been impossible for her. "If Devlin is in the palace, then he's found a better place to hide than I can discover."

"What do you mean 'if?'"

"As you said, Lady Rutland was panicked," Gwynnie murmured as she crawled forward along the beam so she could check the furthest corner of the attic. "She might have seen any man creeping around. If another did kill Jasper Ashdown, then isn't Devlin the perfect scapegoat? All the killer needed to do was break that gate open to make it look like someone had entered the palace. Everyone else's imagination has done the work for them. It would explain why I can't find his hiding place. Wait ... what's that?"

"What is it?"

Something moved in the corner of the attic. The candlelight struggled to reach into the shadows, so Gwynnie slid the candle further along the beam just as a rat shot out from the darkness and scurried across her beam, leaping to another with ease.

Gwynnie flinched back, knocking her head against a supporting timber beam. "God's blood!" she hissed.

"You and that tongue of yours," Tombstone remarked from below.

"Thank you, Ma," she muttered resentfully. "It was just a rat." She pulled herself back across the beam, looking around the attic, but there was no sign of any disturbance. Climbing back down the ladder, she dropped to her feet and promptly handed the candle to Tombstone as she freed her skirt from where she had tucked it into her belt. As she stood straight, she saw Tombstone's face set into a scowl. "What is it?"

"It's just possible, isn't it?" he whispered. "Maybe someone is trying to point the finger at Devlin. He may not be here at all."

"That's what I've been trying to tell you." She coughed on some of the dust from the attic. "It doesn't explain why Jasper Ashdown was in the queen's chambers in the first place."

"I've had an idea about that." Tombstone turned and walked along the corridor, urging Gwynnie to fall into step beside him. "You remember that gambling place on this list?" He patted the pocket of his doublet, where he had put the papers. "What if Ashdown was in debt to someone?"

"You mean, he might have gone to Queen Jane's chambers to steal from her? To repay his debts?" Gwynnie asked. "There were jewels in her rooms, finery too. The queen didn't mention that any of it had been moved, though."

"No, that's not what I meant." Tombstone halted and turned to face her. "If that was his intention, why not steal from an easier quarry than the queen? One of the most guarded people in this palace! He could have stolen from his father, who has many fine things, or any other courtier whose rooms are not so heavily watched. There must be a greater motive for Jasper entering the *queen's* chamber, do you not see?"

Gwynnie jerked her head in acknowledgement.

"I wonder if someone could have held the debt over Jasper Ashdown's head? Maybe they refused to write off the debt any other way, unless he helped them into the queen's chamber," Tombstone murmured.

"Well, if that's the case, maybe all the whispers in this palace are wrong. Maybe Devlin the Devil is not here at all."

CHAPTER 7

"Well? What progress have you made?"

Gwynnie's hand froze on the door handle to Tombstone's room. The voice she heard inside was unmistakable: it was Cromwell.

"We have found little evidence so far for Devlin being in the palace. But if he is here, sir, we shall find him."

"Hmm." Cromwell didn't seem convinced by Tombstone's response.

"Tombstone is the best I have," said Pascal. "He will find Devlin. You can be certain of that."

Gwynnie allowed herself a small smile as she heard Pascal defend Tombstone.

There were footsteps behind her. Gwynnie turned and grabbed a cloth out of her apron, dusting the nearest ledge in the stone wall.

Two clerks walked past, muttering. Neither of them glanced in her direction. The moment they had left the corridor, Gwynnie stuffed the cloth back into her apron and returned to the door.

The conversation had moved on a little. They no longer seemed to be talking about Devlin.

"When are the Duke of Norfolk and Robert Aske due to arrive at the palace, sir?" Tombstone asked.

"Any moment. When they arrive, they will be taken into a meeting with the king and his councillors. Though from the duke's letters…" Cromwell paused. "I fear what he has agreed to put forward from the rebellion's demands. We shall know soon enough." He sniffed sharply. "Nothing can disturb this meeting. An army of thirty thousand peasants may seem like nothing to some, but they have gained an extraordinary following in the north in just one month. We cannot risk that strength of feeling bleeding into the south. We must stamp it out!"

"What is it you wish us to do?" Pascal asked.

"Find Devlin, before he commits another murder within these walls."

"We do not know if he killed Jasper Ashdown. Rumours alone suggest that Devlin was the killing hand." Tombstone spoke slowly.

"Pah! A murderer is seen here, in the palace, mere hours after he threatened to avenge himself on the king. A man is discovered murdered, and you think the events are not linked? The coincidence is unfathomable! It is extraordinary! This Devlin threatened the king. Maybe he decided to take his revenge on the king by making him suffer, by killing his wife, the queen. Who's to say that knife wound wasn't meant for her? The dead man was found in her chamber, after all." Cromwell must have been marching up and down, for his loud steps emphasised every word. "God forbid something were to happen to the queen."

Gwynnie found herself tutting, rather louder than she had intended. It was an irony that the king only abided violence toward his queen if he was the one who ordered it.

"Find him, Tombstone," Cromwell hissed.

"May I enquire as to something, sir?" Pascal clearly did not wish for Cromwell to take his leave just yet. "The Lady Mary. She has been called here this Yuletide."

"What's your question?" Cromwell's voice was tight.

"Well, why has she returned to court? Is she being returned to the line of succession? Should we be writing up the papers —"

"No." Cromwell's reply was firm. "Appearances are everything, Pascal. One of the requests made by Robert Aske and his rebels was to return Lady Mary to the line of succession. It's an impossibility, of course, but bringing her here this Christmas may placate them and make them disperse from Pontefract Castle. If they think Lady Mary is no longer an outcast, it could bring about a change."

"Sir, one more thing." This time it was Tombstone. "The king's son."

"Fitzroy? What of him?" Cromwell asked.

"Forgive me, but the way you sometimes talk about him, the way the king talks about him, I almost wonder … is he truly dead?"

"Of course he is." Cromwell's voice was wooden. "He will not be gracing the corridors of Greenwich Palace again. You can be certain of that."

Gwynnie stepped back from the door. She rather thought Cromwell's last words were not the same as saying that Fitzroy was truly dead in his grave.

She turned on her heel and left the corridor before Cromwell could see her. As she slipped out into the grey afternoon, she wrapped her arms around herself. Cromwell's answer had left her with a growing fear.

"Maybe they are just saying he's dead," she whispered, "to avoid anyone discovering what he did."

It meant that someday, she might see Fitzroy again after all.

Gwynnie yawned as she stepped out of her chamber and closed the door behind her. She didn't bother lighting a candle to lead her way, but moved through the darkness, tucking her loose hair beneath the cloak she had pulled around her shoulders to ward off the cold.

She hadn't been able to sleep. Each time she had closed her eyes, she either saw Emlyn, dressed in man's garb, with a dagger in her stomach, or she was back in the queen's chamber, listening as Queen Jane screamed whilst the man on the bed bled his last.

Stepping into the corridor leading to the staff's chambers, she came to a stumbling halt as she nearly fell over someone's feet.

Ricard was asleep on a chair, his legs stretched out in front of him. A deck of cards and tiny dice were on top of a barrel beside him, along with a solitary candle, though he was looking at none of them for his eyes were firmly closed.

Gwynnie stepped toward him and clicked her fingers.

Ricard awoke with a start and sat up so sharply that he inadvertently kicked his pike. It fell from its position, so that Gwynnie had to hop out of its way to avoid being hit.

"Good evening to you too, Ricard."

"Gwynnie!" he hissed, rubbing his face. "I was just…"

"Resting your eyes?" she teased him. He grunted something in reply then bent down to retrieve the pike. "Since when do we have a guard on the staff quarters?"

"The order came down from a man called Tombstone in the lawyers' chambers." Ricard tried to hide his yawn as he returned the pike to its place. "Do you know a man of that name?"

"I have heard of him," Gwynnie said evasively. The palace was so large and full of people that it was impossible to keep track of who knew who. She didn't think it wise to inform a guard that she was in Tombstone's employment. "You need some sleep."

"As do you." He pointed at her as she tried to hide another yawn. "What are you doing awake at this hour?"

"I need a walk. Beautiful night, isn't it?" she said, gesturing toward the open door and the rain that was coming down.

"Oh, stunning night," Ricard answered gruffly, returning to his reclined position with his feet up on the barrel. "Have a care, Gwynnie."

"I'm always careful."

Ricard laughed then went back to his half-dozing state.

Gwynnie left through the open door and strode out into the rain. She shuddered in the cold, wrapping the cloak tighter around herself. It turned out that it was nigh on impossible to go anywhere alone in the palace, even at this time of night. The inner and middle courtyards were filled with guards marching up and down.

Desperate to find somewhere to walk alone, Gwynnie headed to Friars' Church and its garden. There were two guards here, though they were evidently as tired as Ricard for one was fast asleep and the other was doing his best not to doze on the thorny rose bush beside him.

Gwynnie walked around the church and came across three more guards, all flanking the gate through which Lady Mary had barged her way into the palace.

"Are any of the guards in their own chambers?" Gwynnie muttered aloud. The words had just left her lips when she stumbled to a halt.

It was a good thought. If all the guards were keeping watch over the palace, then their own rooms would be unusually quiet.

Pulling the cloak of her hood over her head, Gwynnie set off back in the direction she had come. She passed through the inner court, keeping Donsen Tower on her left as she headed toward the middle courtyard. If any guard was curious as to what she was doing walking so late at night, they were too tired to stop and ask her.

When she reached the servants' side of the palace, she turned in the direction of the tiltyard, heading straight for the guards' rooms. It was the first doorway she had come across that night that wasn't guarded. The heavy oak door was locked, but Gwynnie was not so easily put off.

Creeping alongside the red-brick wall, she glanced back over her shoulder, but this part of the palace was quiet. As she reached a window, she pressed her fingers against the glass, finding it as unyielding as the door. Dropping down the thin rod she kept inside her sleeve, she pressed it into the gap between the window and the frame, fiddling with the latch. It didn't take long to lift the latch and open the window.

Gwynnie grabbed hold of her cloak and gown, holding them high as she climbed in through the window. She dropped down into the corridor on the other side to find it dark and empty. Unable to see where she was going, Gwynnie reached out with her fingers until she grabbed hold of a table with a tinder box on top. She fiddled, lighting the iron wool. As the flame struck, its orange glow fell on a candle nearby, which she hastily lit.

Lifting the candle, Gwynnie looked up and down the empty corridor. She had never had cause to visit this particular building before. Moving on her tiptoes, she kept the candle outstretched in front of her, guiding each step she took.

This floor held a large chamber filled with tables and benches. It had to be where the guards took their meals.

Climbing a small spiral staircase, she found the bedchambers. There were one or two locked doors, which had to hold more senior sleeping yeomen. There were two larger rooms, each containing about ten beds. In one was a man, who snored so heavily that Gwynnie's quiet footsteps were not in danger of waking him.

She crept on, heading for another spiral staircase at the far end of the corridor. This one was smaller than the last. So much so, that she had to bend down at the top of the stairs in order to avoid hitting her head on a low beam.

She stepped into a bare corridor. Judging by the webs hanging from the ceiling, this part of the palace was rarely occupied. Pikes, halberds and bills had been discarded against the walls. Most were broken, perhaps thrown here and forgotten about long ago. It was more of a dumping room than a chamber.

Gwynnie carefully picked her way around the weapons, doing her best not to catch herself on any of the sharp metal points. She raised her candle high, so that the light bounced back at her off the blades.

At the far end of the chamber was a single doorway, one so small that it was even shorter than Gwynnie. She inched her way toward it. As she reached the door, she opened it and bent her head through the low gap.

It was nothing but a store cupboard, only it wasn't being used to store anything. Inside, tucked into one corner, was a blanket. On the other side were crumbs of bread and even a lonely trencher, dappled with some sort of brown liquid that looked rather like gravy.

Gwynnie hastened to place her candle on a stone ledge in the wall, then bent down to the flagon beside the trencher, giving it a good sniff. It smelled like claret, though every drop had been drunk.

"Is this where you have been hiding?" Gwynnie murmured to herself. For a man to be hiding in this tiny space, either he was not tall, or he was desperate to stay hidden.

Determined to find out who had been using this hiding place, whether it was Devlin the Devil, or perhaps just a guard shirking his duty, she resolved to keep watch. Creeping into a corner of the weapons room, she sank down into a seated position, half hidden behind a breastplate that had been cracked in two and a great helm with the visor torn off. She blew out the candle, watching as a thin vapour spiralled up into the darkness.

If Devlin was in the palace after all, she would wait until he made his appearance.

"You're yawning again. Did you sleep at all?" Samuel asked the next morning.

"Course I did," Gwynnie lied as she watched him knead a piece of dough. He tore a piece off and passed it to her.

"Eat that. No one's looking."

Gwynnie thanked him and sat down on the bench beside him as he worked. It was the early hours of the morning and few people had yet risen. Gwynnie had not slept much. She thought she might have dozed off once or twice during her watch of the store cupboard, but not for very long. It was only a short time ago that she had abandoned her watch. Whoever had been sleeping in the cupboard had not come back that night.

"Did you sleep?" Gwynnie asked as Samuel hid a yawn behind his floured hand.

He shook his head. "I'm worried about Brynne. She's not been the same since that night."

The memory of trying to staunch the blood coming from Brynne's abdomen was enough to make the raw dough stick uncomfortably in Gwynnie's throat. She swallowed it as best she could, just as Samuel handed her some more to eat.

"She's getting worse," Samuel muttered. "It's all to do with this devil man."

"Devlin?" Gwynnie frowned. "Because he's Irish?"

"That's just it." Samuel cast a glance around the kitchen. Few people were around. Od Rudyard loped away to the other side of the kitchen, where he thrust pork legs onto a spit above the fire. Samuel lowered his voice. "She keeps talking about how the Irish are judged here in this land. Called heathens, even barbarians."

Gwynnie frowned. "No decent person thinks such a thing," she murmured.

"You think the world is full of decent people, lass?" Samuel laughed, though it died quickly. "The point is, she's getting worse. She was up half the night muttering —" he looked around again — "muttering Catholic prayers."

This time, Gwynnie choked on the dough. Samuel had to clap her on the back to dislodge it. As it came away in the palm of Gwynnie's hand, old Rudyard looked at them both with interest.

"What if she was overheard?" Gwynnie hissed.

"I know."

"The palace may be changing, but the law hasn't changed that much —"

Samuel sighed heavily and rested his hands on the wooden table. "I know, Gwynnie, but Brynne won't listen to me. She seems too afraid for this Irish soldier."

"Just because he's Irish it doesn't make him a good man," Gwynnie muttered.

Samuel eyed her carefully. "And just because he's Irish it doesn't make him a bad man either."

"You know what I meant," she whispered. "Brynne may be worrying for a man who doesn't deserve her sympathy."

"I know that, too. But is it true what people are saying, Gwynnie? That he's in the palace?"

Gwynnie's stomach knotted tight. She hadn't been convinced until she had found that hiding place in the yeoman's chambers the night before. "He might be here."

CHAPTER 8

Gwynnie checked the corridor of the yeomen's barracks. It was just as empty as it had been the night before. Stationing the guards across the palace made this building the least occupied of all the palace buildings, and the perfect place for an intruder to hide.

Gwynnie blew out the candle in her grasp, leaving it on a windowsill, before climbing the spiral staircase. Taking the same route she had taken the night before, she walked past the yeomen's chambers, heading to the much smaller staircase on the far side of the corridor.

Up in the weapons room, she noticed that another broken weapon had been slung in here during the day: a pike broken in half, the blade bent, as if it had been rammed against a brick wall. Otherwise, the room remained unchanged.

Gwynnie carefully picked her way across the room in the moonlight, heading for the store cupboard she had searched the night before. She reached the door and hesitated.

If this man Devlin was a murderer, then surely he would have no qualms in killing her and leaving her corpse in this room, where it was unlikely to be found until it stank enough for someone to investigate.

Turning away, Gwynnie snatched up a broken basilard from the floor. She kept a small knife in a pouch at her belt, but compared to the basilard it was a feeble weapon. The longer blade sat uncomfortably in her hand. She shifted it between her fingers, so that the base of the blade was nestled in the palm of her hand, then she faced the cupboard door once again.

With shaking fingers, she reached for the door handle, then halted. There was something white shining in the moonlight. A scrap of parchment, no bigger than her thumbnail, had been wedged between the door and the frame. Slowly, she lowered the basilard in her hand.

"He wants to see if anyone opens the door," she whispered to herself. It was a trick she and Emlyn had employed when they had still rented small rooms in the back streets of London, so that if someone opened their door, the paper would drop.

Now confident that whoever had made this their place to hide was not here, Gwynnie reached for the scrap of paper. She took it between her forefinger and thumb before she opened the door an inch, pressing her ear to the gap to check for any sounds of snoring or breathing. She heard none, so she opened the door wider.

The store cupboard was much the same as it had been the night before. There was the blanket in the corner, though the trencher that had been there before had now gone; in its place was an empty flagon and a small wrigglework bowl.

Gwynnie moved toward the bowl and lifted it to her nose. She could smell meat, a luxury indeed considering they were in the middle of the Advent fast. As she returned the bowl to its place, being careful to put it back in exactly the same position, she saw something she had not noticed the night before.

Beneath the blanket was something bound in leather. She reached for it, but in the dark cupboard could not make out what it was, beyond the fact that it was heavier than she had expected. She stepped back into the main room and opened up the leather binding, finding it was a file of sorts. Inside were letters, though the handwriting was so slanted that she couldn't make out the words in the poor light. Tucked into a corner of the file was something cold and metallic. She lifted it from the binding and held it up so that it caught the moonlight.

It was a tiny ornate cross, so bedecked with miniature engravings that it could not possibly be mistaken for a Protestant artefact. This was a staunchly Catholic trinket.

A memory stirred at the back of her mind — something Tombstone had said about Devlin and why he had murdered six men in his barracks.

To enact some vengeance on the king for taking the whole country away from his Catholic God.

Gwynnie thrust the cross back into the file, bile burning the back of her throat. She ran her fingers across the leather, searching for anything else that might be useful. Folded up at the back of the illegible letters was something soft and cloth-like. She pulled it free of its hiding place, finding it was a handkerchief. The white material was a little dirty, though it had clearly been well made, with a delicate embroidered pattern around the edge. In the corner of the handkerchief were two initials, CD.

If she had been in any doubt before that Connal Devlin was the man hiding in this chamber, Gwynnie had her confirmation now. She hastened to fold the handkerchief and return it to its hiding place.

She thought it strange that a man who was capable of murder should carry around something as sentimental as a handkerchief. Gwynnie would guess that handkerchief had been embroidered for him by a loved one, most likely a woman. It seemed the murderer still had enough of a heart to keep it with him.

Gwynnie returned the leather file to the cupboard, being careful to lay the blanket back over it, exactly as she had found it. Before closing the door, she returned the scrap of parchment to its place between the door and the frame, so Devlin would not know that someone had discovered his hiding place.

Hurrying back down the spiral staircase, Gwynnie knew she couldn't afford to lay in wait and watch for Devlin anymore. Now she had seen his initials on that handkerchief, Tombstone had to be told.

She crept out of the yeomen's barracks. The moment she was free of the building, she ran, grabbing hold of the skirt of her gown and sprinting toward the tiltyard. On her way, she nearly collided with two of the guards keeping watch at the tiltyard gate.

"Gwynnie! What are you doing?" Ricard called after her.

"Nothing, there's just someone I have to see. Pleasant evening isn't it?" she shouted back.

"Aye, it is. If you like to be frozen to ice —"

Gwynnie didn't wait around to hear the rest. She kept on running as fast as she could toward the back of the tiltyard. She leapt over the jousting rail, heading for the door to the lawyers' chambers set in the curtain wall, when a figure caught her eye. For one horrifying moment, she thought it was their intruder — Devlin. Then she recognised the tall, broad-shouldered figure. Gwynnie came to a skidding stop in the mud.

"Samuel? What are you doing out here at this time?"

"I could ask you the same." He marched toward her. "Have you seen Brynne?"

"Brynne?" Now he was closer, she could see he was breathing heavily, his eyes darting around. "You mean she's..."

"She's not in our chamber. I woke an hour ago to find her gone, and I can't find her anywhere. I've searched the kitchens, the staff quarters, the orchard and now here." He swept an arm toward the empty tiered seating in the tiltyard. "Have you seen her?"

"No." Gwynnie shook her head. "But we'll find her." Gwynnie clapped his arm. All thoughts of going to see Tombstone were suddenly forgotten. "With two of us looking, we'll find her faster."

"I just don't know why she would leave our chamber in the middle of the night. She hasn't done that since —" He broke off and swallowed hard.

Gwynnie nodded. The last time had been to deliver an urgent message to Gwynnie at the Tower of London. That was the night Brynne had been wounded.

"Have you tried the church?"

"No, not yet."

"Then we'll go that way. I'll search the church, and you search the graveyard."

"The graveyard?"

"I mean she could be wandering around it, not…" Gwynnie waved a hand impatiently then turned to run in that direction, Samuel following behind her.

Gwynnie shot under the main tower of the tiltyard, through an archway and into the orchard, heading for Friars' Church on the far side. A chill wind had picked up and she pulled her coif further down as she reached the church.

Gwynnie tried the door first, looking back over her shoulder to see that Samuel was inching his way through the graveyard, searching for any hiding places where Brynne might be.

When the door didn't budge, Gwynnie walked around the side of the church, trailing her fingers along the stone wall as she searched for the lowest window. Gripping the iron frame, she pulled herself up, pressing her face close to the stained glass. A ray of moonlight fell upon the empty altar and tiled floors.

"Is she there?" Samuel asked, appearing behind her as Gwynnie dropped back down.

"No. Have you searched the dock?"

"The dock? Why would Brynne be there?"

"I don't know, but it's somewhere to look." Once more, Gwynnie led the way.

Gwynnie had reached the inner courtyard when one of the guards stepped in her way.

"What are you doing up at this time of night?"

"We're searching for someone who has gone missing." Gwynnie tried to step around him, but the guard moved to block her, raising his pike.

"Out of our way," Samuel barked as he walked up behind Gwynnie. "You heard me." Despite the fact that Samuel carried no pike or other weapon, the guard clearly thought better of having an argument with a man so much larger than him. He stepped aside, allowing Gwynnie and Samuel to pass by.

Gwynnie dashed through the archway to Donsen Tower, heading straight for the dock.

A line of yeomen sat along the dock itself, while others crouched around lanterns and makeshift fires, trying to stave off the cold. Some of the guards turned with curiosity at their entrance; others continued to blow on their hands to keep warm.

Gwynnie came to a halt. There was someone here who clearly did not belong in this crowd of yeomen. Toward the edge of the riverbank, staring down at the water, was a woman. Despite her coif, Gwynnie knew at once who it was.

"Samuel," Gwynnie whispered as he halted at her side, panting to catch his breath. She nodded toward where Brynne stood.

Samuel straightened his back as he walked toward his wife. When he reached her side, he put an arm around her shoulders. Wordlessly, Brynne laid her head on his chest. Gwynnie saw Brynne's shoulders shudder.

Gwynnie stood awkwardly watching on, uncertain whether she should approach or not. When some of the guards looked curiously at her, she stepped back into the shadows of the tower wall.

Eventually, Samuel and Brynne turned away from the river and walked slowly back toward Gwynnie.

"Is everything … well?" Gwynnie asked.

"Everything is fine," Brynne assured her, forcing a smile. "I just couldn't sleep, that's all."

Samuel put his arm around Brynne's shoulders and steered her back through the archway.

Gwynnie waited, watching them leave, before she approached the nearest guard. He looked up.

"How long has that woman been here?"

"A while," he grunted.

"Thank you." Gwynnie turned to leave.

"I thought she was searching for someone." His words made her turn back again. The guard was already shaking his head. "I was wrong. She just stared at the water instead. I thought she might jump."

Gwynnie recoiled. The mere thought was too painful to contemplate. She thanked the guard once more and left, following Brynne and Samuel back toward the servants' quarters.

CHAPTER 9

"You are certain?"

"I am." Gwynnie poured some beer from a jug into Tombstone's flagon as she stood beside him in the great hall. He was seated with the other clerks, lawyers and councillors at a long table on the far side of the hall. Their feast was a meagre one as it was still the Advent fast, but Tombstone had practically fallen into his dinner from hunger, stuffing the bread into his mouth. "There was an ornate cross, and the handkerchief had Devlin's initials — who else could it belong to?"

Tombstone nodded as he took a swig from his flagon. "I'll tell the yeomen to keep watch, quietly. We don't want him to know we have discovered his hiding place. By God, Cromwell was right, was he not? With Devlin undeniably here ... the coincidence of a dead man being discovered that very same day... It must have been him."

A clerk glanced their way, perhaps curious as to why a maid had been hanging around their table for so long. Gwynnie moved to Tombstone's other side and began to pour beer into other flagons. "It's odd," she whispered.

"What is?"

"If Devlin is here, if you and Cromwell are right and he did enter the queen's chamber that day, then why hasn't he acted since? Why not take the revenge he declared he would take and harm the king or queen?"

"We've increased the guard around the royal chambers, not to mention everywhere else. He'd be hard-pressed to reach anyone."

"Maybe," she murmured. "By the way, where *is* the king?" She used the jug to gesture toward the top table. Lady Rutland sat beside Queen Jane, yet neither of them spoke. A little further down the table, Lady Mary sat with her ladies, talking animatedly. There was no sign of King Henry. The whole display was of a queen isolated.

Gwynnie would never forget the day that Queen Anne had been sentenced to death. Tombstone had been involved in the trial, and was still haunted by it. Neither of them wanted to go through that again.

Gwynnie picked up the jug and moved closer to the top table, the better to overhear any conversation.

Today, the queen looked rather pale as she stared down at her plate. "Please, bring me Cromwell," she urged Lady Rutland at her side. The lady opened her mouth to argue, then closed it and stood from her seat, walking across the hall.

Gwynnie continued to top up flagons as she circled the table, her gaze flitting every so often to the queen. Jane raised her own cup to her lips, then she abruptly recoiled, wrinkling her nose as if there was something foul in her cup. She hastily put it down again and pushed it away.

Gwynnie watched as Jane sat back in her seat. Her hand left the table and rested on her stomach.

Gwynnie's lips parted in wonder. She was so busy staring at the queen that she didn't realise she was topping up someone's flagon too far.

"Watch what you're doing. You trying to drown me in beer?"

"Oh, I'm so sorry, sir." Gwynnie adopted a highly apologetic tone. She used the edge of her apron to mop up the mess. Just then, Cromwell entered the hall with Lady Rutland at his side.

"Your Highness." Cromwell bowed before the table. The queen waved her hand and he stood straight again, his face showing little expression.

"I wish to see my husband, the king." Her words were short and clipped. "Where will I find him?"

"He's in conference with his councillors about the Pilgrimage of Grace. I shall be joining him soon. The Duke of Norfolk is set to arrive at any moment with Robert Aske. Damn fool of a lawyer, thinking he can change the tide of religion in this country by gathering a few friends." Cromwell sneered then lifted his gaze to the queen, seeming to remember who he was talking to. He leaned forward a little, his brow set low. "Discussions are to be had. It is not the time for romances now, Your Highness. This is a matter for the monarchy."

"A queen cannot ask to see her husband?"

"Not at this time, no."

Jane stood from her seat. Her eyes shone with unshed tears as she swept away. Cromwell offered another stiff bow at her retreating back as Lady Rutland scurried after her mistress. The other ladies rose to follow her, but with one swift flick of Lady Rutland's hand they all returned to their seats.

Gwynnie took her empty jug and headed toward the door of the great hall. Neither Queen Jane nor Lady Rutland looked around as she followed them out into the middle courtyard.

"I cannot see my husband now? Is this the way it will be? Is it the way it started for *her*, do you think?" Jane demanded.

"The king loves you." Lady Rutland tried to take her hand. Though Jane gripped it tightly for a moment, she released it again swiftly.

"He loved *her* once, and he loved Queen Catherine who came before her." Jane's breath hitched as she turned in a sharp circle on the cobbled ground.

Gwynnie walked slowly toward the kitchens, her head bowed. Neither Queen Jane nor Lady Rutland looked her way.

"Lady Rutland, I shall need the help of a physician soon." She brushed her hand across her stomach. "You understand me, do you not? Find me someone with … discretion."

Lady Rutland nodded hastily. As Gwynnie disappeared into the kitchens, she pressed her lips tightly together. She could take a guess as to why the queen was talking of physicians, holding her stomach and finding the smell of beer suddenly repulsive.

Gwynnie opened the door to Tombstone's office, not bothering to knock beforehand. He looked up from his desk, where he was searching through papers.

"No one saw anything the day Jasper Ashdown was killed." Tombstone sank down heavily into his chair. He talked easily, apparently not surprised or even irked by her sudden entrance. "It doesn't make sense. How did he get into the queen's chambers without being seen?"

Gwynnie closed the door behind her and arched an eyebrow at him in challenge. "You think it impossible to hide in the shadows?"

"That's different. You have had your whole life to practise the art. The son of an earl has not." Tombstone suddenly looked up from where he was fussing with the papers. "Why are you here? What has happened?"

As soon as she had returned the empty jug to the kitchens, Gwynnie had headed back to the great hall to speak with Tombstone, only to find him gone. She had run the whole way to his room.

"I think the queen is with child." The words fell from Gwynnie's lips.

Tombstone stared at her. "How do you know?"

"She asked to see the king, but Cromwell refused. She recoiled from the scent of beer and even spoke to Lady Rutland about finding a discreet physician."

"Then the king does not know?" Tombstone whispered.

Gwynnie shrugged. If the queen was unable to see her husband, then it was perfectly possible that he did not know he had another child on the way. "If she's with child, then —"

"It means that if Cromwell is right and Devlin broke into the queen's chamber that day to kill her, to enact some sort of vengeance on the king, then he could have taken two lives rather than one." Tombstone swallowed uneasily. "What if you had seen Devlin that day? What would you have done?"

"I would have followed him," Gwynnie said simply. She hesitated, staring at Tombstone. "Jasper Ashdown would not have followed a man like Devlin."

"Why not?" Tombstone shook his head. "I know it's a wild idea, but we must speculate somewhere. Cromwell is right. The coincidence of a murderer breaking in on the same day that a man is murdered is inconceivable. Perhaps Ashdown saw Devlin. Maybe he recognised the face from the ballad sheet. He could have followed Devlin and tried to stop him. Maybe he was murdered for trying to do a good deed."

Gwynnie stepped forward. She searched through the neat stack of papers on Tombstone's desk, knowing exactly what she was looking for. She found the page on which the Earl of York had scribbled down all of his son's known haunts.

"Look at this list," she urged. "Does a man who frequents taverns and gambling houses sound like the sort of person who would do a good deed?"

Tombstone snatched back the paper. "I agree, he doesn't exactly sound like the picture of nobility or philanthropy, but that doesn't necessarily mean he wasn't capable of a good action, Gwynnie."

"Then let's find out. Let's speak to his brothers and see what they can tell us of his character."

"Very well, let's see what they have to say." Tombstone hesitated. "And not a word to anyone about the queen, Gwynnie."

Gwynnie huffed. As far as she was concerned, the sooner someone knew the queen was pregnant, the better. If it was true that the king tired of her already, then he certainly wouldn't execute his wife when she was carrying his child and potential heir.

"What kind of man was he?"

Tombstone's question clearly took both brothers by surprise. Owen and Percy Ashdown looked at one another.

Gwynnie busied herself with collecting the laundry from the brothers' chamber. Though each brother had a privy chamber of his own, they shared a sitting room in their guest wing. Neither brother had acknowledged her presence when she had arrived scarcely a minute after Tombstone in this chamber. She carried out her menial task as they sat with Tombstone around a large mahogany table.

Owen, the elder brother, cleared his throat before replying. "Jasper was a good brother. He would have been the earl one day."

"That will be you now," Percy said lightly, but Owen's sharp glare silenced him.

"He would have made a good earl." Owen spoke woodenly.

"No good comes from making cream out of festered milk now," Tombstone said carefully. "If I am to discover who killed your brother, I need to know the truth about him." His words made both Ashdown brothers shift in their seats. "He was a man fond of a brothel and a tavern. There is a place where I know men go to gamble on the list your father gave me."

Percy leaned forward. "It was only recently that he risked his riches."

"Percy!" Owen barked, but Percy pushed on.

"I don't want you to think our brother was always a gambler. He wasn't. He seemed to lose himself these last few months," Percy explained. "It was as if he was escaping some sadness by going there. Just last week, I asked him why he went. He said that it was where he could feel free."

Owen laughed derisively. "It was indulgence and selfishness, Percy. We both know that."

Percy didn't argue but sat back again in his seat, his back rather rigid.

"Did he ever perform kindnesses for others?" Tombstone asked. "Did he defend others? Did he ever try to protect people?"

Owen sighed. "I do not like to speak ill of the dead, but our brother was not a man of noble character. I once saw my brother run from a tavern brawl after he refused to pay the bill. It was the fastest he ever ran in his life."

Tombstone nodded. "Thank you for your honesty."

Gwynnie stood with the laundry trug and walked to the door. She hesitated on the threshold to listen to the last part of their conversation.

"Before I leave, there is one more thing I'd like to know," Tombstone said. "What has brought you to the palace?"

"We came for the fast and Yuletide celebrations," Owen answered swiftly. "Our father was keen on us coming. Being from York, he doesn't want us to be associated with the

Pilgrimage of Grace. It's a quest to ingratiate ourselves with the king, you could say. We've been in London for a couple of months, but we came to stay at the palace a few days ago."

"I see. Thank you for your time."

Gwynnie hurried off along the corridor and down the nearest staircase, where she waited for Tombstone. When he appeared, he was already shaking his head.

"So, Jasper Ashdown was not the sort of man who would have followed Devlin to that chamber to defend the queen's life?" Gwynnie summarised. "You also have no evidence to prove that Devlin was ever in the queen's chamber. It is only your and Cromwell's speculation that places him there."

"I know. So that still leaves us with the question, why was Ashdown there at all?"

CHAPTER 10

Gwynnie heard the commotion as she crossed the courtyards on her way to the laundry room. Horses' hooves clopped on cobbles as orders were bandied back and forth.

"You there, take the horses."

"The king is coming."

"Stand up straight, lawyer. Is this how you treat your king?"

The reply was drowned out by what started as a murmur and grew to a great buzzing hum, as if a swarm of bees had arrived in the courtyards of the palace.

Gwynnie followed a trail of other maids and staff, passing from one courtyard to another. As they entered the inner courtyard, the crowd obscured her view. Unable to see anything other than cloaks and gable-hooded heads, Gwynnie picked her way through the crowd to the side of the courtyard. Reaching the edge, she dropped the trug she had been carrying on the floor and hurried to stand on a stone windowsill, her head high above the others.

In a small clearing in the centre of the courtyard stood two men. One was unmistakable in his fine black cloak lined with white ermine fur. The Duke of Norfolk had returned to the palace and was currently sneering at a young man beside him.

"It's Robert Aske," a voice whispered nearby.

"That's Aske? That young man?" another voice asked.

Aske looked to be in his thirties, tall and lithe in build, though very thin. He wore demure and formal clothes, with a rather obvious heavy cross hanging from a chain at his throat. He was hardly the picture of a great rebel leader.

"You've seen him then?"

Gwynnie jumped as she heard Tombstone's voice beside her. He had no need to climb onto the windowsill to gain a better view. Instead he leaned against the stonework, his arms folded, watching the Duke of Norfolk and Robert Aske through the crowd.

"He's not what I thought he'd be. They say he gathered the support of thousands in the north. I thought he'd be more of a presence." Gwynnie gripped the window ledge to ensure she didn't fall.

"I'm told he's a man of great charisma and rhetoric." Tombstone smiled rather sadly. "He's a man of great learning too. You'd be surprised how he can turn a crowd to his cause."

"And the king is to meet with him?"

"Cromwell tells me the Duke of Norfolk has brought his request for peace. If the whispers are true —" Tombstone paused and moved a little closer to Gwynnie, ensuring no one could hear him — "then Aske is to be invited here for Yuletide."

"What? As the king's guest?"

Tombstone nodded. "Cromwell is a politician before he is anything else. He knows they must quell the uprising in the north somehow. Extending a hand of friendship to Aske could be a way to pacify the rebels. For now."

Christmas would only last twelve days. Gwynnie rather wondered what Aske's fate would be once those twelve days were over.

A door in Donsen Tower opened and the crowd fell silent as the king and queen stepped out of the building. Henry led the way, with Jane following closely behind, surrounded by her ladies. Lady Rutland stood closest to the queen.

Gwynnie stared in astonishment at the king. He'd been closeted in his own chambers for a few weeks now. Incredibly, he seemed to have gained more weight in that time, despite the fast. His doublet was straining at the laces, and the great cloak he had thrown over his shoulders, embroidered with so much gold that it shimmered like liquid sunlight, did little to disguise his growing girth.

King Henry moved toward the Duke of Norfolk. As he did so, Cromwell stepped forward too. He'd been strangely invisible in the crowd until that moment. The Duke of Norfolk fell to his knee in a deep bow. When Aske did not immediately bow, but stared at the king, apparently in disbelief or wonder, the duke barked at him.

Slowly, Robert Aske also bowed.

"Is he afraid, do you think?" Gwynnie whispered to Tombstone.

"Not enough." As if in testimony to Tombstone's thoughts, Aske stood without being asked to do so by the king.

Gwynnie marked the sharp turn of Henry's head, the white goose feather in his black hat flicking from side to side. He was not happy.

"Gwynnie," said Tombstone, trying to get her attention. "What did you find last night?"

"Devlin hasn't been back to his hiding place in the yeomen's rooms."

"Perhaps he has found somewhere new to hide."

"I do not believe that," Gwynnie said. "He left that cross behind, and the embroidered handkerchief. They are personal to him. No, he'll be back."

"Then we'll have to keep watch." Tombstone stepped forward as the group of men in the middle of the courtyard turned to leave.

Cromwell made a path, the crowd parting as a set of double doors opened in a red-brick wall.

"I'll be needed." Tombstone sighed. "Writing the notes for this meeting is not something I am looking forward to."

He walked into the centre of the courtyard, where he was met by Pascal. As the king and his entourage entered the building, the crowd was plainly reluctant to disperse. They all stared at the doors after they had been closed, and the two yeomen who now stood guard.

Queen Jane was the first to move away. She gripped Lady Rutland's arm and urged her to lead on, the other ladies-in-waiting following closely behind. Margery Lyster and Lady Monteagle hovered for a moment, speaking in low voices as they eyed the closed doors, before they too left.

One of the guards stepped forward: it was clear he now wished for everyone else to depart as well. Gwynnie stepped off the sill but stood her ground, pressed against the wall with the laundry trug in her grasp. She glanced at the closed doors, thinking of Tombstone inside with King Henry, Pascal, Cromwell, the Duke of Norfolk and Robert Aske, as well as all the other councillors. It seemed odd that something as violent as the Pilgrimage of Grace, where so much blood had been shed, could be resolved by something so simple as a meeting.

"Move on there," a voice urged nearby.

Gwynnie looked around. She had heard something in the voice, an inflection in the accent that was not commonly heard within the palace.

Amongst a group of yeomen was the guard who had spoken. His felt bonnet was pulled low over his brow, his eyes impossible to see, as he helped to disperse the crowd.

As the yeomen walked past her, Gwynnie noticed that this particular man's uniform was a little dirtier than the others, the collar frayed and the laces snapped around the neck. The yeomen all looked past her, as if she were invisible. All except one.

The guard with the fraying uniform looked straight at her as he walked by.

Gwynnie had seen that face before — those large eyes, that wide-set jaw and cropped beard. She'd seen it beneath a drawing of short devil horns.

Her palms suddenly clammy, the laundry trug slipped from her fingers and thudded against the cobbles, the contents spilling out.

Dumbstruck, she stared at the face of Connal Devlin beneath the yeoman's bonnet. Now she knew why they hadn't been able to find him. Devlin had been hiding in plain sight.

As she stared into the face of the man who had murdered six men, he looked back at her with curiosity in his eyes, and raised an eyebrow.

"He's —" Gwynnie raised a hand, ready to shout his name and point him out. How had the other yeomen not realised who was amongst them? Had they not seen the same ballad sheet she had seen? Were they so busy looking for an intruder that they didn't notice he was right under their noses?

Devlin moved toward her, cutting her off before she could say any more.

Leaping away, Gwynnie tripped on the laundry trug and fell backwards.

"Woah, there." He reached out and caught her wrist, keeping her upright.

"Move her on, Laurie," another yeoman ordered with a casual flick of his fingers. "We have our orders. No trouble today."

As the other yeomen walked on, Gwynnie tried to catch her breath as she looked up at Devlin. He still had hold of her wrist.

"Good day," he said calmly.

Fear spiked within her and she flung her hands at his chest, pushing him away from her. As she scrambled back, once more in danger of falling over the laundry trug, she was surprised to see that he actually laughed.

"Aye, not had that reaction from a woman before." Then he bent down to pick up all the laundry and dropped it back into her trug.

"Your laundry, flower." He stood straight and held the trug out toward her.

Gwynnie glanced around, but the courtyard was now empty aside from her and Devlin. She flattened her back against the cold brick wall, debating what to do next, whether to attack, fling the trug at him and run, or feign innocence and pretend she had not recognised his face at all.

"You're the first to notice." His words made her look sharply up at him.

He was tall, much taller than her, and strong in build. The pilfered yeoman's uniform was rather too tight across his shoulders. Beneath the felt bonnet, Gwynnie caught a glimpse of dark blond hair.

He raised his eyebrows, clearly waiting for her to say something.

"Scared, flower?" he asked, so quietly that she had to strain to hear him.

It was a strange thing. Gwynnie had expected Devlin to be a monster, an obvious killer. Perhaps she had even thought that he would have the devil horns that had been drawn on the ballad sheet, but this man was softly spoken, gentle even. His eyes were a rich dark blue.

"I won't hurt you," he whispered, offering the trug to her.

With shaking hands, Gwynnie reached out and took it from him. At first she failed and grabbed his wrist instead. His lips stretched into a smile, and she quickly took hold of the basket handle.

"You haven't yet screamed."

"I will," she managed to say. She swallowed past the sudden dryness in her mouth. "I will scream."

"Any moment now?"

"Yes."

"Very well." He smiled again. "I'll wait."

"Shouldn't you be running and hiding?"

He shrugged. "I suppose I'm waiting to see if you'll really do it, or whether you have realised I'm no devil."

"You're a murderer," she whispered.

"And are they always the same thing, flower?" He tilted his head to one side.

She flinched at the words. Her mother had blood on her hands. Gwynnie had shed blood herself, though she had never taken a life.

"You noticed me. No one else has noticed me."

She could have laughed. They were words she had often said herself. "You can't hide in the shadows forever, Devil."

"Devlin, but close enough." He smiled once more. "Now, are you going to call for help, or have you acknowledged I have no intention of hurting you?"

She blinked. He could have hurt her by now. They were alone in this courtyard. Even if someone had noticed them out of a window, he could have easily hurt her, forced her silence, then escaped before anyone came looking for him.

He stepped back and offered a rather formal bow. "Good day, flower," he said softly, then he turned on his heel and walked away. As he disappeared through the arch and into the middle courtyard, Gwynnie came to her senses.

"What the hell is wrong with me?" she muttered angrily. Tucking the trug under her arm, she sprinted after him, but he was not there. There were his fellow yeomen, even a group of gentlemen who were evidently talking of the king's private meeting, judging by the way they gestured toward the palace buildings, but there was no sign of Devlin.

Gwynnie turned on the spot. Wherever Devlin had crept off to, he had done it expertly.

"God's blood," she murmured, throwing the trug down angrily onto the cobbles. "I met the Devil, and I did nothing."

CHAPTER 11

"Tell me you're in jest," Tombstone pleaded, rubbing his temples.

"Of course she's not jesting," Pascal spat angrily as he paced up and down his office, striking his cane against the floorboards.

Gwynnie sat uneasily in front of Pascal's fireplace. It was one of the few times she had been in Pascal's office as opposed to Tombstone's.

"It was him?" Tombstone asked from his seat opposite her.

"It was him," Gwynnie assured him.

"And?" He leaned forward in his chair. One side of his face was bathed in firelight, while the other side remained in shadow, as no one had lit any candles, despite the fading light. In his hand was a glass of port. Gwynnie found herself eyeing it, longing for something to quench her thirst.

"And what?"

"And why didn't you call for help? You could have shouted at the other yeomen. You could have done anything, Gwynnie. It's not like you to stand there and do nothing."

Pascal huffed rather loudly and marched toward another chair. He sat down with such force that the wood creaked ominously beneath him.

"He killed six men," Gwynnie whispered. "What do you think he would have done to me if I had started screaming? He would have silenced me. Think it through, Tombstone. What should I have done?"

He leaned forward a little more, his port glass now balanced on the arm of his chair.

"And is that why you didn't scream?"

"Yes." It was partially true. Fear had frozen her to the spot, but she had also been surprised that the man before her had not seemed like a devil at all. He had picked up her laundry for her.

"You see?" Pascal flicked his fingers in Gwynnie's direction. "This is why your pet can't be relied on."

"This again." Tombstone sat back, turning to Pascal.

Gwynnie saw an opportunity and grabbed the port glass. She downed half the contents in one go, though neither man seemed to notice, for they fell into an argument they'd had many times before.

"She has been invaluable." Tombstone's voice had grown deep.

"She is unreliable. This waif is not the strong spy we need in these corridors."

"She's the best spy because no one notices her."

Gwynnie downed what was left of the glass, thinking about the way Connal Devlin had looked at her. He had noticed her. He'd looked straight at her, even before she had dropped the trug.

"She'll let you down," Pascal insisted. "She's a woman."

"A woman who pulled me clear of the Thames last year when I could have died in its depths. Or have you forgotten that?" Tombstone asked.

Gwynnie slyly returned the empty glass to the arm of Tombstone's chair as Pascal spoke again.

"I did not say she hasn't proven herself useful on occasion."

"Oh, be still my rapid heart," Gwynnie said, her tone thick with sarcasm. "I believe that was a compliment."

"Enough." Pascal rubbed his brow tiredly as Tombstone reached for his port glass. It was halfway to his lips when he noticed it was empty.

"I was just singing your virtues," Tombstone hissed at her.

Gwynnie shrugged. "I was thirsty."

Tombstone stood to top up the glass, but rather than drinking from it himself, he passed it to Gwynnie.

"Stay here," he said.

"What? Why? Where are you going?"

"I am going to take the yeoman guards, and we'll search for this Devlin. Now we know he's hiding as one of them, we'll examine every face wearing that uniform. We'll check his hiding place too."

"It won't do you any good." Gwynnie's words made Tombstone halt before he reached the door. "If Devlin is half as good a soldier as he should be, he'll have chosen a new hiding place and a new disguise. My silence wasn't going to last forever. He knows that."

"I'm still going to try. We have to start searching for him somewhere."

"Yes, yes, we must." Pascal stood up. Striking the ground with his cane, he reached the door first. "I shall inform Cromwell that Devlin has been seen inside these walls. I daresay Cromwell was right after all. What cruelty, to avenge yourself on the king by trying to murder his wife. This poor Ashdown man must have been in the wrong place at the wrong time."

Gwynnie clutched the port glass in both hands.

"What is it?" Tombstone asked, eyeing her carefully as Pascal departed from the chamber. "You don't believe that possibility?"

"I worry it is not the truth. I have heard this theory from Cromwell and you, because of the timing of the murder. You and I heard from Jasper Ashdown's own brothers that he was not a man of noble character. They said he was a man likely to flee from a brawl. That description does not paint a picture of a man who would follow Devlin in order to protect the queen. So, why was Ashdown in her chamber in the first place?"

Slowly, Tombstone closed the door again and walked back toward Gwynnie.

"What did Devlin look like?" he asked carefully.

"You know what he looked like. You have seen the ballad sheet."

"Yes, but you have seen the real man. What is his colouring? His complexion?"

"Dark blond hair," she said. "Blue eyes. He has stubble, here." She trailed a hand along her jaw. "He's tall, too. Taller than you, and rather … strong in build."

"I think I need another drink before I begin this search." Tombstone reached for the carafe on Pascal's table, but rather than pouring it into a glass, he swigged directly from the carafe itself. Gwynnie had never seen him do anything of the kind before. He was usually so proper. "Did you like him?"

"He's a killer."

"That doesn't answer my question. From your description, it seems you rather liked the look of this Devlin."

Gwynnie took another sip of her port, aware of a sudden dryness in her mouth. "He was not what I expected. I thought he'd have the face of a monster, and, well, he didn't."

"Stay here." Tombstone put down the carafe and marched toward the door.

"You already gave me that particular order."

"Then abide by it for a change. I don't want you to get hurt if you bump into him again. I also don't want you flinging yourself at his feet."

"Flinging myself...? All I said was that he didn't look like a monster." Gwynnie stood up in protest, but Tombstone was already halfway out the door.

"You forget, I know what it's like to fall for a handsome face that is forbidden, Gwynnie. Don't do it," he warned.

"I didn't even call him handsome!" she shouted after him, but Tombstone had gone. She groaned in frustration. "Jesu, save me from Tombstone and Pascal." Then she put her empty glass on the mantelpiece and sat down in one of the chairs.

She didn't spend long looking into the fireplace before she knew she didn't want to wait for their return. If Tombstone and the yeomen guards were about to commence a search, then Devlin would be on the move, looking for somewhere new to hide. If the two lawyers wanted to know where he was going to hide next, then they needed someone to watch him from the shadows.

Gwynnie clung onto the church bell in the tower. The wind whistled through the open archways on either side of her, making her shiver. She pulled her woollen cloak tighter around her shoulders as she pressed herself against the stone wall of the church. It was an old cloak now, far too thin for purpose, but she'd had it since she had lived in the attic rooms in London with Emlyn, and she was reluctant to buy another.

From this vantage point, she could see most of the palace grounds. The garden and orchard extended far to her right, the cemetery was behind her, and up ahead were the inner and middle courtyards, surrounded by Donsen Tower and the various turrets of the palace building. In the distance, Gwynnie could just make out the rooftops of the yeoman's buildings. Even from this far away, she could hear the hollers of the search. Men were demanding that every inch of the building was turned upside down, that every man would be forced to strip his uniform in order to find Devlin.

Gwynnie peered around the edge of the stone wall to look down at the garden. She knew that in Devlin's shoes, she would look for somewhere quiet to hide now. Somewhere that no one would think to look for him.

"Come on, come hide this way," she murmured into the cold December air.

Not a shadow moved in the myriad of lantern lights that were scattered across the courtyards. She shifted her focus to the orchard instead, watching for any sign of movement. There was nothing. Gwynnie slid down the wall and sat with her legs hanging over the edge of the bell nook, looking out across the grounds. The wind had picked up, making her reluctant to stay outside for much longer.

Gwynnie laid her head against the stonework, thinking back to the last time she had hidden herself in a church tower. It was some years ago, not long after she and Emlyn had started stealing to survive. One of the first places they had ever robbed was a church.

Gwynnie had not wanted to do it, but Emlyn had insisted that people were slowly turning against the tide of Catholic frippery. She was confident the fine altar pieces would not be missed.

Gwynnie, still a child, had kept watch from the top of the tower as Emlyn had broken into the vestry and prised open a coffer where all the altar pieces were hidden. They had never made it out of that church with their loot. Gwynnie had seen men coming and rung the bell, warning her mother to get out before they were caught. To avoid being caught herself, Gwynnie had scrambled down the roof of the church. How they had escaped being caught that night, Gwynnie still didn't know, but they had run for what felt like miles through the streets of London before their pursuers had given up.

"*Keep on running, miting,*" Emlyn had said. "*And never stop hiding.*"

Gwynnie's thoughts were broken by the sound of a gate swinging open. Peering down, she caught sight of a figure inching forward through the graveyard, clearly trying their best not to make a sound as they picked their way cautiously toward the church.

Much as she had done, they found the front door locked. She could hear them trying it, then quiet footsteps followed as they walked around the church.

Gwynnie scrambled on her knees to the other side of the bell tower, watching as the figure appeared on the other side of the church. They found the same side door she had managed to pick the lock of, then they slipped inside.

Cursing, Gwynnie scrambled to her feet. She tiptoed toward the spiral staircase reaching down into the belly of the church and as quietly as she could, crept down through the darkness.

She pushed the door at the bottom of the stairs open an inch, just enough to allow her to look through. The pale moonlight that shone through the stained-glass windows bathed the nave in an eerie blue glow. Gwynnie jolted when she saw a figure in a black cloak move. They glanced behind them as they approached the altar.

Halting before it, they delved a hand underneath the table, pulling out a hessian sack and laying it out on the altar cloth. The blue light fell on the items they took out, revealing food, what appeared to be a clean shirt, and even a corked flagon. The figure tipped back their hood, uncorked the flagon, and drank in quick gulps. Their face briefly caught the light, and Gwynnie saw that it was Connal Devlin.

She watched as he chugged most of the drink before reaching for the food, his hunger evident. He sat down on the front pew, devouring a chunk of bread.

Gwynnie focused on the back of his head. Devlin would be unprepared for an attack now. If she could catch him unawares, perhaps strike him down, he would be stopped. She'd ring the church bell, Tombstone and the guards would come running and Devlin would be taken back to the gallows.

Slowly, Gwynnie slid the metal rod that she so often used for picking locks out of her sleeve. It was small but heavy in her hand. If used correctly, it might just render a man unconscious.

Gwynnie pushed the door open just enough to allow her to slip through the gap and into the side aisle of the church. Unaware of her presence, Devlin kept on eating, ripping open a new muslin pack that someone had tied neatly for him. The scent of cheese and ham filled the air as Gwynnie tiptoed closer.

She was once more struck by how innocent the man before her looked. His dark blond hair was thrown forward as he bent over his meal. He didn't appear to have a weapon with him. He was just a starving man who someone had shown kindness to by leaving him food.

Gwynnie stepped into the space behind his pew, inching closer. She raised the rod in the air, reminding herself that this was no innocent man. He was a murderer. He had killed not just one man but many. She inhaled, raising the rod higher.

Then his head jerked up.

CHAPTER 12

Gwynnie didn't have time to move away, even when she realised that she had betrayed herself by making a noise. Devlin was already on his feet. His muslin pack was thrown aside, the ham and cheese tossed onto the tiled floor as he whipped around. Gwynnie's wrist was grabbed tight and she was pulled forward over the back of the pew. She landed on her back on the wooden seat, staring up into the shocked face of Devlin, who prised the rod out of her hand in one swift movement.

"You!" The Irish accent was suddenly plain as Devlin reared up above her. All at once he dropped the rod — the metal clattering loudly against the tiles. He released her wrist and staggered back.

Gwynnie stared up at him in amazement.

"You dropped the rod," she whispered. He could have easily turned the rod back on her to silence her, but the moment he had seen it was her, he'd cast it aside.

"You shouldn't sneak up on a hungry man, flower. Least of all with a weapon in your hands. Are you trying to kill me?" He ran a hand through his hair as he picked his food up off the floor. "Next time, don't breathe before you strike. It gave you away."

Gwynnie rubbed the old wounds in the base of her back. She had earned them when she had first come to the palace, and though they had long ago healed, there was a weakness there. Being thrown over a pew hardly helped.

"Why are you trying to kill me anyway?" Devlin wiped the cheese and ham on the clean shirt then ate it.

Gwynnie wrinkled her nose. "I'm no murderer. Unique in this company, I know." Her voice was tart.

He stopped chewing. "What are you doing here, flower?"

"Stop calling me that."

"Something you should know about me." Devlin stepped forward and Gwynnie shrank back on the pew, aware of just how much stronger than her he was. He had flicked her over the back of the pew as if she was nothing more than a straw doll. "I don't follow orders easily."

"I thought that's what soldiers were supposed to do."

"Aye, a grand soldier, aren't I?" He laughed, though the sound was forced. "I have torn shirts for my uniform, boots that are falling apart, and a weapon that, well, leaves a little to be desired." He held up a small dagger from his belt that Gwynnie hadn't seen before. It looked rather old and blunt.

When she flinched at the sight of it, he turned and laid it down on the altar.

"Surely you've realised by now that I'm not going to hurt you."

Gwynnie nodded and rubbed her hand along her back again, checking if she would be able to sit up well enough. Devlin stepped toward her.

"Wait!" She raised her hands sharply in the air. "Did I say come closer?"

He backed off, holding his hands up too. "I was going to offer to help."

"Oh yes, and you are the man I'd ask for help, Devlin the Devil."

"Is that what they called me? Aye, grand name. Though I would have credited those ballad sheet writers with a little more imagination." He turned and sat on the edge of the altar table, beside the wooden cross that somehow looked both

Catholic and Protestant. Though it was made of wood, it was heavily carved and very ornate. "What else did they write about me?"

Gwynnie sat up, blinking at him. It was as though they were talking in a tavern or in the street, not in a church they had both broken into in the middle of the night.

"Done talking, flower?" he asked when she did not reply.

"I thought I told you not to call me that."

He shrugged. "You haven't given me your name."

"What a wonderful idea. I'll happily tell a murderer my name."

"You call me a murderer, but *you* were the one about to strike *me* down." He gestured at the rod, which was still on the floor.

Gwynnie's hand itched to take it up again. As she slid along the pew toward it, Devlin watched her warily, his blue eyes rather bright in the moonlight.

"Don't make me take it off you again," he said, his voice sombre and low. "I vowed long ago never to hurt a woman."

"Yet you would kill six men?" Gwynnie countered hotly.

He shook his head. "I see you've read the ballad sheets and believed them."

"What person wouldn't?"

"Ah, you can read then, flower."

"I thought I told you —"

"Give me your name, and I'll stop." He reached for the flagon and took a gulp.

"Someone in the palace is helping you. Who?" Her words met with stony silence. Devlin cast a glance around the church.

"Anyone know you're here, flower?"

"Yes." Gwynnie's answer was so quick, he actually laughed. It softened his features.

"So that's a no, then."

"I thought you were a soldier, not a sorcerer who can read minds," she muttered, moving to stand. She bent down, reaching for the rod. Devlin made no move to take the rod off her, though he watched her carefully, never once looking away.

"Why did you try to attack me?" His voice deepened.

"Because a man died in the palace. No one here wants another death —"

"I had nothing to do with it." Devlin stood up and walked toward her. Gwynnie backed up. She collided with the edge of the pew, winced, then scuttled around it.

"You know what death I'm talking of, though, don't you?"

"I was told about the death of Jasper Ashdown."

"By whom?" Gwynnie asked. She turned and walked along the pew. Devlin continued to follow her.

"I had nothing to do with it. I was nowhere near Queen Jane's chamber that day."

"Why deny it?" she asked, now walking around the end of the pew. "You're already going to hang for the six murders you did commit. Why not add one more to the list?"

"You're supposing I did the first six," he said, taking hold of the back of the pew and leapfrogging over it to cut off her path. Gwynnie yelped and scuttled back. "And as you say, why bother denying the seventh murder if I had done the first six?"

"Step aside," she ordered, finding her back against a stone pillar.

Devlin made no effort to close the gap but stood with his arms folded, blocking her path. "Now, why would a maid want to avenge the death of a man like Jasper Ashdown? Were you…" Devlin hesitated. "His lover?"

"No!" Gwynnie barked the word so loudly that Devlin chuckled.

"Good. From what I hear, Ashdown wasn't a nice man. Don't give yourself to a man like that."

"Just what I've always wanted," she declared with thick sarcasm, "advice on taking a lover from a murderer."

"So, if you weren't his lover, then why try to kill me?"

"I wasn't trying to kill you."

"Stun me then? Enough for the guards to come running and arrest me? Aye, I can see it in your eyes — that's what you wanted." He fixed his gaze on her. "No ordinary maid would go to such lengths. Who are you?"

"I'm just a maid," she insisted tightly. It was all she could ever admit to if she wanted to keep her head. The one man who knew the truth, Tombstone, now held her life in the palm of his hand.

"And I'm a jester at the king's court," Devlin replied wryly. "Shall I prance around for your pleasure now? Aye, a grand idea." When he performed a rather flamboyant bow, Gwynnie fought back a smile. "Were you laughing?"

"No. I wouldn't laugh at a murderer."

"But you might laugh at a man who wasn't?" he said, stepping forward. She mimicked his movements and stepped back, flattening her body against the pillar. "You haven't called for the guard yet."

"Believe me, I will."

"That makes twice you haven't called for them." Devlin held up two fingers. "Maybe you don't see the devil in me after all, eh?"

"I know men need not wear the faces of devils to have their hearts." She'd heard enough. Whatever Devlin's charms, she couldn't let a murderer escape again.

She scuttled around the pillar.

"Where you running off to, flower?"

Gwynnie sprinted for the door leading up to the bell tower.

"Stop!" he shouted, suddenly alert, but Gwynnie didn't. She shut the door loudly behind her and felt him rattle it just as she slid the bolt across in the darkness. "Don't ring that bell," he ordered through the door. "Don't do it, flower. Please!"

"Please? You're actually pleading with me?" Gwynnie grabbed her skirt and hitched it high as she escaped up the spiral staircase. "Oh yes, that will make a huge difference."

"It should do. Just listen to me!" he bellowed, but Gwynnie ignored him.

Devlin was now throwing himself repeatedly at the door, trying to break it down.

As she reached the top of the stairs, Gwynnie heard the unmistakable sound of splintering wood followed a moment later by Devlin's feet on the steps. She spun around fast, reaching for the bell ropes. She unravelled the first from where it was tied around a wooden beam then tugged on it heavily. Even as she pulled, she caught sight of Devlin behind her. He caught the rope and pulled it roughly out of her hands.

"No!" Gwynnie cried, trying frantically to get it back from him, but it was little use. He just held the rope up out of her reach. She looked around wildly and saw that in their tussle, they had managed to make the bell swing. Larger than a carthorse and made of solid bronze, it was heading their way fast.

"Get down." Devlin grabbed Gwynnie and flung her to the ground. She was pressed to the boards as overhead, the bell swung. The first ear-splitting chime seemed to reverberate through Gwynnie's skull. She lay as flat as she could, aware that Devlin's arm was stretched across her stomach. He lay beside her, gritting his teeth as the bell rang above their heads.

Then it swung the other way, releasing them from their trapped position.

Gwynnie rolled over first and crawled out of the bell's reach. Devlin followed her and they both scrambled to the wall, falling against it just as the bell came back toward them. The lip of the bronze stopped just inches from their noses, before it was pulled back by momentum. The chime rang out again, so loudly that they both covered their ears with their hands.

Devlin suddenly had hold of her arm again, and it took her a moment to realise he was dragging her to her feet, pushing her toward the staircase. They both fell onto the steps together, with Gwynnie in the lead, running down in an effort to escape the bell.

As she burst through the broken door, she inhaled sharply. Her ears felt numb, as if both eardrums had been pierced. She leaned against the nearest pew as Devlin stopped beside her.

"Wait..." Gwynnie tried to speak above the ringing in her ears. "Why did you do that?"

"Do what?" Devlin was staggering away, thumping the side of his head with one of his palms. He reached for the items that had been left for him in the church and stuffed them back into the muslin pack.

"You pushed me down!" Gwynnie shouted. "You stopped the bell from hitting me. Why?"

Devlin turned to her, half of his face hidden by shadows, the other half bathed in silver moonlight. "Maybe I'm no devil, flower."

There was a loud whistle beyond the church walls and the sound of raised voices. Gwynnie looked around at the church door. Someone was hammering on it, trying to force it open.

Gwynnie turned back in time to see Devlin slip out of the side door in the vestry through which they both had come.

"Until next time." He performed another flamboyant bow, then vanished.

Gwynnie thought about chasing him, but the pain in her head was so severe that she slumped down into the nearest pew.

The front door was broken open and palace guards filled the space. They sped up and down the aisles, and some searched under the altar, one finding the pieces of cheese Devlin had left behind. Others focused on the broken door leading to the bell tower.

Ricard saw Gwynnie and moved toward her.

"Gwynnie?" His voice was muffled. She wondered for a moment if some of the lost cheese had ended up stuffed in her ears, but she knew it was absurd. That clanging bell had impaired her hearing. "Gwynnie, are you all right?"

"He was here, Ricard. Devlin was here."

CHAPTER 13

"You lost him again?" Pascal asked as Gwynnie placed a trencher down in front of him in the great hall. Furious at his tone, she flicked a particularly bony chicken leg onto his lap as she stood straight.

"Oops," she squeaked. Pascal brushed it onto the floor with a tut.

"What happened?" Tombstone cut into the conversation, serving himself from the trencher. There were few others around, but even so, they kept their voices low.

"I went to the church to keep watch." Gwynnie placed down a wrigglework bowl full of bread. "It seemed to me that if you were going to turn the yeomen's barracks upside down, Devlin was going to look for somewhere new to hide, and he did. He came to the church. Someone had hidden a bag for him there."

"A bag?" Pascal stopped eating and looked up at her.

"You know, something you carry things in." Her reply made Tombstone laugh, though he pretended to be choking when he saw Pascal's expression. "There was some food, and even a clean shirt. Someone is helping him."

"Who?" Tombstone seemed to have lost all interest in his food.

"I don't know." A wild idea crossed her mind, but Gwynnie dismissed it. Brynne could not be the only Irish member of staff in the palace. There had to be others, and just because she was also Irish, it didn't mean she would help Connal Devlin.

Gwynnie quickly described what had happened, even telling them how Devlin had pushed her down and stopped her from being hit by the bell.

"Well, perhaps this devil may have some decency in him after all," Pascal muttered.

Tombstone was eyeing Gwynnie with interest and she shifted nervously. She hastened to pick up some empty dishes from the table.

"How did he get away this time?" Pascal asked suddenly.

"I am a thief and he is a soldier," Gwynnie reminded him coolly. She looked away. At the top table, Queen Jane still sat alone. She stared down at her plate, making no conversation with the ladies around her, not even Lady Rutland. Further along the table sat Lady Mary.

"Interesting," Gwynnie whispered.

"What is?" Tombstone looked up from his food, and Gwynnie nodded toward Lady Mary.

With a fixed and pointed expression, Lady Mary was staring at the queen.

"Why is the king still not dining with his wife?" Gwynnie asked, pretending to tidy the table so she could spend longer talking to them.

"He's still closeted with the Duke of Norfolk and Cromwell. I think he even intends to dine with Robert Aske tonight," Tombstone explained.

"Dine with him? Well, I imagine that will be rather like a cat sharing dinner with a mouse."

"The cat at that table will be Cromwell." Tombstone nodded slowly.

"I imagine it is all at Cromwell's suggestion," Pascal added as he stood up. "I shall meet you back at our rooms." He tapped Tombstone on the shoulder and departed.

Gwynnie stole Pascal's seat. When a nearby lawyer glowered at her, she chose to ignore him, turning to face Tombstone, whose eyes were still fixed on Lady Mary.

"What do you make of her?" asked Gwynnie.

"Queen Jane or Lady Mary?" Tombstone shrugged and continued without waiting for an answer. "The queen is demure and mild. She doesn't speak her mind as the last queen did. As for the Lady Mary…" He paused, his eyes narrowing a little. "She has her own opinion. I think she just chooses carefully when to give it." Tombstone pushed away his plate. "I've had enough. Come, let's go to my chamber. We can talk about what happened last night."

Gwynnie stood, wincing a little at the pain in her ear. It had been hurting since the bell had clanged over her head. The ache seemed to radiate through her skull and into her neck, especially when there were loud noises around her.

Not in the mood to argue, she followed Tombstone out of the great hall, rubbing the side of her head. She discarded the gathered flagons and trenchers on a ledge outside, then hurried after her employer, heading toward his rooms. They had been walking for some minutes when she felt Tombstone's eyes on her.

"You're unusually quiet."

"Maybe I'm just not in the mood for talking." She rubbed the side of her head again, adjusting her coif to try and cover her ear. Tombstone eyed her with such interest that she let her hand fall away.

He led the way through a door and into the corridor outside the lawyers' offices and chambers. Gwynnie followed, adjusting her jaw in the hope it would relieve some of the pressure she was feeling in the side of her head.

A woman's voice caught her attention, startling her. Tombstone shoved his cloak into her hands.

"What is this for?"

"So that you have a reason to be here without too many questions."

"Questions from who?" Gwynnie asked, as Tombstone halted very suddenly in the corridor.

Standing outside Pascal's room was a woman.

She was of a similar age to Pascal, perhaps a few years younger, her hair white as snow. Her face was lined, the crow's feet heavy, as if they had been engraved with a chisel, and the blue veins beneath her pale skin made it look as if it was covered in ice.

"Ah, he's still here then." The woman's voice was as cold as her appearance as she released Pascal's arm and walked toward Tombstone. She didn't incline her head in acknowledgement of the bow he gave her, nor did she offer a smile. "When I decided to come and see you today, Neville, I had rather hoped to find he was no longer here."

"Yes, I'm still here." Tombstone matched her cold tone as he stood straight.

"Elric, how you've changed." She looked up at his face, pulling at her cloak in a way that made the quality of the material rather obvious, flashing the silken interior and the embroidered rose edging. "You're looking older. Rather … gaunt."

It wasn't an expression of concern for his health. For the first time, she smiled, as if pleased with her insult.

"My dear, Elric is doing well here." Pascal moved to her side. It was the most placid Gwynnie had ever heard the magistrate. Determined not to just stand there and gawp, she busied herself fluffing the collar of Tombstone's cloak, as if she was there for a purpose.

"Hmm." The lady was not convinced.

"My dear, let us leave Elric to his good work. I shall show you around the palace. You were so eager to see it before the celebrations for Christmas begin, after all."

Gwynnie sneaked a glance at them. From the way the lady took Pascal's outstretched arm, Gwynnie presumed she had to be his wife.

"Yes, show me." Yet her eyes remained on Tombstone. "I still remember what you were like as a boy, Elric. You had the same habit then of finding your way into places where no one wanted you."

Pascal took his wife's arm and steered her away. "Elric, we shall talk later."

Tombstone nodded but said nothing.

As Pascal and his wife disappeared down the corridor, Tombstone released a long breath and marched toward his office. Gwynnie hastened to follow, slipping inside before he could shut the door.

"Is Pascal your father?"

"Gwynnie!" Tombstone rounded on her so fast that he managed to knock an inkwell off his desk. She caught it before it could hit the floor then returned it to the desktop.

"You look alike."

"He is not my father."

"If you were born from another mother, illegitimate, that would at least explain why that woman dislikes you so much."

"I am not having this conversation. Now, sit down."

Gwynnie huffed, though she was in no mood to deny him. She sat down on one of the chairs, and rather than discarding his cloak, she laid it across her lap to keep warm. With her ears still ringing, she leaned back, resting her head on the soft cushion.

"Do your ears hurt?" Tombstone asked.

"Oh, my ears are perfect. I can hear the most beautiful music all the time."

"Gwynnie."

"Yes, they bloody hurt."

She heard a click of wood and opened her eyes to see that Tombstone had pulled out the medicinal box from his buffet cabinet. He retrieved cotton wool, then lit a candle.

"Why didn't you tell me how much this hurt last night, Gwynnie?"

"What does it matter?" she asked tartly. "I'm your shadow, remember? I'm not human. Not flesh and blood at all."

"Well, this certainly looks like blood." He had pulled her coif off her head and was now peering into her ear with the candle close to her face.

"I'm bleeding?" she murmured.

"It's dry." Tombstone wiped the blood away with some dampened cotton wool. "By the looks of things, that bell burst your eardrum last night." He walked around her chair to check the other ear. "This one might be all right. Can you hear well?"

"Most things sound like they're underwater."

"Nothing to do about it, I'm afraid. Most heal within a few weeks or so. Just keep your ear out of water for the time being."

"Water? Why?" She winced as he wiped away the last of the blood from her ear.

"Something my mother said," Tombstone muttered thoughtfully. "Water can carry infections more easily, and your ear right now is effectively an open wound. Keep it dry if you can."

Gwynnie nodded and then regretted it, holding her head as still as she could in the chair.

"Your mother," she began carefully, watching as Tombstone took the chair opposite her and leaned back. "You speak of her, and yet you say so little."

"I tell you what." Tombstone closed his box and blew out the candle. "I'll tell you a secret about my mother, if you tell me a secret in return."

"Well, I would agree, except you already know all of mine."

"Not anymore." Tombstone shook his head. "You have a new secret."

"What?" Her voice grew high. "What secret?"

"You have met Devlin twice, Gwynnie. Neither time have you been able to stop him —"

"Because I'm built like a bear, have multiple strings to my bow and can fire any arrow at will. Yes, that sounds about right."

"We both know you have your ways."

"Not with a killer like him," Gwynnie muttered gravely. "This is different."

"And?" Tombstone tilted his head to the side, watching her closely.

"And what?"

"And he saved you from being struck by that bell." Tombstone nodded slowly in thought. Gwynnie began to shift in her seat. The chair creaked loudly beneath her. "One secret of yours for one of my own." He held up one finger. "Are you developing a soft spot for Devlin the Devil?"

"No." Gwynnie's answer came so fast that he dropped his hand back down onto the arm of the chair. "But —" she knew she wouldn't find out any more about Tombstone's life without offering up something — "I can't deny that he's not what I thought he would be. I thought he'd be a monster to look at, and he's not. He's handsome. I thought he'd be a demon when he spoke, and yet he laughs. He has charm; he even picked up my washing for me when I dropped the trug."

"He offered you a simple kindness and you're willing to forgive all his sins?"

"Never." Gwynnie's voice deepened. "I will not be turned by a handsome face, nor tricked by a nice smile and easy wit. I rang the bell last night. I went to the church to look for him, and I sent up the alarm when I found him. Never think I would risk everything I have for a man who has a nice face."

Tombstone let out a sigh. His relief was palpable as he leaned back in his chair again. "Good, Gwynnie. We don't all have the freedom to love who we want in this world. If I'd seen you'd set your heart on a murderer —"

"I said he had a nice face, not that I was about to run up the aisle with him, thank you." She waved her hand impatiently at him. "Now, it is your turn. I have offered you my secret; it is time to tell your own."

"Very well." Tombstone looked at the medicinal box that still rested in his lap. "Pascal is not my father. He knew my mother, though, and when she died, Pascal became my guardian." He grimaced at the words. "It's not a particularly apt description. I was never acknowledged under his guardianship, not really present in his household at all. When my mother passed, I was just ten years old. My life changed, and though I will not claim Pascal is a perfect man —"

Gwynnie snorted.

"I do know him to be a good one." Tombstone held her gaze. "Now, is that enough sharing secrets for one day, do you think?"

"Yes, I think so."

Tombstone stood. He returned the box to the cabinet as Gwynnie trailed her fingers around her ear, thinking of the dried blood that had been there all night. Was it possible that Devlin had the same wound?

"There's one thing more," she said as Tombstone closed the cabinet.

"Yes?"

"Something Devlin said. He claimed he did not kill Jasper Ashdown. In fact, he claimed he was nowhere near Queen Jane's chamber that day."

"I see." Tombstone folded his arms. "And do you believe him, Gwynnie?"

She looked down in thought. Maybe she did wish to believe that the man who had stopped her from being hurt by that bell wasn't a killer, but to believe it would be a weakness indeed.

"I know people lie. How do you think I have survived my whole life?" Gwynnie replied coolly. "No, I don't believe him."

CHAPTER 14

The yeomen's shouts could be heard in the great hall as they began yet another search. Gwynnie knew Tombstone was with them, instructing where to search. Despite his insistence that they'd leave no stone unturned, she had little confidence that they would find Devlin.

"Someone is helping him," she muttered to herself as she cleared some flagons from the long tables.

Despite the meagre feast, the hall was full. Gwynnie overheard more than one person complain that the fast lasted too long, while others had different things occupying their thoughts.

"Do you think that's who they're searching for?" one young woman said to an older lady. "That devil?"

"Who else would they be looking for?" The lady patted the younger woman's hand. "Do not fear, child. They will find this man. They will not let a murderer run free from the palace."

Gwynnie looked around at the words. She knew more than one murderer had left Greenwich Palace without facing justice. Fitzroy was one; their own king was another.

As Gwynnie turned to leave the great hall, others departed too. Queen Jane led the way, with Lady Rutland and her other ladies behind her.

"I need some time," Jane said as they all moved through the doorway and into the courtyard. "Please, give me a few minutes alone."

"We shall hang back, Your Highness," Lady Rutland assured her dutifully.

Gwynnie followed, casting a quick glance back at the top table where King Henry's chair remained firmly empty. Yet again, he had not joined his wife for dinner.

"No. Do you not understand?" Queen Jane's voice was sharper than Gwynnie had heard it before. She tiptoed her way around the group of ladies, keeping her head bowed. "I do not wish to be watched. I do not need to have you all standing a short distance away from me, staring as you would at a squirrel in a tree. I just need a moment alone, please." She grasped Lady Rutland's hand desperately. "Just a few minutes."

"Well, I..." Lady Rutland looked around. "I suppose we could head to your chambers. Where will you be?"

"The gardens. I will breathe the cool air of this winter and pray it clears my head." Jane adjusted her gable hood, pushing back the long train of blue material as she pulled a white ermine cloak around her shoulders. At once, she took off through the courtyards. At first, her ladies trailed behind her, though they kept their distance.

Gwynnie looked down at the empty flagons in her hands and made a decision. "She should not walk alone," she whispered to herself, remembering what had happened to the last man who was alone in her chamber. If Cromwell's wild insistence was right, and Devlin had gone to harm Queen Jane that day as some sort of twisted religious revenge on the king, then what was to stop him harming her now?

Gwynnie took off at a run. She burst into the kitchens, startling one of the young boys turning the spit in the fire. He dropped it, and the fresh fish he had been cooking fell into the flames, the silver scales blackening in seconds.

"Careful, lad!" old Rudyard snapped at him. The boy mumbled his apologies, picking up the spit as Gwynnie dropped the flagons onto the nearest table.

Samuel looked around from where he was pulling fresh bread out of the stone oven.

"What is it, Gwynnie?"

"Nothing, it's just…" She looked around frantically. "I need to go."

"Gwynnie, wait!"

She didn't wait. She sprinted through the kitchen, heading out of the other door. She ran past storerooms of grain and mead, then stumbled onto the path that led to the tiltyard. As she sprinted through the yard, she slipped more than once on the dewy grass, though fortunately, no one was around to notice. She kept on running until she reached the tower in the tiltyard wall that led to the gardens and orchard.

Catching her breath, Gwynnie leaned against the wall, wishing she had brought a cloak as the icy wind ruffled her hair.

At first, she could see no one. The orchard looked empty, the trees swaying in the wind like skeletal hands reaching up from their graves.

Gwynnie crept forward. To her left, the formal garden stretched out. In the summertime, these lined borders were full of flowers and rich green leaves, but now they were barren patches of land. Most of the bushes had lost their leaves and what greenery did remain was very small and uninviting.

Gwynnie pressed her back against the nearest tree and peered around the trunk.

Apparently, Queen Jane was unaware of the danger she had put herself in. She walked freely with no guard nearby, no weapon at her hip to protect herself should Devlin make an appearance. With her blue gable hood framing her delicate features, her white fur and her elegant, embroidered boots that could just be seen beneath the elaborate skirt, she was not a woman ready for battle.

"What are you doing, Your Highness?" Gwynnie whispered into the cool air.

Queen Jane walked around the nearest bush, reaching out with white-gloved hands and trailing her fingers through the branches. As she turned to walk back through the gardens, Gwynnie caught sight of her expression. The queen's thin lips were pressed together, her face even paler than usual, and her eyes darted from side to side.

The crunch of gravel beneath someone's boot made Gwynnie whip her head around. She searched for a weapon. The rod she had nearly struck Devlin with was tucked so far up her sleeve, it was a struggle to get it back down again. She stepped forward, prepared to use it, until she saw who it was that approached the queen.

"Your Highness?" Lady Mary's voice rang out loudly.

Gwynnie shot back behind the tree before anyone could notice her, breathing heavily. She tucked the rod back up her sleeve, straining to listen to the conversation.

"Your Highness, what are you doing out here?" Mary called again as she marched toward her stepmother, her dark green cloak billowing behind her.

"I live in this palace, do I not? It is my home," Jane said simply. "Am I not permitted to wander in it?"

"Did your ladies-in-waiting not think to warn you of the dangers of walking alone at this time?"

Jane did not answer.

Gwynnie took the opportunity to peer around the tree once again, watching the two women together. She saw straight away that Mary was taller and had a more commanding presence.

"A man was found dead in your room," Lady Mary went on, her deep voice resounding loudly around the garden. "If the killer's intended target was you, do you think it wise for you to give him the opportunity to kill you by walking alone?" Lady Mary tutted. "If you must walk, then I shall accompany you. You must have someone here." With a flick of her head, Lady Mary walked on through the gardens. Jane parted her lips, clearly wanting to argue, but she seemed to think better of it and hastened to catch up with Mary.

The two women walked on with such haste that soon enough, Gwynnie could not hear their conversation. Forced to move from her hiding place, she darted from one tree to the next, being careful only to move when she was certain that neither of the ladies were looking in her direction. With each trunk she pressed her back against, her gown became increasingly damp. The cold seemed to reach into her bones and made her shiver all the more.

"Thank you for coming this Yuletide, Mary." Jane's voice was soft and musical. "I understand that it cannot be an easy thing for you to come here —" She broke off as Mary looked at her, a harsh glint in her eyes. "I understand —"

Mary stiffened. "No one can truly understand another, for we can never know how another's mind works, can we?"

"I suppose not, no. I was offering sympathies. I apologise if I offended you."

"You did not offend me." Yet Mary's voice was sharp. She eyed her stepmother curiously as they turned and walked back through the bare borders. Gwynnie stayed perfectly still, not daring to move, for it would give away her location. "I am curious, though. I have been informed that it was you who persuaded my father to welcome me back to court."

"I do not wish to see a family divided," Jane said gently. "It is right that you should be with your father at Christmas, Mary."

"Hmm." Mary's tone gave little away. She stopped walking just as the wind picked up. Gwynnie wrapped her arms around herself, trying to stay warm as she arched her neck, listening to their words. "As we are trying to *understand* one another, let me ask you something." Mary fixed her eyes on Jane. "Why was Jasper Ashdown in your chamber?"

Jane shifted, her white gloved hands pulling at the ermine fur on her cloak. "That I do not know. I was shocked to find him there."

"Curious." Mary tilted her head to the side. "For I heard your dear friend Lady Rutland say to Lady Monteagle that you knew this man. You knew the Earl of York's son."

"Knew him? Not exactly." Jane spoke fast. "I knew his name. I had seen him in passing at court. If Lady Rutland said I knew him, she was probably speaking of our shock that in his death, none of us could recognise his face as being one that belonged at court."

"That is what she meant, is it?"

"Yes, I'm sure of it." Jane raised her chin. "Unless you would like to insinuate anything about my conduct, Mary?"

"No. I have instead come to offer you a warning, Your Highness. He will be rid of you too. You are aware of this, are you not?"

"Who?"

"Save me from foolishness and naivety," Mary scoffed and turned away, walking on through the garden.

With their backs turned, Gwynnie saw her opportunity. She crept out from behind her tree and moved to another. She narrowly reached her hiding spot, just as Mary turned back to face Jane.

"He was rid of my mother. He was rid of Anne Boleyn in just three years." She waved her hand impatiently. "How long before he is rid of you too?"

"If you seek to warn me, to put me on my guard, then it is not needed," Jane declared, though her voice quivered a little as she did so. "I am nothing like Anne."

"Perhaps not." Mary nodded solemnly. "Yet the truth and lies get muddled in my father's head. You would be wise not to let the tale of a man being in your chamber reach my father's ears. Not if you wish to keep your head."

Silence followed this statement.

"Now, I suggest we return to your chambers, Your Highness," Mary said. "It is right that you should have more to guard you than I." She waved her hand toward the exit of the gardens.

Jane hesitated, then gave a small nod and moved to lead the way out of the gardens. With an imperious flick of her head, Mary followed her.

As the two women vanished through an open gate, Gwynnie sighed and stepped away from the tree. She was now shivering and her fingers had gone numb.

"Does she like her ... or hate her?" she wondered aloud, trying to make sense of Mary's behaviour.

The light had started to fade, the shadows around the garden growing longer. For a moment, Gwynnie thought the shadow behind her was her own, before she realised she was not alone.

"You look cold, flower."

CHAPTER 15

Gwynnie spun around so fast, she nearly lost her balance.

Connal Devlin stood before her. He wore a clean doublet, which Gwynnie assumed must have been provided for him by his accomplice, and his blond hair looked freshly washed. Devlin looked quite smart, despite the obvious rip in his doublet, which may have explained why someone no longer had need of it.

Gwynnie looked around frantically. There was no guard nearby, and Queen Jane and Lady Mary were now out of earshot.

"What are you doing here?" Gwynnie demanded. "Were you watching the queen?"

"Was that the queen?" Devlin frowned. "Which one?"

"What do you mean, *which one?*"

He turned and looked at the gate through which the two women had just left. "I was hiding back there." He pointed at a clump of trees that Gwynnie had not been near. "I was here before they came, and before you started darting between the trees like a mad woman —"

"Oi!"

"Aye, well, was it was the action of a sane woman?"

Before Gwynnie could reply, Devlin took off his cloak and flung it around her shoulders.

"What are you doing?" she asked in surprise.

"It's called a cloak. Keeps the cold off." He waved his hand through the chilly air around them. "Now, are you going to attack me again, or can we have a civilised conversation?"

"I will not stand and talk with a murderer." She backed away from him and cupped her hands around her mouth.

"This again," he sighed.

"Help! Help!" Gwynnie shouted as loudly as she could through her cupped hands. "I've found him — it's De—"

His hand flattened over her hands, muffling her cries.

"Well, flower, I can't say it's not been entertaining to meet you again. Keep the cloak." He turned on his heel and ran.

"What? No!" Gwynnie sprinted after him.

Devlin was a fast runner. He fled the orchard, speeding toward the church and graveyard. He glanced back at Gwynnie, and though she was losing ground, he didn't let up.

As he veered left around the church, she headed to the right, looking out for any sign of a yeoman guard.

"Where the hell did you station them today, Tombstone?" she muttered aloud, dismayed to see there wasn't a single guard by the church. As she dashed around the building, Devlin appeared from the other side and they almost ran headlong into each other. At the last moment, Devlin jumped out of the way.

"You're quicker than I thought!" he shouted as he took off across the graveyard, with Gwynnie in pursuit.

She was no longer afraid of him. He had proved he wouldn't hurt her. It gave her the freedom to chase him without fear.

She darted between the gravestones, trying to cut corners through the undergrowth and shorten the distance between them. Her lungs burned with the effort of trying to keep up with him.

The curtain wall of the palace could be seen in the distance. Gwynnie smiled when she caught sight of the tops of two pikes leaning against the wall. It wouldn't be long before Devlin appeared in their path, and he would be caught.

Devlin leaped over two gravestones, dived to the left and headed straight toward the pikes. Gwynnie saw an opportunity and jumped down a small bank of earth, halving the distance between them.

As she reached him, the pikes appeared before her. She had barely acknowledged the fact that there were no guards at all, only two pikes propped up against the wall, when she reached out for Devlin's arm.

"No!" she cried, grabbing hold of him. As she tried to jerk him backward, the two of them lost their balance and fell down another small embankment. As they tumbled down the cold, hard earth, they became entangled and Gwynnie ended up on top of Devlin.

"Oomph," he huffed, his breath stolen.

Gwynnie stared at him for just a second before she acted. Winded, he seemed in no hurry to move, his arms splayed out on either side of him. Gwynnie reached into her sleeve and pulled out the rod, but she was too slow. Devlin took hold of her wrist, recovering fast, and prised it free of her grip. It was thrown away — she heard the clink of the metal against the stone wall.

"No more, flower, no more," he said in a hoarse whisper, holding his hands up in surrender. "I need to catch my breath if you're to chase me again."

Gwynnie realised she was still on top of him and scrambled off with a growl. She could hear him chuckling, even as she crawled away toward the pikes leaning against the wall. She took hold of one and tried to swing it toward him. It was so long and top-heavy, however, that the blade instantly buried itself in the ground.

"Well, I'm terrified now," Devlin said with a grin from where he still lay on his back. "Hold the staff further up."

She did as he told her, enabling her to lift the blade of the pike higher.

"That's better. Widen your stance too. As you are, I could disarm you in seconds."

Unsure why he was giving her this advice, Gwynnie planted her heels wider.

"Why tell me this?" she hissed at him. Devlin slowly sat up, cracking his back and shoulders. As he stood, Gwynnie shifted her grasp on the pike, making it plain he wasn't going to run from her again.

"Because you can do with the advice." He shrugged and stepped toward her.

Gwynnie backed up, moving to stand in front of the gate in the wall, so he could not escape through it. When she spied the second pike, she knew there had to be guards somewhere nearby. Tombstone would never have left orders for a gate to be unmanned.

"Help! Devlin is here!" she called.

Devlin halted. He folded his arms and cast a glance at the yew trees and stones in the graveyard behind them. They both waited in silence to see who would come, but nothing happened. Devlin raised an eyebrow.

"They won't come," he said eventually.

"Why not?"

"Because of the two guards who were keeping watch here." He pointed at the gate. "One is back at the palace, hanging over his privy — he's been doing it all morning. And as for the other ... well, you're looking at him."

Gwynnie cursed. "You mean that even after the search of the yeomen's barracks and every guard, you are *still* pretending to be one of them?" she asked in disbelief.

"Aye, now they know me as a guard, that's all they see when they look at me." He flashed her a smile. "It was simply a case of hiding from the chief of the guards."

"Why are you here?" Gwynnie stepped forward with the pike.

"Would you really like to know?" Devlin's voice turned sombre. "Or do you just want to run me through with that pike?"

When she didn't answer, he took a cautious step toward her.

"Don't," she warned, pointing the blade of the pike at his face.

"You don't strike me as a woman who causes bloodshed."

"Then you do not know me," she warned.

He moved sharply forward. He took hold of the wood below the blade and tugged it hard. Gwynnie tried to hold onto the other end, but it slipped out of her grasp, pulling her forward so that she stumbled toward him.

Devlin drove the base of the pike into the earth beside him as Gwynnie found her balance.

"Aye, you're right there, flower." He stood straight, smiling once more. "But I know this much. No maid creeps about watching the queen unless she is up to something. And no maid tries to stop a man accused of murdering six people. So, who are you?"

"I will not answer your questions." She stepped back to block the gate, her arms stretched against the stone wall on either side, refusing to let him past. "You will not escape."

"Ah, I see I must explain something more." He picked up the other pike off the wall and drove it into the ground beside the first. "I've had plenty of opportunity to escape. I've stood guard on many gates, and I could have slipped out of any one of them. And yet…" He held his arms out wide. "I'm still here."

"If you have come to harm the king and queen, we will not let it happen."

"We?" Devlin raised his eyebrows. "You say we, but in all the time I've been here, you're the only one to find me." He pointed a finger at her. "You're the only one to even look at me. Most don't look too hard here, do they? Most see what they expect to see." His eyes narrowed a little. "You did not, flower."

Gwynnie inched away from the gate. "You'll be taken to gaol when the guards arrive."

"No one's coming."

"They will come. Someone will have heard me shouting." She looked around, but there was no one in sight. "They'll hang you for the murder of that man."

"Jasper Ashdown?" Devlin leaned against the wall beside the gate, picking up a yeoman's bonnet from where it had been left slung across a hook. Pulling it down over his brow, he said, "Tell me, what did the man look like?"

"Are you in jest? You know what he looks like, you —"

"I have never been in the queen's chambers." Devlin calmly folded his arms across his torn doublet. "This Ashdown … tall man, was he?"

"He was tall."

"Dark hair, beard?" He pointed at his own chin. "A rather measly one?"

Gwynnie blinked. The dark hair on the dead man's chin had indeed been a rather feeble attempt at a beard.

"Well dressed?" Devlin continued.

"Yes."

"Blue doublet?"

"Yes…" Gwynnie stiffened. "And yet you claim you are not his killer?"

"I saw him." Devlin raised the hat a little, looking Gwynnie in the eye. "When I broke into the palace, I saw him. He was walking toward Donsen Tower. He was not alone. There was another beside him, trying to get his attention."

Gwynnie blinked. She didn't know whether to believe him. There was something sincere about Devlin's words, and yet…

"You're a killer. Why should I believe a word you say?"

"Because I didn't kill Ashdown, flower." His voice had softened. "I could tell you more about my life, if you were interested, but you already think me as guilty as every other who has read the ballad sheets, don't you?" He cursed and shook his head. "Well, it was good to meet you again, flower. And as I don't doubt that you're about to run off and find a guard to arrest me, it's time to say goodbye again." He moved toward her.

For some reason, this time, Gwynnie didn't back up. When he reached her, he flicked the collar up on the cloak he'd given her.

"Careful in this cold. You'll catch your death." He adjusted the collar of his own doublet, breathing into the lining. He smiled and turned toward the graveyard. "Oh, one last thing — " he turned back to face her — "your name?"

Her mouth turned dry. Against her better instincts, she found her name falling from her lips.

"Gwynnie."

"Gwynnie," he repeated with another smile. He bowed, another one of those flamboyant bows he'd offered before. "Until next time, then." He vanished into the graveyard.

Gwynnie stared after him. The light between the yew trees was fading, and it would not be long before it was dark.

"God's wounds," Gwynnie muttered, shaking her head as she wrapped the cloak tightly around herself. "What has happened to me?"

CHAPTER 16

"Well?" Gwynnie asked as Tombstone marched in from the cold. He blew on his hands as Gwynnie broke off from her sweeping of the ground floor of Donsen Tower.

"Nothing. They can't find him anywhere." Tombstone cursed loudly and flung himself down on the bottom step of the tower.

"You couldn't find him?" Gwynnie sat down beside him, almost knocking over the candelabra beside them in her haste. The candlelight flickered, casting shadows across the floor.

"No. The guard who was supposed to be at that gate still denies it was Devlin with him. He's convinced it was a man by the name of Laurie. He says that whichever maid claimed to see him there is wrong." Tombstone eyed her carefully.

"Oh yes, because a man could not possibly have made a mistake!" Gwynnie retorted hotly.

"That's not what I meant, Gwynnie."

"Devlin is a soldier. Disguising himself as a guard comes naturally."

"Well, we've still found no sign of him. You're the only one who has seen him."

"I didn't make him up."

"I know you didn't." Tombstone's voice was serious. "My worry is that even if the guards do see him, it will take some heavy persuasion for them to believe it's Devlin and not this Laurie. Especially if this man has as much charm as you claim he has."

"Tombstone," she growled in annoyance, but he held up a hand, showing he wasn't looking to pick a fight.

"Is there anything else that might be useful in finding him?"

"He has an accomplice in the palace, of that much I am certain." Gwynnie suddenly sat up straight on the step. "He had bathed and had clean clothes, but the doublet was torn, here." She laid a hand on her chest. "It was the kind of thing that might be left in the laundry, forgotten about. Someone in the staff could have easily taken it and given it to him."

"Who?"

"I don't know." Once again, Gwynnie thought of Brynne. Other than feeling sad about a fellow Irish person's fate, Brynne had not spoken of Devlin in particular. She could have no reason for wishing to help him. "There is something else. When I was watching Queen Jane and Lady Mary together, the lady said something of interest."

"What?"

"She claimed that Lady Rutland said the queen had been seen in the company of Jasper Ashdown."

Tombstone's grey eyes narrowed. "In what sense?"

"I don't know, but the queen denied it." Gwynnie stood and picked up the broomstick. "She said she may have seen him in passing since he came to court, but she had not recognised him in death. His face was ... altered."

"Death does that to people."

"I know. It's just that..." Gwynnie trailed off and returned to sweeping the floor.

"What is it?" Tombstone asked.

"Their conversation confused me." She halted, the broomstick gripped tightly in both hands. "Regarding her father, Mary asked, 'How long before he is rid of you too?' I couldn't tell if it was a threat, or if she was actually trying to warn the queen."

"From what I hear," said Tombstone, "Lady Mary has little sympathy with others. She holds onto her anger too much, her fury at her and her mother being ousted from the palace."

"Maybe she's not quite the woman you think," Gwynnie murmured. "Is it possible that Lady Mary fears it happening again, do you think? That King Henry will ... kill another wife?"

"Careful," Tombstone hissed and glanced over his shoulder, but they were quite alone. "We can never confirm what we heard about Queen Catherine's fate."

"They say her heart was black," Gwynnie muttered angrily. "Daundelyon said that Queen Catherine's maid saw the king's own physician forcing vials of liquid down her throat when he thought no one was watching. That he murdered Catherine on the king's orders."

"Hearsay." Tombstone stood, his voice firm. "And don't forget, Gwynnie, that the man you are accusing of murder is a king. If either of us told anyone what we knew — or thought we knew — we'd both go to the gallows quicker than Devlin."

"All I'm saying is that we can't let it happen again."

Tombstone held up his hands. "Believe me, Gwynnie, I know. That is why we need to find Devlin, before he does the job for the king."

"He didn't recognise her."

"What?"

"Devlin didn't recognise Queen Jane. He asked which one she was."

"So? Just because he does not know what she looks like, that doesn't mean he was not in her chamber."

"Hmm." Gwynnie nodded. After all, Tombstone could be right. "Is the king yet done with his discussions about the rebels?"

"No." Tombstone sighed heavily. "Not yet."

Gwynnie leaned on the broomstick, thinking of Queen Jane sitting alone at the top table in the great hall. She was still lost in thought when a scream pierced the air.

Tombstone wheeled around and sprinted up the steps of the tower as fast as he could. Gwynnie dropped the broom and went after him. The screaming continued, accompanied now by the sound of doors being opened and footsteps running across the landing above them.

As they reached the top floor, it wasn't difficult to make out the source of all the commotion. The screams came from Queen Jane's chamber.

Two yeomen sprang ahead of Gwynnie and Tombstone, as three ladies-in-waiting scurried forward. Margery Lyster, Elizabeth Tyrwhitt and Mary Zouche were all in their nightshifts, with cloaks thrown haphazardly across their shoulders.

"Open that door," Tombstone ordered as they reached the queen's chamber.

One of the yeomen tried the handle, but it did not move.

"Knock it down!" Tombstone shouted impatiently as the screams from within continued.

The two yeomen threw their shoulders against the door. At first, it didn't budge, but the second time, it gave way under their weight. One of them barrelled through into the queen's chamber as the other stepped back, allowing Tombstone in first, with Gwynnie and the ladies-in-waiting behind him.

"What is this?" a voice cried. "Get out. You cannot be in the queen's rooms." It was Lady Rutland, brushing aside a curtain that divided the queen's bedchamber. "You broke the queen's door!"

"What is happening?" Mary Zouche cried, her voice shaking. "Is there another dead man?"

"Do not be so foolish, child," Lady Rutland snapped at the young woman.

Tombstone moved toward the private bedchamber. The queen was no longer screaming, but they could hear her great heaving cries. Lady Rutland stepped in his way.

"No man may enter the queen's chamber," she warned.

"Then accompany me," Tombstone said impatiently.

"What is happening in there is private," Lady Rutland said firmly, then her eyes landed on Gwynnie. "You." She flicked her fingers urgently at Gwynnie. "You can come. As for you three —" she motioned to the ladies-in-waiting — "pull yourselves together." Lady Rutland turned and strode into the private chamber, brushing aside the curtain to allow Gwynnie to follow.

As Gwynnie stepped in, her stomach knotted. She knew this scent. She had smelled it before in another queen's chamber. She looked toward the bed.

Queen Jane, her fair hair loose around her face, was moaning and clutching her stomach.

"It's gone, isn't it?" she murmured through gasping cries as Lady Rutland knelt down before her. "I've lost the child."

"Your Highness, we do not know —"

Gwynnie moved away from the bed. She acted on instinct, remembering everything she had done the last time. Queen Jane was not so far along as Queen Anne had been when she had lost her child, but the blood was all too familiar.

Gwynnie reached for a buffet cabinet, pulling out spare sheets. She tossed them onto the bottom of the bed to mop up the blood, then pulled out a chamber pot from underneath the bed and handed it to Lady Rutland.

"She will need it," Gwynnie whispered. "I've seen it before. She will also need a physician."

"He will need to be discreet," Lady Rutland said sharply. "I know of none in these walls who would not tell the king."

Gwynnie nodded. She didn't question why the king didn't know about his wife's state, but she knew how bad it would be were he to discover that Jane had lost their unborn child. The last woman to lose his son before he could be born had found her head on the chopping block.

"There is someone," Gwynnie murmured as Jane fell back down on the bed, crying heavily and clutching her stomach. "Someone with medical training, though he is no physician. He is a good man. If you wish for secrecy, he will give you that."

"Who?" Lady Rutland urged. "Tell me."

"He is the man you just forbade to come in here. The lawyer, Tombstone."

Lady Rutland glowered. "You expect me to allow a lawyer to look at the queen?"

"You asked for a discreet man with medical training, and I have offered him to you." Gwynnie glanced back at the bed. The poor woman had curled up into a ball. Great gasping cries wracked her body.

Lady Rutland rested a comforting hand on Jane's back.

"It's gone," Jane wailed. "It's gone!"

"Your Highness —"

"Stop calling me that!" she screamed.

"Ask him," Gwynnie whispered to Lady Rutland. When she shook her head yet again, Gwynnie hissed, "Queen Anne's lasted more than a day."

"What?" Lady Rutland's top lip trembled. "You are certain?"

"I was there," Gwynnie replied. "She passed the child, but she was unwell for some time. Unless you want to lose our new queen, I suggest you get Tombstone in here now. He can be trusted, believe me."

Gwynnie turned away. She found a fresh bowl of water on a table nearby and moved it closer to the bed, hoping to try and clean the queen up a little.

Lady Rutland breathed heavily. She must have resolved the argument in her own mind, for the next moment, she marched back toward the curtain and swept it aside.

"You." She pointed at Tombstone. "Your maid says you have medical training."

"I do," Tombstone replied.

"And you will not speak of what you are about to see?"

"You have my word." His voice was firm.

Lady Rutland pulled the curtain back, allowing him to enter the chamber.

Tombstone stepped in. His eyes met Gwynnie's, before they flicked down to the blood on her hands.

"How far along was she?" Tombstone asked Lady Rutland quietly.

Lady Rutland took his cloak as he shrugged it off. "Maybe two months ... nearly three." She gulped as Tombstone stepped toward the bed.

Jane gave no sign of acknowledging his presence. She cried out in pain as Gwynnie tried to mop her brow with a cloth.

"Can you help her?" Lady Rutland whispered behind Tombstone.

"I can make her more comfortable. I cannot bring the child back, though."

Queen Jane's cries became even more piercing.

CHAPTER 17

Gwynnie didn't dare sit down in one of Queen Jane's fine chairs. Instead, she slumped against the windowsill, breathing heavily as Mary Zouche brought forward a tray of drinks. She passed small chalices of port and claret to Tombstone and Lady Rutland but hesitated before handing Gwynnie one.

"Is there a reason you do not think a maid worthy of a drink after what she has just done for your queen?" Tombstone asked coolly. The lady, who was now dressed in a formal gown, glanced at Lady Rutland.

"By this light, give her a drink," Lady Rutland said crossly. "Without them, I do not know what we would have done this night." She was sitting in a chair opposite Tombstone, the once-white apron she had thrown over her fine gown now stained with dried blood. She rested her forehead in the palm of her hand as she nursed the glass on her lap.

Gwynnie looked uneasily at Tombstone. They both knew he had stretched what medical knowledge he had to make the queen comfortable. It had taken hours to calm her. Now the sun had risen, she was sleeping peacefully. She had eventually allowed Gwynnie and Lady Rutland to clean her up and settle her in fresh sheets. She'd drunk spiced caudle and soothing tonics, after she had passed what was unmistakably her lost child.

The three of them fell into silence as they waited for Mary Zouche to leave. Only when her footsteps could be heard on a distant set of steps did Lady Rutland lift her head and speak again.

"No one can know of this," she said, looking between Gwynnie and Tombstone. "I beg of you, please do not say a word to anyone."

"If the king knew his queen was in pain, he may come to her—" Tombstone began.

"And what happened to the last queen who lost his child?" Gwynnie asked, cutting him off.

Tombstone shook his head. "I never want to see that again," he whispered, his face pale.

"I imagine you have to report to Cromwell in your duties, sirrah." Lady Rutland sat tall. "Are you prepared to keep this secret from him, too?"

"I am." Tombstone spoke without hesitation. "I am a man used to keeping secrets, my lady. My office demands it."

Gwynnie drank from her glass. She knew how many secrets he kept close to his chest. She rather suspected that Cromwell barely knew him at all.

"If it will keep the queen safe, then rest assured he will not hear of what passed here from me." Tombstone placed the glass down on the arm of his chair. "I take it that the king did not know his wife was with child?"

"No." Lady Rutland shook her head sharply, tears in her eyes. "He has not seen the queen in days. He thinks only of the rebellion and his treaties."

Gwynnie huffed under her breath. Both Tombstone and Lady Rutland glanced at her.

"And you will keep this secret too?" Lady Rutland asked, though she spoke more lightly. Clearly, she was already prepared for Gwynnie's assent.

"You have no need to doubt it," Gwynnie assured her. "I'll take the secret to my grave."

"Then I thank you both." Lady Rutland sat taller, perhaps trying to regain some composure. "The queen would thank you herself, were she able to do so."

"Do not think on that." Tombstone finished his glass. "What did the queen do yesterday?"

"What do you mean?"

"I mean that some miscarriages have no causes. Others ... have definite causes. What are your thoughts?" Tombstone gestured to her with his glass. "You are always at the queen's side, my lady."

"When she came back to her chambers yesterday evening, there was a gift of sweetmeats here. We assumed they had come from the king, an apology for his long absence." She stared into space. "What if it was not the case after all?"

"What are you supposing, my lady?"

"I'm supposing..." Lady Rutland stood from her chair. "But, no, surely not." She dismissed the idea with a shake of her head. "When I was young, I was told there were ways to be rid of a child. I heard rumours, of yew berries and other toxic plants." She pointed at an empty rosewater bowl that had been placed on the mantelpiece nearby. "The queen described the sweetmeats as tasting fruity. Do you think it possible that they were tampered with? That someone could have *forced* the death of this child?"

Gwynnie moved toward the bowl and took it down, sniffing its contents, though she could discern nothing but the heavy sweetness of sugar and fruit.

"There are ways to do such a thing, but it is highly dangerous," Tombstone murmured. "Sometimes, they kill the mother as well as the child." He too stood from his seat. "But who would do such a thing?"

Lady Rutland's voice trembled as a tear ran down her cheek. "Is it not what they said? That Devlin the Devil spoke of vengeance on the king and his family? Perhaps he saw this as his opportunity. He saw a way to be rid of both the king's wife *and* his heir, but for the grace of God … she has survived." She bent her head in prayer.

"You cannot believe such an accusation, surely?" Gwynnie said as she followed Tombstone down the steps of Donsen Tower.

"Lady Rutland and Queen Jane were the only ones to see these sweetmeats. We do not even know who delivered them. You can't be certain that it wasn't Devlin or his accomplice." Tombstone waved a hand in the air as he hurried on.

Gwynnie gripped the banister as she sprinted to keep up with him. As he reached the bottom step, she darted in front of him, cutting off his path. "Your blind insistence on following Cromwell's speculation has become absurd. Lady Rutland claims that only they knew of the pregnancy. The king did not know. So, if it was not known at court, how on earth would a man like Devlin know?"

"*You* knew, Gwynnie." Tombstone thrust a finger toward her. "You knew when apparently no one else did. If one person can notice it, why cannot another?"

"How about the fact that he didn't even know who the queen was? When he saw her with Lady Mary, he asked which one she was."

"And did you tell him?"

"No!"

"Shh." Tombstone urged as a guard looked curiously at them from the doorway. "Come, we need to get cleaned up before the whole court rises and sees us covered in blood."

Gwynnie followed him out into the courtyard, but rather than heading to the lawyers' rooms, she persuaded him to follow her to the laundry room instead.

"This is closer," she assured him. "There's also something I have to check." They left the icy courtyards and entered the brick building, both shuddering at the cold.

"Christ, it's as cold in here as it is outside."

"Do you imagine they keep a maids' room warm?" she scoffed, moving toward trugs of fresh water that had been brought in the night before. She plunged her hands into the nearest one, splashing her face and arms as Tombstone did the same in another.

"It can't have been him," Gwynnie said as she took off her bloodstained apron and threw it into a basket full of dirtied clothes.

"Just because you were charmed by his manner —"

"It isn't that."

"Really? Are you certain?" Tombstone asked. "Because logic still says it could have been him. What other man has a motive for harming the queen, other than the very man who threatened just days ago to take vengeance on the king and has been seen in the palace walls by *you*?"

"I didn't want you to calmly make very good points."

"What did you want?"

"I wanted you to believe me," Gwynnie mumbled. As Tombstone arched his eyebrows at her, she threw her hands in the air. "I know it sounds mad, but I do not believe he did it."

"Then I suggest you were turned much more by his handsome face than you claim you were."

"I was not!" She marched across to a cupboard. "The queen would not be the first lady to lose a child without cause or reason. It happens to many. It's tragic, awful, but it does not mean that what she ate last night was poisonous. Besides, has she not recovered rather well if she was poisoned with something like yew berries?"

"I do not believe it was yew berries." Tombstone shook his head. "My mother used those once in medicine. The effects were … horrific." He grimaced. "They were not the cause of what happened last night."

"Then you admit it could have been natural?"

"It could have been," he admitted, plunging his head into the cold water. When he blew bubbles at the shock of cold, Gwynnie couldn't help but laugh. He pulled his head back out, shuddering.

"Pleasant, was it?" she asked as he glared at her.

"What did you want to check in here?"

"This." She turned back to the cupboard, flinging the doors wide so she could peer inside. "Here is where we keep the clothes that have been unclaimed. The courtiers are usually happy to throw out a doublet or gown if it's ripped. The seamstress sometimes offers to mend them." Gwynnie pulled out a basket, dropped it to the floor, and searched through. There were torn coifs, spare shifts, and even a fine kirtle that had a nasty pull in the thread, but there wasn't a single man's item.

"Why are you looking in there?"

"I think that whoever is helping Devlin is supplying him with clothes from here." She pointed at the basket. "Which means it has to be a member of staff. Who else would know about this store of clothes? Who else could get into the kitchen to get him food?"

"Who, Gwynnie?"

"I don't know." Gwynnie sighed. She'd put it off long enough. She had to speak to Brynne.

Tombstone stepped back from the trug and sat down heavily on a bench, his head in his hands. Gwynnie looked up at the sudden display of emotion. "Are you all right?"

"Fine," he muttered, unconvincingly.

"Yes, I know what you mean. An ideal way to spend a night, wasn't it?" Her sarcasm made him peer up at her. There was pain in his expression.

"Will you ever forget what you saw?"

Her energy vanished as she closed her eyes. "Never." Opening her eyes, she moved toward the bench and sat down beside him.

He nudged her shoulder softly. "We carry our wounds with us, Gwynnie. As my mother used to say, some wounds are not so easy to forget."

"A wise woman, your mother."

"She was."

"I don't doubt she would be impressed with you today."

"Impressed?"

"What you did for the queen." Gwynnie nudged him back. "It was a kindness. You didn't have to help her, but you did. Well done for that."

Tombstone smiled. "Thank you." He bent his head forward. "Little comfort it gives me, though. If that man, if that Devil —"

"Devlin." When Gwynnie corrected him, his smile vanished.

"If he is behind the queen's pain, then we are to blame for not having captured him sooner."

Gwynnie swallowed uncomfortably then nodded. She couldn't argue with that.

"We need to find him." Tombstone stood up.

"We've been saying that every day since he arrived. What more are we supposed to do?"

Tombstone halted beside the bowls of water, staring into them.

"Where would you hide now?" he asked. "If it was you, Gwynnie, where would you hide?"

"In plain sight. If he's as clever as I think he is, he will have put on a new disguise by now."

"And where would you sleep?" Tombstone asked. "Where would you go at night to make sure no one could find you?"

Gwynnie sat forward. An idea had formed that she couldn't dismiss. "I'd go somewhere you have already looked."

CHAPTER 18

Gwynnie blew on her hands to warm them up. She'd once had a pair of gloves, but they were now threadbare after long hours of work.

She looked out from the bell tower, peering toward the opposite end of the palace estate and the yeomen's building. Tombstone was keeping guard in the weapons room, watching to see if Devlin would return to the store cupboard he had made his chamber, whilst Gwynnie kept watch from the church.

"Come on," she whispered, searching the moonlit grounds for any sign of a moving shadow. It made sense to her, to hide in a place that had already been searched, believing no one would look there again.

The moon rose higher in the sky, and yet no one moved in the grounds.

Gwynnie leaned against the wall of the tower and stared up at the bell high above her head. She rubbed her sore ear, thinking of the pain she had suffered the last time she had been here. The sound had radiated through her skull as Devlin had pushed her down to the boards, out of harm's way.

"Why did you do that?" she murmured aloud.

Something creaked deep within the belly of the church.

Gwynnie leaned forward, straining her ears. For a minute, there was only silence. She was beginning to believe it had been her imagination when there was another sound. This time it was a low thud, the sound of a door being pressed back into its frame.

Grabbing hold of the tower wall, she leaned out as far as she could, trying to peer down into the church grounds to see who had caused the noise, but all was still.

Then another creak came, this time from inside the church, far beneath where she stood.

Gwynnie slowly inched toward the spiral staircase, her hand outstretched in the darkness. Someone was inside the church. They were moving things around. It sounded rather like pews being pushed together, then something being dropped. Someone cursed and must have picked the thing back up again, returning it to its place with a dull thud.

She edged her way down the steps, trying not to make a sound. At the bottom, Gwynnie stood by the closed door and pressed her good ear to the wood, listening intently to the sounds within.

She couldn't tell who it was. It could have been the priest, though she doubted he would come into the church at this time of night. It seemed more likely that it was either Devlin, collecting another parcel from his accomplice, or it was that accomplice, hiding the food they had taken from the kitchen stores.

Reaching for the latch, Gwynnie lifted it just enough to push the door open a crack and peer into the apse of the church.

In a scene similar to a few nights before, she saw a hooded figure moving around the church. Only this time, he seemed more anxious than before, marching up and down, unable to settle. As he lifted a flagon to his lips and took a heavy gulp, the hood of the cloak slipped back far enough to reveal his face.

"Devlin," Gwynnie mumbled. It was small comfort to be proven right when she saw how restless he was. He marched back down the main aisle, looking repeatedly at the doors, as if he expected someone to arrive at any moment.

Gwynnie held her place, hoping that if he was indeed expecting his accomplice to appear, then it would only be a matter of time before she knew their identity.

Yet the main door remained firmly closed. Devlin cursed and turned away again, marching all the way to the altar where he abruptly dropped to his knees. He disappeared from view, masked by the pews, forcing Gwynnie to move back a step on the staircase so she could glimpse the top of his head.

Devlin started to mutter. Some words caught her ears; others were whispered too quietly for her to hear.

"God —" he had to be praying — "help me now. Help us both…" He raised his hand to cross himself in the Catholic fashion and Gwynnie stiffened at the sight. "Get me out of here," he continued, then he bent his head forward in supplication.

Gwynnie stepped down, moving toward the door. There was something strange in the prayer. Why would a murderer who had come to harm the king pray to God to get him out of this place?

She pushed the door open a couple of inches, reaching for the weapon that Tombstone had insisted on giving to her. Tucked in her belt was a small dagger. She gripped the handle tight and held it behind her back, preparing to use it if necessary.

Gradually, she crept down the side aisle of the church, being careful to keep Devlin in view at all times. He was still on his knees in front of the altar. As she drew level with the side of the altar, she paused, the dagger poised behind her back.

"Flower, you really need to work on creeping up on me."

Gwynnie froze. "How did you…?" she began.

He raised a hand and pointed at the large gold altar plate on the table. Propped on its side, what little moonlight had bled through the stained-glass windows had fallen on the shiny surface, creating a distorted reflection of the church.

Gwynnie moved, watching as her reflection shifted from side to side.

"Let me guess." Devlin stood up and turned to face her. "That friend of yours is waiting somewhere in this church?"

"Friend?"

"The lawyer that seems to follow at your heel like a pup." He raised his eyebrows questioningly.

"Wait … you've seen us? You've been watching?"

"I may have glimpsed you once or twice."

"And you think he follows at my heels?" She couldn't help but laugh at the idea. The grip on her dagger loosened a little, until Devlin stepped forward. "He's here," she said in a low voice.

"Where?" Devlin swept his arms out wide. "Show him to me. Call him. He can arrest me. That is why you're here, is it not? To arrest me at last?"

"He's here," Gwynnie lied, though she knew it would be fruitless to shout for Tombstone. He was far away in the yeoman's quarters, watching the store cupboard in case Devlin returned there.

"Then call him." Devlin took another step toward her. "Or has he just left you with a better weapon this time?"

Gwynnie adjusted her hold on the dagger.

"Flower, if you were going to hurt me, we both know you would have done it by now."

"You're a murderer."

"Am I?" He cocked his head to the side. "Then you should have no qualms about killing a killer, should you?"

155

Gwynnie fell silent. If she advanced toward him now, he would surely be able to stop her. He was a trained soldier, and she nothing more than a thief who had been handed a dagger.

Yet she had no choice. If she did not try, she would be letting him walk free through the palace, where he might hurt someone.

She took a step forward. He acted immediately, reaching out and grabbing her arm. He spun her around so fast that she yelped in surprise, before he tore the blade from her grasp and threw it away. It clattered against the altar pieces, knocking the plate and a candlestick over so that they clanged noisily. He released her just as quickly, and she staggered away, colliding with one of the pews.

"Now, can I finish my prayers before you try to kill me again, Gwynnie?"

She faltered, for it was odd to hear him using her Christian name. "I wasn't trying to kill you —"

He was already turning away, though, sinking down in front of the altar again on one knee. He bent his head forward, speaking so quietly that she only caught the very end of his prayer.

"...and protect this woman," he whispered. "We both know she is no maid, aye, she's something more. And being something more within these walls cannot be safe."

"I don't need your prayers!" she exclaimed suddenly.

Devlin glanced over his shoulder at her. "Oh, and God, can I at least win one argument between us?"

"I can answer that prayer for you." Gwynnie huffed and glanced toward the doors behind her. She and Tombstone had made a deal. If either one of them saw Devlin in the night, they were to send up a signal, but if Gwynnie went to ring the church bell again, she knew everything could go as wrong as it had done before.

Devlin stood up before she had time to debate her next action. He turned to face her, folding his arms across the ripped doublet that must have been stolen from the laundry.

"Did you do it?" The question fell from her lips on instinct.

"Do what?"

"Queen Jane…"

"I was nowhere near the queen's chamber when that man was killed," he said plainly. "I told you that before. Have you lost your hearing?"

"Mostly, thanks to you." She motioned to the roof and the bell.

"That wasn't my doing."

"It wasn't mine."

"I beg to differ."

"Did you hurt the queen and her…?" Gwynnie trailed off before she could mention the unborn child whose life had now been lost.

"Jesu, what in God's name are you talking about? Is the queen unwell?"

"Should a devout Catholic man like you be swearing in here?" She gestured toward the altar behind him.

Devlin took a deep breath. "What is it I am supposed to have done now?"

"On top of being a murderer seven times over?" she hissed.

"You may remember something, flower." He stepped toward her. "I never confessed to such a thing, did I?"

"That is what a guilty man would say."

"And an innocent one."

Gwynnie took a step back, eyeing where the dagger had fallen. It would be impossible to reach it without him

157

intercepting her. If she was going to summon help, then she had to either send a signal to Tombstone or the nearest guards. She inched away a little, glancing at the doors. Devlin's eyes narrowed and he cocked his head.

"Not impossible, flower."

"Stop calling me that!"

"Very well. Then I bid you good day." He bowed to her. "Maybe this will be the last time I say goodbye to you."

"What?" She watched him walk away, heading toward the vestry door. "Where are you going?"

"You're clever enough for me not to tell you." He began to run, heading for the door.

Gwynnie looked between him and the dagger. She bolted forward, snatched it up, then hurried after him.

By the time she emerged from the church, Devlin had crossed the graveyard, heading in the direction of the outer curtain wall. The wind had picked up. A storm was brewing, the rain lashing against Gwynnie's skin. She grabbed her skirt, tucked it into her belt, and ran after him, gripping the dagger tightly in her hand.

"Devlin!" she barked when she saw him disappear behind a yew tree. "You can't hide in the palace indefinitely. You know that."

He didn't answer her, but there was a snap of twigs uncomfortably close. Gwynnie whipped around, seeing that there was in fact another shadow moving between the nearby trees. At first, she thought she was mistaken — the wind was buffeting the tree branches so much that it could have been an illusion, yet the figure was abnormally still compared to the swaying branches around them. She stumbled toward them, mistaking the figure for Devlin, but then she saw that it was in fact a woman. The figure was wearing a long cloak and gown.

They froze, staring back at Gwynnie, their face impossible to discern in the darkness. Gwynnie stepped forward and the woman scurried back, like a frightened cat, then turned and bolted into the darkness.

"Who's that then, do you reckon?" Devlin's voice sounded much closer to Gwynnie's ear than she was prepared for.

She raised the dagger high in the air as she found Devlin standing behind her. He tore the dagger from her grip in one swift movement. Yet again, he tossed it away, the blade burying itself into the trunk of a nearby tree.

Suddenly an ominous crack pierced the air as a branch overhead snapped.

"No!" Devlin barked and Gwynnie was pulled off her feet as he dragged her out of the way. The heavy branch came down swiftly, the impact scattering leaves and twigs as it landed exactly where Gwynnie had been standing.

CHAPTER 19

Breathing heavily, Gwynnie became aware that Devlin's hand was still on her arm. He was on his knees, holding onto her, his breathing as loud as her own.

"You…" she whispered.

"Are you all right?" he murmured in her ear, his grip on her arm slackening.

She jerked her head upward to look at him. His brow was furrowed.

"What kind of murderer are you that you would save a life?" The words spilled out of her in a rush. "You're supposed to be a devil."

He released her and sat back, still trying to catch his breath. The moonlight shone on his face as he leaned against one of the tall gravestones, marred with lichen and age.

"I'd ask is it because I am a woman, but the queen —"

"I have never raised a hand to hurt any woman," Devlin declared with sudden vigour. "I spoke the truth. I have not been in the queen's chamber. I am not the man who left that dead body in there, and if the queen has been hurt now, then I give you my word that I am not the one who caused that pain."

"You're supposing your word is worth something."

"Is it worth nothing?" He nodded at the fallen branch as others above them quaked in the storm.

Gwynnie's mouth turned dry as she stared at the twigs. She could have been crushed, but Devlin had saved her.

"Maybe it is worth something," she said, a little reluctantly. He chuckled, and Gwynnie fought back a smile, planting her palms on the damp ground as the shock of how close she had come to death washed over her.

"I'm a soldier, Gwynnie. I'm no murderer." Devlin leaned his head back on the stone, his laughter leaving him. "I didn't kill that man in the queen's chamber, just as I didn't kill any of the soldiers in my barracks that day."

Gwynnie's stomach knotted tight as she whipped her head around to face him fully.

"You didn't?" she whispered.

"I didn't." He levelled his gaze at her. "I was there. I won't deny I was in the barracks when it happened. But I didn't do it."

"Then what did happen?"

Devlin looked away.

"You deny the accusation, but the moment I ask what happened, you fall silent? I thought you were quite fond of talking."

"You barely know me."

"And yet each time I've met you, you've refused to stay quiet." Her words made him smile briefly.

"Aye, a grand opinion you have of me. Would you believe me if I did tell you what happened?" he asked slowly.

Gwynnie swallowed but didn't answer.

"Exactly." He stood up, slipping a little on the wet ground. "So what would be the point in telling you anything, flower? I'm Devlin the Devil, aren't I? And you'd believe what's written on a ballad sheet over the man who saved your life, wouldn't you?" He raised his voice to be heard over the wind and rain.

Gwynnie hurried to stand as Devlin turned and walked away, heading toward the curtain wall. She raced to catch up, her damp hair now sticking to her head beneath her coif.

"Tell me then," she urged.

"What?"

"Tell me what really happened that day."

"You won't believe me." He stared ahead as he wound his way through the gravestones and trees.

"How do you know unless you try?" she insisted, pulling on his arm. "I know the ballad sheets do not always speak the truth. I know they lie." How many times had she seen the Shadow Cutpurses' names in the ballads, and how often had they portrayed Emlyn and herself as something they were not? The ballad sheets even thought they were men. "Explain what happened."

They stepped out of the treeline and moved down a bank toward the curtain wall. Gwynnie baulked when she saw that the gate was once more unmanned except for two lonely pikes against the wall.

"Are you acting as guard tonight?"

"I am." Devlin pulled out a stool and sat down on it, hiding under the eaves of the wall to shelter from the rain. The stool beside him bore dice from some sort of game that had been etched into the wood.

"Where's your friend?" She gestured toward the second pike, also standing under the eaves. "In the privy again?"

"Visiting the maid he spends his nights with." Devlin shrugged. "He gets what he wants, and I get to sit here alone. It is a good deal for us both." He folded his arms and leaned back against the wall, apparently signalling an end to their conversation.

Gwynnie swept the dice off the stool and dragged it forward, sitting herself down heavily in front of him. Devlin watched her every move.

"Well?" she urged.

"Well what?"

"I would not choose to sit out here for my own amusement. What happened that day in the barracks?"

Devlin grimaced and looked away. He reached into the neckline of his doublet and pulled out a thin set of rosary beads. They were not half so ornate as those Gwynnie had seen hidden around the palace by fine ladies who tucked them up their sleeves. She recognised the cross she had seen hidden in the cupboard that Devlin had made his bed.

"You were there," she prompted. "You saw it happen. Why were you in the barracks that day?"

"For these." He held up the rosary. "I was being disciplined for holding onto them. When I came to this country, all the battalions wanted Irish soldiers. I suppose tales of barbarians made them think I'd be vicious in a fight. They didn't think about the fact that it meant I was a Catholic, a man of the old religion." He spoke with resentment as he wrapped the rosary around his hands and bent his head forward, the raindrops running down his face.

There was something vulnerable about his manner. Gwynnie found it hard to believe that the man before her was the same one she had seen depicted with horns and a tail.

"I was reprimanded for holding onto these. They demanded I get rid of them, on pain of being ousted from my battalion."

"And?" Gwynnie urged.

"And I refused." He wrapped the rosary tighter around his palm. "Cassian Wightwick, my captain, was a good friend. He kept trying to persuade me to give them up. He warned me that the army might not just exile me, but could arrest me and maybe hang me for it." Devlin's breath hitched. "Cassian was one of the men killed that day."

Gwynnie stared at him. Either Devlin was an excellent actor, or he was truly hurt by this man's death, for he blinked rapidly, quelling tears.

"Who killed him, Devlin?"

"My name is Connal." He sat up straight. He stuffed the rosary beads back beneath the neckline of his doublet and looked straight at her. "Don't call me Devlin anymore."

"Why not?"

"Because I don't like it, flower."

"And I don't like being called flower," Gwynnie reminded him, her eyebrows raised. He smiled, though it vanished in an instant. "Who killed him, Connal?"

He swallowed uneasily, then shook his head. "You wouldn't believe me." He sat forward. "You work here, in the palace. All you know is what you read in the ballad sheets and what you hear whispered by the gossipers. That is your world," he hissed. "And it's a blind world."

"You think me blind?"

"I know it."

"Then you don't know me," she said. "Let my lawyer friend speak to you. He is a good man. If you have a tale to tell, he will hear you out."

"Why do you trust this lawyer?" He leaned forward. "How can you trust a man who is at the beck and call of a man like Cromwell?"

"Because once, a while ago now … Tombstone listened to my tale. He believed me. He is the reason why they didn't hang me when many wanted to."

Slowly, Devlin reached toward her. She wasn't sure what he was going to do, but held herself completely still. His fingers brushed her chin, ever so gently. She could not remember feeling such a soft touch before.

"Why would they hang you, flower?" His voice was so low, she nearly missed it.

"Because they thought I had killed man." She held his gaze. "You want to be heard? You wish to be believed? Then talk to my friend."

His hand fell away. Oddly, she missed his touch.

"Find your friend, Gwynnie." He folded his arms. Despite his words, something in his manner had stiffened.

"You mean it?"

"Find him."

Gwynnie stood and walked a few steps, before turning to look back at him. "You'll trust me? You'll meet him?" she asked.

"Find him," he urged her again.

Gwynnie smiled. At last, perhaps they were going to get some answers. If Devlin could reveal the truth about the murders, then maybe they could work out what was really happening within the walls of the palace.

As she scrambled up the bank, she took off at a run, sprinting through the palace grounds. She cut across the orchard and formal garden, then headed through the tiltyard, where Ricard was half asleep at his post under the tower. He jumped when he saw her.

"Careful, Gwynnie!"

"No time!" she shouted back.

As she reached the yeomen's barracks, she didn't slow down. Up the spiral staircase, she found Tombstone, slipping more than once on the steps in the darkness.

"Tombstone? Tombstone!"

"Shh," Tombstone hissed. "Are you trying to bring every yeoman in this building running?" He stood beside a discarded suit of armour.

"I found Devlin. He's here. He's guarding the outer wall on the other side of the church."

"Wait, you talked to him? Again?" He clambered over the discarded armour and broken weapons. The metal clattered and rang loudly as he stumbled toward her. "Where's that dagger I gave you? Why didn't you use it?"

"When you see the size of him and the size of me, you might understand why that's rather difficult. He's a trained soldier. He took it out of my hands. Come, he wants to speak to you." She dragged Tombstone toward the stairs.

Within moments, they were back in the palace grounds. "What did he say?" Tombstone asked as they cut through the orchard.

"That he's an innocent man. He didn't kill the man in the queen's chambers."

"And why do you believe him?"

"Because he said he didn't kill those soldiers either. There was another to blame. He talked about a friend." Gwynnie spoke quickly as she ran, breathing heavily. "A captain in the army, Captain Cassian Wightwick. Tombstone, he's grieving his friend."

"You think men don't kill their friends?"

"Would you just listen?" She grabbed his arm and steered him across the graveyard as they reached the church. "He saved my life again. He pulled me out from beneath a branch."

"What branch?"

"A falling branch."

"You're barely making sense, Gwynnie."

"I know!" She stumbled down the bank. "It's just that something's amiss, Tombstone. That man has saved me twice now. Why would he do that if he was a cold-blooded killer? I am the only one in the palace who can point him out. A sharper devil would have killed me by now, or let the branch or the bell do it for him. Not Devlin."

"Damn it, Gwynnie. You like the man."

"So what if I do?"

"Liking him is dangerous." Tombstone caught her arm and pulled her to a stop. "A judge found him guilty and sent him to the gallows, Gwynnie. Do not give your heart to a man like that."

"I'm not offering my heart up on a platter. I'm telling you that something is wrong here." She released herself from Tombstone's grip, yet as her eyes swivelled toward the curtain wall, she found it empty. The two pikes were leaning against the stone wall, the dice returned to the stool. The only signs that she and Devlin had been there at all were a few muddy footprints in the ground. Devlin had gone.

Gwynnie turned on the spot, frowning deeply. "Tombstone, he was here. Trust me, he was here. I talked to him."

"Are you inventing this man?" Tombstone muttered, planting his hands on his hips and shaking his head.

Gwynnie scrambled back up the bank again. "Come, look at this." She hastened through the gravestones, rushing to the spot where the branch had fallen. As she reached it, she glanced at the trees, remembering the figure of the woman she had seen. It now seemed such a strange memory. She half wondered if she had imagined it.

"Look," she called as Tombstone followed her, pointing at the branch. "Devlin saved me from that. What kind of murderer would do that?"

She expected another tart reply, but Tombstone was silent. He stared at the large branch, clearly thinking as Gwynnie had done before that she might have been crushed.

"Well?" she prompted impatiently.

Tombstone crouched down, looking at the branch. "You chased him out here, then he stopped and pulled you back from this?"

"Yes," Gwynnie replied.

Tombstone stood again. "Why would he bother?" he murmured.

"That's what I've been trying to ask you!"

Tombstone scratched his jaw, deep in thought.

"What do you know about his crime?" Gwynnie asked. "What exactly happened to those six men he supposedly killed?"

"Let's check my paperwork." Tombstone lifted his head. "Come, let's get out of this cold rain. You're shivering."

Gwynnie realised that she was still wearing the cloak that Devlin had given her and pulled it tighter around herself.

"Here it is." Tombstone stepped forward from his desk, clutching some papers in his hand. "And drink that up — it will warm you quicker than the fire."

Gwynnie sat beside the fire, still shivering a little as she nursed a cup of hot water. In the cup some herbs were steeping, which Tombstone had collected from his medicine box. Gwynnie was hardly in the mood to question what they were. She just trusted his knowledge and sipped the water.

Tombstone sat down in the chair opposite her, bending close to the fire to better read the papers.

"That doesn't look like a ballad sheet," she murmured, pointing at the top paper.

"It isn't. It's a report from the constable who investigated the killings at the barracks. I asked for a copy of it." He flattened the paper and read aloud. *"The soldier, Connal Devlin, was called to the office of the lieutenant and major of his corps to be disciplined. His Captain, Cassian Wightwick, was also present —"*

"That's the name he told to me," Gwynnie cut in. "Devlin said he was being disciplined for holding onto his rosary. Cassian Wightwick was trying to persuade him to give it up."

"It seems the lieutenant and major had other ideas," Tombstone murmured, looking over the report. "They were threatening to discharge him and send him back to Ireland. It seems that he refused to give it up. This much was overheard by another soldier, who soon left the barracks. Last he saw, there were just seven men in that room. As well as Devlin, Wightwick, the major and the lieutenant, there were two other soldiers acting as witnesses, and a sergeant." Tombstone turned the page. "It's not known what was said, but then there's this." He read aloud: *"Half an hour later, there were multiple reports of shouts and cries going up from the major's office. It is not known how, but Devlin managed to overpower six men. He killed them all."*

Gwynnie tried to picture Devlin in a fight with six men, killing them all in cold blood. "How?" she whispered.

"It goes on: *As soldiers tried to get through the door, other men saw Devlin break out through the window. He was seen running across the courtyard, yelling about vengeance. How he would see justice done, and how the king would pay for what he has done to them all. He was stained with blood."* Tombstone handed the paper to Gwynnie to read.

Soon enough, she laid it back down on her lap, shaking her head. "It doesn't sound like the man I met."

"The man you met could just be a good actor."

"And what if there is some grain of truth in what he said?"

"Gwynnie, he was alone in the room with six men." Tombstone pointed at the paper. "What more do you want?"

"I want to be certain." Gwynnie thrust the report back toward him. "You asked me to be your eyes and ears, to see things and discover things you can't. I am telling you now, not all is as it seems with Connal Devlin."

Tombstone sighed. "Very well," he murmured. "Then I suggest that tomorrow, you and I visit Devlin's barracks."

CHAPTER 20

"You're going where?" Samuel handed Gwynnie the bag of bread he'd just made, though he appeared to regret it and tried to take it back again.

"We're just going to a soldier's barracks. That is all." Gwynnie took the bag again. "Trust me."

"Trust you?" Samuel scoffed. "I know very well you don't tell me everything, Gwynnie."

"And do you tell me everything?" She glanced about, but those in the kitchen were busy going about their duties, and not one of them was paying attention to her. "How is Brynne at the moment?"

"I know, I know." Samuel shook his head. "But what good does it do to tell you that Brynne is up at night, muttering about prejudice against the Irish?"

Gwynnie shrugged as she tied the bag of bread together. "I'll be back later today."

"The lawyer is going with you?" Samuel asked uncertainly. "Are you going to tell me exactly what it is you do for him?"

"Maybe someday," Gwynnie murmured. As Samuel turned his back, she took an apple that had been left on the workbench and dropped it into a pocket in her pale blue woollen gown.

When he turned round again, Samuel looked at the empty space where the apple had been.

"Gwynnie, that was mine."

She hastened to pull the apple out again and offered it to him, but he chuckled and shook his head.

"Keep it. But do me a favour." He glanced around, much as she had done, though he was clearly just making sure that Brynne was not nearby. "Tell me what you discover, but don't tell Brynne."

"You have my word." Gwynnie nodded and turned to leave, taking a bite out of the apple as she went.

"Oh!" Gwynnie gasped as the cart came to a halt. Tombstone paid the driver as he climbed down. Gwynnie was in no hurry to follow; she stood on the back of the cart, staring at the soldiers' barracks stretching out before her.

There were multiple rows of red-brick buildings, all lined up neatly and adjoining one another. Some of the windows had bars over them rather than glass, as if they were prisons rather than barracks. Despite the chill in the air and the light rain, only a few chimneys puffed with smoke. The rest were empty, betraying the lack of fires within.

In the yard, there were young soldiers running drills. They carried pikes and staffs, moving them to various positions according to the barked commands of a rather small soldier with a high-pitched voice.

"I'm reminded of a little yapping terrier," Gwynnie whispered to Tombstone as she stepped down from the cart. He smiled a little then put a finger to his lips.

"Don't let any man of high rank hear you talking like that here. If anyone asks, you are my maid accompanying me for the day."

"I'd better carry your bags then." She took a satchel off his back and wound it over her shoulder, huffing at the weight. He helped her to adjust the satchel, but when she saw one of the soldiers eyeing them suspiciously, she shrugged him off. "No man of high standing would stoop to help a maid."

"You mistake me for an arrogant pig," he muttered. "Come, let's see what we can discover."

Tombstone led the way across the yard, walking past the soldiers. Most didn't even glance their way, though some looked with mistrustful eyes.

"Sir." Tombstone bowed to the terrier-like man. "Where will I find your major?"

"In the quarters behind you, sir." The soldier saluted Tombstone. "Ask for Major Harold Widgeon."

"Thank you." Tombstone inclined his head and turned away, leaving Gwynnie to scurry after him.

They entered the building, where Gwynnie felt even smaller than she usually would have done. Across the walls, pinned high above her head, were various weapons. There were some ornamental swords, lots of daggers and basilards, and even halberds. Amongst all the weapons were paintings, including a particularly large and dominating portrait which was twice the height of Gwynnie. The figure on the canvas was supposed to be King Henry, but Gwynnie had to bite her tongue to avoid laughing at the image.

"The likeness is uncanny, is it not?" she said drily to Tombstone, who coughed to cover up his own laughter as some soldiers walked by. The painting displayed the king as a great warrior with a fine sword at his hip, broad shoulders, and such a wide and powerful stance it was a wonder he hadn't ripped his hose. It was a rather stark contrast to the real man, who had seen over forty-five summers and had a receding hairline and growing stomach.

"Stay here whilst I find out where we need to go," Tombstone said.

Gwynnie flattened her back to the wall as a long line of soldiers walked by. They marched two abreast, all carrying various bags and boxes under the orders of a tall soldier who led the way.

"Quickly now. All must be ready for the new major's dinner tonight. Stop staring at that maid, Bernard. You'd think you had never seen a woman before."

Gwynnie looked around to see that one of the soldiers was indeed staring at her. When she pulled a face at him, it sent him scurrying on even faster than the tall soldier's orders had done.

Two soldiers at the back of the group were lugging a long, heavy box. Neither one of them glanced Gwynnie's way, both too caught up in their own conversation.

"I still don't believe it," the shorter of the two muttered. He was clearly struggling with the weight of the box and had to readjust his grip more than once.

"You heard him shouting about vengeance yourself," said the other. "You were in the courtyard."

"I don't remember hearing him say the king's name." The shorter soldier dropped the box.

"Urwin!" his colleague barked. "We need to hurry. I'm not about to risk another disciplinary; this fast is killing me as it is. Come, hurry." They both bent down to pick up the box.

"Well, tell me what *you* heard that day in the courtyard. Go on."

"Devlin roared about vengeance," the taller soldier said hurriedly, clearly much more concerned with retrieving the box.

"Yes, he did. He shouted about vengeance — how justice had to be served."

"He said the king's name."

Urwin spat as he stood straight, not helping his friend with the box. "He said, 'By king and country, I will have vengeance.' Does that sound like a threat on the king's life to you?"

"Right now, I just want to make sure I get my dinner tonight. Pick up the damn box, Urwin."

Urwin grumbled but bent down and lifted one end of the box. "I just think something is wrong about that day."

"You've said the same thing every day since. Find someone else who will listen, Urwin."

As they disappeared out of the door, Gwynnie looked up. She was breathless with what she had heard.

Hurrying to the door, she watched as all the soldiers carried their boxes into a room in a different building across the courtyard. Urwin and his colleague disappeared inside along with the rest of them.

"Gwynnie?" Tombstone's voice made her jump. "This way. I have an audience with the major."

She nodded and hastened to follow him through the corridors, though she glanced back more than once, thinking about what she had overheard.

They were forced to wait outside the major's office for quite some time. Gwynnie and Tombstone had finished their bag of bread by the time the door opened.

A thin and rather rodent-like soldier stepped out. His brown hair was slicked back, as if he had just bathed, and the fresh cuts on his jaw showed that he had recently shaved. Unlike the men in the barracks, he carried a floral scent that contrasted sharply with the smell of sweat.

"Major Widgeon will see you now." The thin soldier gestured for them to follow him inside.

Tombstone led the way, with Gwynnie following dutifully behind him. As they stepped into the room, he took off his cloak and handed it to her. She tried not to struggle under the weight of the cloak, the food sacks and his satchel.

"Your maid can wait outside," a rather sharp voice commanded.

"My maid stays with me, Major, for I have already seen your soldiers' eyes wandering over her. I will not leave her in a place where she is vulnerable."

Gwynnie looked up, rather startled to see the major looking straight at her. He was younger than she had expected and so large in girth that she doubted he had ever seen battle or run the drills that were being performed outside in the yard. He looked down his long nose at her then dismissed her with a wave of his hand.

The younger rat-like soldier pulled out a chair for her and purposefully placed it as far away as possible, in the corner of the room. She moved to take the seat, biting her lip to stop any tart words from escaping her lips.

The soldier moved to his master's shoulder and stood dutifully behind him as the major adjusted some maps on his desk before looking at Tombstone.

"I understand you have come to ask questions about Connal Devlin, lawyer."

"I have." Tombstone offered a light bow. "My name is Elric Tombstone. I am in the service of the magistrate of London, Neville Pascal, who in turn reports to Lord Cromwell."

The mention of these names had a marked effect on the major.

He stood from his seat behind the desk and adjusted his uniform over his rotund belly. He carried the same floral scent the younger man wore, seemingly in an attempt to distance themselves from the other soldiers.

"Well, if Lord Cromwell wishes to know more…" He cleared his throat. "What can I do for you, Tombstone?"

"We believe this Devlin is trying to get into the palace." Tombstone's words made Gwynnie's head jerk up. Apparently, they had so far managed to keep it a secret from the rest of London that Devlin was already within the palace walls. "We wish to know what sort of man we are dealing with."

"Very well. Then you shall have the information you so desire." Major Widgeon nodded at the younger man, who moved off to a corner of the room. He reached up toward some shelves stacked high with rolled-up scrolls and searched through them. "Devlin was a rather revered soldier."

"Revered?" Tombstone repeated.

"A fine fighter. Even honourable. He had many friends here. Before I took on the role of major, I was more closely associated with the men. I heard many good reports of him." He held out his hand for one of the scrolls and his soldier passed it to him. "You can take this with you. It details his successes in training and battle."

"How long had he been here?"

"Just under a year. Not long. He said he'd come from Ireland at the request of someone in his family." Major Widgeon scratched his jaw, deep in thought. "Well, I may have misremembered that. They all come for one reason or another."

Tombstone handed the scroll to Gwynnie. She was tempted to unroll it and read it for herself, but instead she tucked it away into his satchel.

"And the day the incident happened?" Tombstone asked.

"He was being reprimanded. He was Catholic. I know many men try to keep their true faiths hidden, but Devlin's prayers and rosary were a little too obvious. He was called into this very room by my predecessor, Major Frederick Allaway."

Gwynnie stiffened and looked around the room. Was it possible they were in the same chamber where the murder of six men had taken place?

"It happened here?" Tombstone asked, clearly thinking the same thing.

"It did." Major Widgeon looked a little uncomfortable, pulling on his blue uniform and trying to loosen it a little. "I was just about to pull out of the yard on horseback when the shouts went up. Devlin broke through this window here." He pointed to a glass window behind him. It had been fixed rather haphazardly and clearly let in a considerable draught that ruffled Widgeon's hair.

"He was running, screaming about vengeance, cursing at the top of his voice." Major Widgeon shook his head.

"What did he say, exactly?" Tombstone asked.

"Oh, I don't remember. Some guff about justice being served. He mentioned the king." Tombstone flinched and Gwynnie shifted in her seat, longing to tell him what she had just overheard.

"Who else saw what happened that day?"

"There were many soldiers in the yard. You're welcome to question them." Major Widgeon gestured toward the window behind him. "Though it will do little good, I imagine. You're dealing with a zealous madman, Tombstone."

"Strange…" Tombstone murmured. "How did a madman manage to overpower six men?"

"He was chained up as well," the rat-like soldier said suddenly. Major Widgeon's eyes bulged so wide, Gwynnie thought it a wonder they didn't fall out of their sockets. "My apologies, Major." He saluted his superior. "But when Devlin was in here, his wrists were chained. I helped secure him myself before I was dismissed from the room."

"Then how did a chained madman overpower six men?" Tombstone asked, looking between the two of them.

The younger man had no answer and shook his head, as Major Widgeon huffed.

"I thought you were here to find out more about this man, not to question his guilt."

"Indeed, Major, but I want to discover the truth about what happened."

CHAPTER 21

"His name is Urwin." Gwynnie pointed at the room the soldier had gone into with the others. "Ask him what he saw and heard that day."

"He didn't think Devlin threatened the king?"

"No, he thought it was part of a curse. By king and country, you know, that sort of thing." Gwynnie hissed in Tombstone's ear as they stepped out into the courtyard and only narrowly avoided being trampled by a line of marching men.

"Why is Devlin moving about the palace like a shadow? If he were the madman they say he is, then he would surely fight his way past the guards to reach the king." Tombstone shook his head. "Something doesn't make sense."

He paused beside the next building along and handed Gwynnie the key they had just received from Major Widgeon. Rather reluctantly, the major had agreed to hand over the key to Devlin's room. Unusually, he'd had a room of his own rather than being in one of the more public rooms. No one had been in since.

"You search Devlin's chamber whilst I talk to this Urwin. Something tells me that despite what Major Widgeon says, he doesn't want us talking to many people."

"Why not?" Gwynnie asked.

"These barracks are currently at peace." Tombstone looked around the yard. "Imagine trying to keep control of so many trained fighters if you told them that there could still be a murderer amongst them."

"How I envy Major Widgeon that particular task."

"Exactly. Now, go search the chamber whilst I speak to Urwin." Tombstone stepped into the building as Gwynnie walked along the edge, heading toward an archway and a set of steps that led high into the rafters of the building.

At this time of day, the staircase was quiet with all the soldiers running their drills. It meant Gwynnie could climb the stairs unseen, wandering the corridors until she found a room that had evidently not been disturbed in some time. She took a step back when she saw that people had carved words into the wood of the door.

The first message was plain: *Do not enter.* Yet there were others that looked more superstitious, scribbled by soldiers in stolen moments. Some had etched crosses into the wood, as if they could keep the devil from entering. Others had written *Damned spirit, Devlin the Devil,* and even a blessing to drive out his curse: *May he never walk amongst us again.*

Gwynnie checked the corridor. Seeing she was alone, she turned the key in the lock and stepped inside, closing the door behind her.

The stench of must and damp was so strong that she held a hand over her mouth as she faced the room. There had to be a leak in the building, for all around the window grey mould was growing. It was a foul place to be.

Gwynnie tiptoed over the floorboards in an effort not to make them creak.

On a small table beside the bed was a plain wooden cross and a candlestick holder. A toilette box contained a shaving brush and a blade. On the bed was a weapons belt, with two daggers held in tiny scabbards. Under the bed were boots that had been kicked away.

"It's like he just left it," Gwynnie whispered to herself.

She moved toward the coffer at the bottom of the bed and lifted the lid, unable to muffle the loud creak of the wood. Inside were uniforms and spare doublets, along with extra boots and clean white shirts. Uncertain what she was looking for, Gwynnie searched through the box, but she could find nothing of interest. Abandoning the coffer, she moved toward the edge of the bed and the apparent leak.

Either Devlin had been forced to live here when it was still leaking, or the damage had happened since. She placed her palm on the damp wall, finding that the water went all the way to the pillow. She lifted it up, finding a small hessian purse that had been tied up with string and tucked underneath. She pulled it free and loosened the strings.

Inside the small purse were what at first looked like coins. As Gwynnie poured them out onto her hand, she saw they weren't coins at all, but little pewter trinkets, the size of buttons. Emblazoned on each one was a shamrock.

At the back of Gwynnie's mind, a memory of where she had seen it before surfaced.

"That's not possible," she mumbled aloud.

"I'm telling you, I know what I saw." The sudden loud voice coming from outside caught Gwynnie's attention. She moved closer to the window.

The voice belonged to Urwin, the soldier. He had staggered into the courtyard, looking wild and desperate, with Tombstone following him.

"Calm yourself," Tombstone pleaded, his hand outstretched. "All I want to know is how certain you are."

"I am completely certain. With God as my witness." Urwin threw both arms at the sky. "He didn't threaten the king's life. He was just cursing."

Gwynnie pressed her face closer to the window, but Tombstone had managed to calm Urwin down now. He approached the soldier and laid a hand on his arm. Their conversation continued in such low whispers that she had no chance of hearing another word.

Gwynnie dropped the hessian purse into the pocket of her gown and slipped back out of the room, taking care to lock the door behind her before she hurried down the stairs. As she reached the courtyard, Urwin was walking away, leaving Tombstone staring after him.

"Well, it looks like that went well," she said as she reached his side. "Clearly you have a good questioning technique to make a man shout at the sky."

"Thank you for the compliment," Tombstone sighed. "Something isn't right, Gwynnie."

"Why? What did he say?"

"He said that Devlin's hands were still chained when he ran across the courtyard." Tombstone shook his head. "How can a man, even a skilled soldier, overpower six others when his hands are chained? He didn't break free; he was still bound when he escaped — it makes no sense."

Tombstone beckoned for Gwynnie to follow him as they made their way back to the entrance of the yard. "Urwin claimed Captain Wightwick and Devlin were great friends. Why would Devlin turn on Wightwick just because he pleaded with him not to wear his rosary? It's an extreme reaction."

"Perhaps he didn't do it." Gwynnie's words made Tombstone stop walking. He turned to face her, his lips pursed.

"Perhaps," Tombstone admitted evenly. "There is more. Urwin heard the glass smash as he was working in the next yard. He came into this yard to see what was happening, and only then did he see Devlin climbing out of the window."

"What are you saying?"

"I'm saying that there was enough time for someone else to smash the glass and get out of the room before Devlin was seen climbing out of the same broken window." Tombstone walked on, heading for the cart that had returned to collect them. "How about you? Did you find anything?"

"He was a neat man, rather like you. He kept his room nice, but there's been a leak and there's heavy mould around the window."

"Anything else?" Tombstone asked.

Gwynnie thought of the small hessian purse and the pewter shamrocks hidden in her pocket. She knew she should say something, but then she remembered where she had seen one once before and found other words slipping from her lips.

"No, nothing."

Gwynnie entered the kitchen. Darkness had long since fallen and all the staff had gone to bed, even Samuel, who was often seen up at this time, either drinking with old Rudyard or preparing dough for the next day's bread. Glancing around, she looked for somewhere she could hide, her gaze falling on the dark fireplace. It stretched the full width of one wall, so large that it could have fitted ten people inside it. Seeing an opportunity, Gwynnie slipped into the fireplace and pressed herself into the corner, masking her whole body in the darkness.

"Now, I wait," she whispered, sinking down to her haunches and watching the kitchen.

For long enough, she had kept watch for Devlin around the palace grounds, but there was another that needed hunting tonight. There was another who was sneaking about, who could lead her straight to Devlin.

Gwynnie reached down and pulled the hessian purse out of her pocket. She didn't know what those trinkets meant, but they had to mean something.

She craned her neck, staring into the darkness, but no one came. No one crept about the kitchen, stealing food for the escaped killer. It was so quiet that Gwynnie felt her eyelids grow heavy. Slowly, her head nodded forward, and she fell into a deep sleep.

In her dream, she saw Emlyn. She was a child again, walking at her mother's side through the busy streets of London. She held onto Emlyn's hand as they crept through the crowds.

"Our hunting ground, miting," Emlyn said and smiled warmly. *"We have to steal to survive now. You know that, don't you?"*

She nodded at her mother's words, watching in awe as Emlyn bumped into a stranger, apologised profusely, and managed to lift the leather purse he kept at his hip.

"It's the only way to survive, when life deals you a poor hand."

Gwynnie reached out to take the leather purse from her mother. She gripped onto it hard, aware that it felt like hessian rather than leather.

There was a light thud.

Gwynnie's eyes shot open. She was still holding Devlin's purse as she looked frantically around the kitchen for the source of the noise. A figure moved in the moonlight.

For a moment, Gwynnie thought it was Devlin. She sat forward, straining to see, and soon realised it was a woman, but it was not the woman she had spied standing between the trees that night by the church. That shadowy figure was taller than this one. The woman was busy opening storage drawers, pulling out fresh bread. She constantly looked around, checking that no one was about to discover her. She flicked the dark hair falling down from her coif back over her shoulder.

Gwynnie silently climbed from her hiding place and walked across the kitchen. The woman was now so busy decanting mead into a fresh flagon, she didn't notice Gwynnie approaching from behind, not until Gwynnie upturned the hessian purse and let the shamrocks fall out onto the workbench beside her.

Brynne jumped so much that she nearly collided with Gwynnie.

They both froze, staring at one another in the moonlight. As the silence stretched between them, Gwynnie pointed at the shamrocks, forcing Brynne to look at them too.

"I saw one like that once. It was here, in this kitchen. You were turning it over in your fingers." She picked up one of the shamrocks and held it high. "I used to think it was just a symbol of your Irish heritage, but it means something more, doesn't it?"

"We hold onto them," Brynne whispered, staring at the pewter shamrock. "They signify one that was loved and lost."

"Do you know who these belong to?" Gwynnie asked.

"No," Brynne answered. She returned to her task of putting bread in a sack.

"Then maybe I should ask you instead who that bread is for?"

"Pray, do not, Gwynnie." Brynne squeezed her eyes shut.

"The answer to both questions is the same — Connal Devlin."

Brynne gasped and stepped away. She looked ready to run, but Gwynnie couldn't let her. They were friends, and she certainly wasn't going to let all of that come crashing down now with this discovery.

"Why are you helping him?" Gwynnie asked. "It cannot simply be because you share the same heritage. That is not it, is it?"

"Pray, Gwynnie, no more." Brynne's eyes filled with tears.

"You know him, don't you?"

"Of course I do," Brynne practically squeaked as she held her hand over her mouth. "I've known him his whole life."

Gwynnie thought quickly. If Devlin hadn't come for vengeance on the king after all, then there had to be another reason why he was at the palace. "He came to see you?"

"He came to me for help." Brynne dropped the bag and held both hands against her chest. "I'm the only family he has in this country. Where else was he supposed to go?"

Gwynnie stepped toward her. "Who is he to you? Tell me, Brynne, please," she pleaded.

"I can't."

"Why not?"

"Because he asked me to tell no one. He was afraid that if anyone knew we were related, by association I would be in danger."

"Brynne, listen to me." Gwynnie kept her voice soft as she took her friend's shoulder. "You are already in danger. If anyone else in the palace discovers that you are the one who has been helping him —"

"No!" Brynne yelped.

"Hush," Gwynnie begged, her eyes darting about the room. "We need to get out of here, before anyone comes running." She scooped up the shamrocks, returned them to the purse and stuffed it back in her pocket. Then she grabbed the hessian bag and Brynne's arm, pulling her out of the kitchen.

"Where are we going?"

"Away from here," Gwynnie said. They hastened down a passage just as Gwynnie heard the sound of footsteps. She pushed Brynne into an alcove and held a finger to her lips, silently urging her not to say a word. Brynne nodded and held both hands over her mouth.

They waited until the footsteps had passed, then Gwynnie took hold of Brynne's arm once again. She led her out of the passageway and into a tiny courtyard nestled between the food stores.

"Brynne, I need you to take me to him," Gwynnie said.

"I can't." Brynne's voice hitched. "I promised I wouldn't."

"I need you to trust me." Gwynnie offered up the hessian sack. "You can give him his supplies. I won't raise the alarm for his arrest, but I need to see him. Please, just take me to him."

Brynne hesitated, her eyes filling with tears. "He's no killer, Gwynnie. I know he's not."

"I know."

"You do?" Brynne's eyes widened. She reached out and grasped Gwynnie's hand. "Oh, Gwynnie. He's my son."

CHAPTER 22

Gwynnie followed Brynne as they tiptoed their way through the palace. They headed all the way to the church and the graveyard. As they passed the place where the branch had fallen the night before, Gwynnie paused for long enough to look at the spot among the trees where she had seen the woman in the darkness. Whoever that woman was, she had been taller than Brynne and most determined not to be seen.

"Quickly," Brynne pleaded. "Before we are seen by anyone."

They went down the bank and toward the outer curtain wall. Gwynnie eyed the two pikes resting against the wall and the abandoned game on the stool.

"He's not here, Brynne. I've seen him keep guard here, but he's not here now."

Brynne halted at the bottom of the wall and pointed upwards.

Gwynnie looked up, her eyes tracing the top of the curtain wall. The crenellations stretched far and wide around the trees, every now and then offering a glimpse of a walkway at the top.

Brynne whistled, one high note followed by a low note. Slowly, from behind one of the crenellations, a figure emerged, standing tall.

"God's blood," Gwynnie hissed. "You mean all this time, you were just up there?"

"Good evening, flower." Devlin leaned forward on the stone wall, his face bathed in the moonlight filtering through the tree branches. "Aye, I take it there's a reason you have brought my new friend, Ma."

"Your new friend?" Brynne said, her Irish accent suddenly strong. "Never mind that, I brought you food — look." She held up the hessian sack.

At once, Devlin jumped up onto the edges of the curtain wall and leapt out. Brynne gasped and Gwynnie threw her hands over her face, but Devlin didn't fall. He grabbed easily onto a branch from the nearest tree, his feet swinging through the air before he reached out for the main trunk and climbed down. As he hit the ground, Brynne shot forward, running into his arms and embracing him tightly.

"You're getting thinner," she said, leaning back and holding his face between her hands.

"I'm well enough," he assured her. His eyes flicked from Brynne to Gwynnie. "Is someone going to start explaining a few things?"

"It's your turn for that." Gwynnie stepped forward. She picked up the hessian sack Brynne had dropped and passed it to him. "Eat, drink, do as you need to. I want to know why you are here in the palace."

"You mean…" He paused as he took the sack, raising his eyebrows. "You believe I'm not here to hunt the king and queen?"

"I believe the man who fled from the army barracks that day with his hands chained could not possibly have murdered six men," she said.

Devlin smiled. It was so sudden that Gwynnie couldn't quite believe the difference it made to his face.

"You believe him? Oh, Gwynnie. Oh, thank God!" Brynne now flung herself at Gwynnie, only Gwynnie was not as strong as Devlin and was nearly knocked off her feet.

"I want an explanation, Brynne. I'd also like to be able to breathe."

Brynne promptly released her. As Gwynnie caught her breath, she watched as Devlin opened the sack and tore into his fresh cob.

"What really happened that day?" she asked. "I've been to the barracks. I've seen the major's room, the window you broke out of. I've heard how you didn't threaten the king's life but cursed instead. Tell me the truth, Devlin."

"Connal," he corrected her, stepping forward. "It's my name, remember?"

"I'll call you that if you tell me everything."

He glanced away, looking at the trees nearby. "Is your friend the lawyer here?"

"No." Gwynnie shook her head. "Tombstone is not here tonight."

When Brynne looked around fearfully, Gwynnie gently took her arm and steered her toward one of the guards' stools. "Sit, Brynne. Calm yourself."

Devlin gestured for Gwynnie to take the other stool, but she refused, standing straight and waiting for him to begin his tale with her arms folded.

"What I told you was true," he said, swallowing the chunk of bread he had been eating. "I was in the major's office to be reprimanded for my faith, for holding onto my rosary too much."

"And then what happened?"

"They put me in irons." He looked down at his wrists, clearly remembering the feel of the cold metal. "They were disciplining me when it happened. Cassian was so worried. He urged them not to dismiss me, saying I was one of his best men." There was the ghost of a smile on his lips, though it vanished all too quickly. "They were mid-argument when he came in."

"Who? When who came in?" Gwynnie urged impatiently.

"His name is Henry Magner." Devlin stared down at the bread in his grasp. "It all happened so fast. He killed Cassian first. Cassian's back was to him as he pulled out the blade and…"

Brynne wiped her face. Whether she was crying or not, Gwynnie didn't know, for she couldn't look away from Devlin. The man seemed to be in agony.

"I couldn't get to him," Devlin croaked. "My irons were fastened to the chair. I tried to stop Magner, but he just…" He coughed and looked away. "Magner turned on the other soldiers. He left the lieutenant and major for last. Neither one of them were very skilled in battle. They had only ever sat behind desks and given orders."

He looked down at the ground as Gwynnie thought of the rotund man who was now the major. She could easily believe it.

"Why didn't he kill you?" The words escaped Gwynnie's lips in a rush. "You were chained up. It would have been easy for him."

"I'm not certain." Devlin shook his head. "I was breaking free of the one chain that kept me bound to the chair when he turned to look at me. Perhaps he planned to do it, then cut his losses and decided to run. Maybe somewhere in the midst of his madness he realised that leaving one man alive would allow him to shift the blame elsewhere. He ran as I made it to my feet, my wrists still chained together." He stopped, his breath catching in his throat. "There were some good men in that room. He only managed to kill them all because of the shock.

He was too quick as he yelled about how he wanted to know who had given the order."

"What order?" Gwynnie asked.

Devlin took a deep breath and turned his eyes to the sky. "One of the battalions was sent to quell the Lincolnshire uprising last month. The uprising led to the Pilgrimage of Grace itself." He chewed his lip for a moment. "Many dispersed when they found out an army was on the way. Others did not. Lives were lost in that battle. Henry Magner's brother, Lucius, was one of those who fell. The order for the battalion to march without backup and a lack of ammunition came from Major Allaway. He'd believed that peasants wouldn't put up much of a fight. He was wrong." Devlin reached for the flagon and tried to take the lid off it, but in his distraction he couldn't manage it.

Without thinking, Gwynnie moved forward and took the flagon out of his hands, removing the lid for him.

"Thank you," he whispered as she handed it back to him. He took a large gulp. "I don't know if he wanted to take out as many soldiers as he could in anger, or if it was the only time he could break into the major's office, but he killed them all. And I … I could do nothing to stop it. By the time I'd broken the leg off my chair to release my irons, he'd smashed his way out of the window. I tried to save Cassian, but he was gone. There was so much blood… I ran after Magner, I tried to stop him, and yes, I screamed about vengeance and justice: I called for vengeance on Henry Magner … and I cursed a few times. I may have mentioned the king then."

Gwynnie's mouth fell open as Brynne covered her face.

"Did you just shout out Henry? Or did you say Magner too when you made your threat?"

"I can't remember." He sat down heavily on the stool beside his mother.

Gwynnie suddenly understood why so many had thought Devlin had threatened the king. The man he had actually threatened shared the same Christian name — Henry.

Brynne laid a hand on his arm. The love she clearly bore for him made Gwynnie's heart ache.

"What happened after that?" Gwynnie moved to sit on the side of the nearby bank of earth.

"I was tackled to the ground by soldiers before I could reach Magner." Devlin stared into the flagon. "I was found guilty by a judge and convicted to hang at Tyburn."

He pulled down the neck of his doublet. Gwynnie caught sight of a thin red line across his throat from where the noose had cut his skin.

"The hangman should have taken better care of his charge," he said, gravely. "The rope was too thin, and it snapped when they tried to hang me. I tore it free from my throat, used it to stun the hangman, then ran. I didn't kill him, Ma," he added hastily to Brynne, who was already nodding.

"Then you came here?" Gwynnie asked. "You thought a palace surrounded by guards would be a safe place for a convicted murderer?"

"I knew my mother was here." His voice had softened. "Gwynnie, I have no money. I only had the few possessions they let me take to the noose with me. My rosary, and —"

"An embroidered handkerchief," Gwynnie murmured, looking at Brynne.

"When did you go through my things?" Devlin sat forward.

"It doesn't matter." She waved at him to carry on.

"I'm trying to get him on a ship home to Ireland, Gwynnie," said Brynne. "Passage isn't cheap, but I nearly have enough money. Ships leave from Southampton all the time. If I can get him the money, he can leave. They can't take him out of Ireland once he's safely home."

"What brought you to England in the first place?" Gwynnie asked, watching as Devlin took his mother's hand.

"When I received a letter saying my ma had been stabbed, I had to come."

Gwynnie hung her head. All at once, she felt it was her doing. She was the reason that Brynne had been hurt that night. If Brynne hadn't been hurt, then Devlin would never have come to England in the first place.

"I didn't tell anyone because Samuel doesn't know," Brynne whispered. "When I ran from Ireland, I was escaping my first husband. He was a cruel man."

"*Is.* He is a cruel man." Devlin spoke sharply. "My father doesn't have a kind bone in his body."

"Samuel doesn't know I was married before," Brynne said in a rush. "If he had known, he wouldn't have married me."

Gwynnie's eyes widened. "Brynne, are you a bigamist?" she asked.

"I had to escape that life," Brynne said desperately. "The only good thing in my life was Connal." She clung to his hand. "He helped me to get away."

"It was the only way," Devlin mumbled. "I know that."

"So, Samuel has no idea?" Gwynnie stood. "God's blood, Brynne. Samuel is out of his mind with worry for you. He finds you wandering the palace at night, looking lost and scared. He's thinks it's all because of what happened the night you were hurt."

"No, no. It's because…" Brynne looked at her son. "At first, I feared my first husband would find me here. That he would follow me to England when Connal came. Now, all my fears are for Connal's safety."

"God's death."

"Does she always curse like that?" Connal asked Brynne with interest.

"Always," Brynne replied with a nod.

"Are we actually having this conversation?" Gwynnie marched toward them. "I stand before a bigamist and a convicted murderer —"

"An innocent one," Devlin reminded her.

"And we're talking about my cursing tongue? God's blood!"

"Gwynnie!" Brynne protested, clutching the cross she wore around her neck.

Gwynnie paced up and down as she thought about what to do next. She would have to try and persuade Tombstone to believe this tale. Without his help, there was nothing she could do, but she also knew Tombstone wouldn't believe it until he had met and spoken to Devlin himself.

"Queen Jane." She turned back to face Devlin. "You never went anywhere near her chamber?"

"No." Devlin was firm.

"We were making a plan for where he could hide when the news broke of the body discovered in the queen's chamber," Brynne hastened to add. "He was with me the whole time, Gwynnie."

"I saw that man, Jasper Ashdown, walking toward Donsen Tower after I had crept into the palace. I swear to you, Gwynnie, that is all I know."

She nodded distractedly, returning to her pacing.

"Do you believe us?" Brynne asked. She released her son's hand and slowly stood. "Gwynnie?" She moved into Gwynnie's path. "Please, tell me you believe us."

Gwynnie halted, her hands on her hips as she glanced at Devlin. The man who had given her his cloak when she was cold, who had even saved her life. There was only one possible answer she could give.

"I believe you," Gwynnie declared. Brynne clapped her hands in delight as Devlin sighed with relief. "But getting everyone else to believe it may be a tall order."

CHAPTER 23

"This is where you have been hiding?" Gwynnie dropped a second sack of provisions that she and Brynne had brought. Buried deep within the curtain wall was a tiny chamber, barely large enough for Devlin to sleep inside. It was an old store cupboard in the tower wall, perhaps once used for guards who kept watch over this part of the palace. The mould and damp ceiling suggested it had long fallen out of use. It was so small that Gwynnie and Brynne stood outside of the cupboard as Devlin hesitated in the doorway. Gwynnie handed him the food as Brynne kept watch from the window in the corridor. It was early morning, and the sun was already beginning to rise.

"Not every night." Devlin reached into the sack and pulled out the food. "I had to find a new hiding place when my first was discovered by you." He eyed her suspiciously. "How did you find it?"

"I know where shadows hide," she said in a low tone, though Brynne gave no sign of having heard her.

Devlin stared at her. "What kind of maid are you?"

"It doesn't matter." She moved to the window in the corridor beside Brynne and peered out. "It seems to me that sneaking you aboard a ship bound for Ireland is risky in itself."

"Why?" Brynne jerked her head around.

"Because if I can recognise your son from a ballad sheet, who's to say someone at the dockyard won't?" Her question made Devlin grunt as he pulled a fresh shirt from the sack. He raised his eyebrows.

"How small do you think I am?"

"It was all the laundry had. What a strange way that is to say thank you." At her dry words, he smiled and mouthed, *thank you*. As he retreated into his store cupboard to change, Gwynnie looked out across the graveyard with Brynne. "Were you here two nights ago to see your son?"

"No." Brynne shook her head. "I always left his food in the church. He doesn't want me caught in his company in case the palace officials punish me."

Gwynnie nodded slowly. She was now sure that the woman she had seen in the trees was not Brynne after all, but another woman entirely.

"If we can't get him to a ship, what do you suggest, Gwynnie? What else can we do?"

"I was thinking it would be wiser to clear his name."

"And you think that possible?" Devlin's voice was abruptly deep. She turned to see him emerging from the cupboard as he tucked in his shirt. Gwynnie tried not to stare at his broad shoulders and looked away hurriedly.

"With the right help, I think it is possible, yes," she continued. "First, if Tombstone and I can discover Jasper Ashdown's real killer, then that will clear you of one accusation levelled at your head. We'll also see if we can find Henry Magner."

Devlin didn't look convinced, but he nodded all the same.

"We'll also need more help," Gwynnie said. "If you keep bringing food parcels, Brynne, then sooner or later you will be seen. If we can at least switch up the deliveries, then we stand a better chance of keeping him hidden. I'll bring some, and I think Samuel should too."

Brynne stared at Gwynnie. "Oh, Gwynnie, we cannot tell him. What would he say about my sin?" Brynne covered her face with her hands.

"In case you hadn't noticed, Samuel adores you," Gwynnie assured her. "If you tell him the truth, he'll forgive you anything. Even a little thing like bigamy."

"A little thing?" Devlin spluttered with laughter.

"You're not helping." Gwynnie waved a hand at him to be quiet. "We need to tell Samuel, Brynne. He can help us. I'll also talk to Tombstone and persuade him to meet with you, Devlin."

"Connal," he reminded her. "Why is that so difficult, flower?"

"Gwynnie. Why is *that* so difficult?" She tossed his words back at him, rather distracted by how handsome he looked when he smiled. They stared at each other for a moment before Brynne broke the silence.

"I'm not sure I can do this, Gwynnie. I can't tell Samuel the truth. He'd hate me. I could not stand it if he hated me —"

"It's not possible for Samuel to hate you." Gwynnie took Brynne's shoulder. "He loves you too much, and right now we need to buy more time. We need time to discover who really killed Jasper Ashdown. If Devlin —"

"Connal," he cut in.

"If your son is caught before we can find the real killer, then who's to say that he would even make it to a prison or Tyburn again? The palace is under the rule of Cromwell as much as it is King Henry. I wouldn't trust him not to order the death of a man on the spot."

Devlin nodded in agreement. "We have to try, Ma," he urged.

Brynne's voice broke as she crossed herself. "May God and Samuel forgive me for what I have done."

"I am not certain about this." Brynne wrung her hands as she and Gwynnie made their way toward the kitchen.

"Do you have a better idea, Brynne?" Gwynnie asked. "How many times have you nearly been caught delivering food to your son?"

"A few times," Brynne confessed in a whisper.

"Then we need to take more precautions. Come, I'll help you tell Samuel." They halted outside the kitchen.

"What is wrong now?" Gwynnie asked when Brynne hesitated.

"Just something I saw ... between you and Connal..." Brynne began slowly.

"I beg your pardon?" Gwynnie's voice grew high.

"I have been on this earth far longer than you, Gwynnie." The smallest of smiles lit up Brynne's face. "I know when two people are drawn to one another."

"Pah! I cannot laugh loudly enough to dismiss such a claim." Gwynnie went to lead the way into the kitchen, but Brynne barred her path.

"You can laugh all you like, but I know what I saw. You forget, I know my son well —"

Gwynnie stared at Brynne. "I disappear into the shadows, Brynne. People do not notice me. I highly doubt your son has taken much note of me beyond me being the annoying woman who keeps finding him in his hiding places."

Brynne shook her head and cast a quick prayer to heaven as she turned and marched into the kitchen.

"What are you praying for now? My soul?"

"Patience to bear with your stubbornness."

"I'm not stubborn." Gwynnie followed her into the kitchen.

They were suddenly surrounded by noise and activity. All around them, the palace staff were at work preparing breakfast.

Spit boys scuttled past them, heading toward the fireplace that was now bright with roaring flames. Cooks took fresh bread out of the ovens as maids churned butter, and others started laying out what meagre food was allowed during the fast in trenchers and bowls.

"Brynne, what you said, you cannot be right —" Gwynnie caught her arm and whispered in her ear.

"Gwynnie, dear, you smile every time you look at him."

"I do not."

"No? I remember smiling like that. It was the first few days that I knew Samuel." Brynne pulled her arm free and walked across the kitchen, searching for her husband.

Gwynnie stood still. Tombstone's teasing about her head being turned by Devlin was easy enough to ignore, but for Brynne to make such comments was too much. She swallowed hard and followed Brynne across the room.

No good could come from thinking too much of Connal Devlin. That much she knew already.

"Samuel?" Brynne said as they reached his side.

"Ah, there you are." Samuel had just pulled a tray of fresh cobs out of the oven, the crusts nicely bronzed. His face was red from being so close to the flames as he laid them down and turned to face Brynne. "Where have you been?" He took hold of his wife's shoulders. "I woke this morning to find you gone."

"I couldn't sleep so I went for a walk."

Gwynnie's rather loud tut made Brynne glower at her.

"Brynne has something to tell you, Samuel." Gwynnie stepped forward. "Though here may not be the best place to do it."

Samuel looked ready to argue as he glanced around at all the food being served up for breakfast.

"Please, Samuel," Gwynnie said. "This is important."

He looked at Brynne, who nodded. "Follow me," he said. As he turned away, Samuel flicked his fingers at old Rudyard. "Keep an eye on my next batch in the oven."

As the three of them walked out of the kitchens, Rudyard's curses could be heard following them.

They wandered down two corridors and into a small passageway, well away from anyone who may overhear their conversation. Samuel rolled out a barrel of cheap mead kept for the staff and placed it on its end, gently steering his wife to sit.

"You look exhausted," he said, kneeling down beside her. Brynne's frightened eyes softened as she smiled at him, extending her hands toward him. He took both, kissing the back of each one. "Are you going to tell me what's going on? Why you have spent so many nights creeping out of our chamber? Have you ... found another to love?"

"What? No!" Brynne moved forward and kissed him firmly on the lips.

"We need to speak," Gwynnie said, interrupting their intimate moment. "And we do not have long. Brynne?"

"I don't know how to begin." Brynne looked between them. "First, my dearest Samuel, know this. You are the love of my life. I have never loved another as I love you. What I have done ... know that I did it out of desperation, a will to survive. That is very important for you to understand."

"Just tell me what is going on," Samuel said in a gentle voice. "Please."

Brynne nodded. "When I was in Ireland, something happened. Something I never wish to talk about again. It meant I had to come here, to England."

"Brynne, you're not making much sense." Samuel leaned toward her.

Gwynnie glanced over her shoulder. She caught sight of two footmen walking past the end of the passageway. It wouldn't be long before someone appeared and asked why they weren't at their tasks.

"I cannot say it. I cannot." Brynne flung her hands over her face.

"We do not have long." Gwynnie waved her hands behind them. "Just say it, Brynne. Samuel will understand."

"What if he doesn't?" Brynne cried, her breath hitching.

Samuel turned to Gwynnie. "Will someone please tell me what is going on?"

Knowing they would soon be out of time, Gwynnie moved to Samuel's side and bent down to whisper in his ear. "Brynne was married before. In Ireland. She married a man she did not love, a man who was cruel. She ran away to England to be free of him, but not before she had given birth to a son."

Samuel stiffened, his hands gripping the barrel.

"That boy's name is Connal. Connal Devlin."

Samuel stood abruptly and ran a hand through his hair.

"Please, forgive me," Brynne pleaded. "I never meant to deceive you…"

"This explains why you have been sneaking out at night," Samuel said. "You've been going to see him. You're protecting your son, a murderer."

"No!" Brynne stood, taking hold of Samuel's arm. "He's innocent. He has not committed either crime they accuse him of."

"I believe him to be innocent too," Gwynnie cut in.

Samuel sat down on the barrel that Brynne had vacated. Brynne fussed around him, hopping from one foot to the other.

"I am sorry I did not tell you the truth," she said hurriedly. "I feared that if you knew, you would leave me."

"Is your first husband still alive?" Samuel's face was contorted with pain. Brynne didn't need to answer for him to sense the truth. "Dear God, I never thought a woman with your religious fervour would do such a thing, Brynne."

"I was trapped." She took hold of his shoulders. "I had to get away from him. My son helped me to escape Ireland and come here. I fell in love with you, and I married you because I wished to. It felt as if God had dealt me a good hand at last. What is so awful about that? Pray, tell me!"

"Why tell me now?" Samuel clearly sensed there was more to this.

"If we are to prove Devlin's innocence and keep him hidden, we'll need your help," Gwynnie explained. "Will you meet him?"

Samuel hesitated.

"Please, Samuel," Brynne begged. "He is a good man. If you still believe there is an ounce of goodness in my soul, please believe in my earnestness now. My son is innocent of these crimes."

Samuel took her hand, though he remained silent for a few minutes. He seemed to be turning everything over in his mind as Gwynnie once more checked the corridor behind them.

"Please," Brynne begged. "Just meet him."

"As you wish. I will meet him." But as he spoke, he released Brynne's hand.

CHAPTER 24

Tombstone froze as he opened the door of his office. Gwynnie was already inside, having picked the lock. She sat in his chair with an apple in her hands, chewing away as he kicked the door shut behind him.

"I wonder why I even bother to lock this door anymore," he mumbled as he strode across the room. "Can I have my seat or has that gone, as my breakfast has?" He pointed at the apple in her grasp.

"There's another." She passed him a second apple, showing no sign of moving from his seat. "There are things you need to know."

Tombstone took a bite out of the apple and gazed at her face. "Did you sleep at all last night?"

"Do I look that bad?" She wiped her tired eyes with the sleeve of her gown.

"Perhaps it's better that I don't answer that question."

"Wonderful. So kind, as always, Tombstone." She continued to rub at her eyes.

"So, what has happened that I need to know?"

Telling Tombstone what had happened the night before turned out to be an easier task than telling Samuel. He sat on the windowsill, eating his apple and staying quiet for the most part. When Gwynnie revealed what she had discovered about Brynne, he sat taller on the stone sill, suddenly alert.

"Why didn't you tell me about those shamrocks?" Tombstone asked when she had finished her tale. "You say you found them yesterday at the barracks — why not tell me?"

"Because Brynne is my friend," Gwynnie explained as she placed her apple core down on the desk. Tombstone stood up at once and brushed it off into a bowl, wiping his desk with his sleeve. "I wanted to protect her."

"I'd say your loyalty does you credit, but you once declared you were my friend too." Tombstone raised his eyebrows. "What happened to that?"

"I'm telling you now, aren't I?" Gwynnie cocked her head. "And you still keep many secrets from me."

His grey eyes narrowed, but he said nothing. Instead, he returned to his place on the windowsill. "You wish me to help clear Devlin's name?"

"Why not?" Gwynnie sat forward. "You cleared my name when they accused me of murder."

"That's different."

"How?"

"I knew you were innocent."

"Do you honestly think that Devlin is guilty?" she asked.

"His innocence is much harder to prove. However —" he held up a hand before Gwynnie could interrupt him — "if we could find out who did kill Ashdown, it would be a start. Perhaps if I could find any evidence against this Henry Magner, that would help Devlin's case at the barracks too."

"So, you will do it then?" Gwynnie asked eagerly.

Tombstone stood up. "First, take me to meet him."

Brynne and Gwynnie led the way through the churchyard, Samuel and Tombstone behind them.

"Who are you, exactly?" Samuel asked Tombstone as they walked.

"Elric Tombstone, clerk and lawyer to the magistrate of London, Master Pascal."

"Yes, yes, I have heard all that before." Samuel waved a hand impatiently. "What I want to know is why are you so much in Gwynnie's company?"

"Do we have to do this now?" Gwynnie said over her shoulder.

"She's right. We have other business to attend to." Brynne pointed ahead at the curtain wall where they knew Devlin was hiding.

"Have you made her your mistress?"

"Samuel!" Gwynnie nearly walked straight into a gravestone as she spun around. "I am not his mistress."

"I have to ask, Gwynnie. Someone has to look out for you here."

Despite the fading daylight, Gwynnie could see just how red in the face Tombstone had become.

"Let me assure you," Tombstone said, "I have not taken Gwynnie or any maid as my mistress. I wouldn't do that."

Gwynnie had to bite her lip in order not to laugh. She rather wondered what Samuel would say if Tombstone revealed the truth: that he was much more likely to take a footman for that position.

"Hmm." Samuel grunted. "Come, let's get this over with."

Brynne took her husband's arm as they walked down the bank together, but there was clearly tension between them.

"He has not forgiven her then?" Tombstone whispered to Gwynnie as they fell into step beside one another.

"I think he's still in shock," Gwynnie said. "He still loves her." She pointed as Samuel helped Brynne down the bank when her foot was caught in a mound of earth.

Tombstone nodded, clearly deep in thought. "The webs marriages can weave…"

Gwynnie looked up at him. "What do you mean by that?"

"Nothing." He looked away at the curtain wall. "Now, where is this man?"

Gwynnie sighed when she saw the two pikes leaning against the torch-lit wall, with no sign of Devlin or the other guard who was supposed to be watching the gate.

Brynne halted by the gate and gave the same whistle as the last time they'd been here. At once, a figure appeared above the crenellations. He flinched when he saw it was not just Brynne and Gwynnie this time.

"Come down, Connal, please," Brynne urged softly. "You can trust these men." She laid a hand on Samuel's shoulder.

Devlin's eyes flicked toward Gwynnie, before turning in Tombstone's direction.

"I trust him with my life," Gwynnie called out. She felt Tombstone flinch in surprise at her side. She turned to him, seeing him smile. "Flattered?"

"A little." He looked back up at Devlin. "I do not believe you killed those soldiers, Devlin."

Abruptly, Devlin moved. As he had done before, he leapt out from the curtain wall and gripped onto the nearest tree branch. Brynne gripped Samuel's shoulder tightly, clearly fearful that her son would fall, but Devlin had done this too many times. He climbed down the rest of the tree with practised ease, landing on the ground with his feet spread wide.

Brynne took Samuel's hand and steered him forward.

"Samuel, meet my son. This is Connal." She smiled, looking at her husband hopefully.

"Not much family resemblance, is there?" Tombstone mumbled to Gwynnie.

If she looked really hard, Gwynnie could see a little similarity between the pair in the set of their jaw and nose, but Devlin had to look far more like his father than his mother. "There's more similarity between you and Pascal," she murmured.

Tombstone did not comment.

Devlin bowed. "I wish we had met another way," he said to Samuel. "My ma has told me much about you."

Samuel jerked his head in a nod. "She said you helped her to escape Ireland, when she ran from her first husband. Is that true?"

"Aye, sir."

"Then I thank you for that." Samuel suddenly extended his hand. They all stood frozen, watching as Devlin raised his hand and shook it. The tension cracked, and Brynne began to cry happy tears.

"It's a wonder she has any tears left," Gwynnie whispered to Tombstone.

"You are innocent, then?" Samuel asked rather impatiently as he and Connal released one another's hand.

"I am, sir. I am no murderer. Of that I can assure you."

"I'd like to ask you more about that," said Tombstone, taking a step forward. Devlin bowed once again as Tombstone approached him. Gwynnie hastened to Tombstone's side. "Gwynnie told me everything you said about that day. About this Henry Magner."

"And do you believe me, sir?"

"There's one thing I'd like to know." Tombstone gestured toward Devlin's throat. "How did you escape the noose?"

Devlin reached up to the neckline of his doublet and pulled it open, revealing the red scar across his skin. "The noose broke as the hangman kicked away my stool. I don't know why, sir. Perhaps it was an old rope. When the hangman came for me again, I turned the rope on him to get away. I didn't kill him," he hastened to add.

Tombstone nodded. "Then you came here?"

"Aye, sir. I came to find my ma and work out a way to be free of England." He glanced at Brynne. "We didn't think it possible to overturn my conviction. Flower here seems to think otherwise."

"Flower?" Tombstone repeated.

"He means me." Gwynnie sighed heavily. "I thought I told you not to call me that, Devlin."

"Likewise." He smiled and Gwynnie found it rather hard not to smile back. "Do you think it possible, sir?"

Tombstone scratched the coppery stubble across his jaw. "I wouldn't say it is a definite thing."

"She says you cleared her name when she was accused of murder." Devlin gestured toward Gwynnie. "She's also rather reluctant to tell me whose murder that was."

"She's good at keeping secrets," Tombstone admitted.

"Was that a compliment?" Gwynnie asked, standing taller.

"Perhaps." Tombstone turned back to Devlin. "I need you to tell me everything in detail. I know you have already told Gwynnie, but I need to hear it from you, from start to finish." He reached into the lining of his doublet and pulled out parchment. He also handed an inkwell and a quill to Gwynnie to hold.

"Are you planning to twist my words into a confession?" Devlin asked suspiciously.

"No. I'm going to write up your defence and hand it to the magistrate of London, my superior," Tombstone said, unfurling the parchment.

"And you're asking me to trust you? A man I have just met? The same man who has sent yeomen guards to search for me for days on end?"

"How about you trust the woman who hasn't yet been able to stop you?" Tombstone inclined his head toward Gwynnie. "She trusts me."

Devlin began tying up the neckline of his doublet once again, his eyes fixed on Gwynnie.

"Please," she whispered. "This could be the only way to clear your name."

Devlin gestured toward the two stools by the wall. "Then shall we take a seat? Telling you everything may take a while."

Tombstone handed the parchment to Gwynnie to read, but she found it almost impossible to decipher his cursive handwriting. She could make out a few words here and there, but she wished he had written it a little plainer if he desired her to read it all.

"This is everything?" Tombstone asked Devlin, who now stood against the curtain wall, one of the pikes in his hands, just in case another yeoman guard walked by. Beside him, Samuel and Brynne were sitting on the stools, hand in hand. They had scarcely said a word to each other as Devlin had recited his tale in the darkness, but Gwynnie was relieved that Samuel had at least listened to everything Devlin had to say with perfect attentiveness.

"It is," Devlin muttered. "I don't know what else to give you."

"Then it will have to do." The way Tombstone stared down at the parchment told Gwynnie everything. He didn't think it was enough to clear Devlin's name.

Her hands clenched into fists. "What more do you need?" she asked, turning to face Tombstone.

"We need someone else to have seen Henry Magner near the major's office, but we didn't hear his name mentioned when we were at the barracks." Tombstone folded up the parchment. "We'll have to see what we can do with this."

"You're not hopeful, are you?" Devlin's deep voice sounded strained.

"I'll go and see Pascal now." Tombstone began to walk away, stopping to beckon Gwynnie to follow him. "Gwynnie, I may need you."

"Are you in the lawyer's employment?" Devlin asked as she turned to leave.

"That's what we've been questioning for months," Samuel muttered, though he didn't quite meet Devlin's gaze.

"Don't ask questions you don't want to know the answers to," Gwynnie replied as she followed Tombstone. He was halfway across the churchyard, and as she scurried up the bank she heard footsteps behind her. She turned to see that Devlin was following. He drove the pike into the ground beside him.

"You're taking a risk, flower, bringing that lawyer here."

"Do you suppose taking a risk is new to me?" Gwynnie said, trying to sound more confident than she felt.

"Aye, perhaps not." He eyed her carefully. Ordinarily, no one looked at her with such acute attention. "Well, you know all my secrets now. Care to tell me one of yours?"

"Devlin —"

"Connal."

"Connal, what is it you want to know?" Gwynnie's stomach knotted tight, fearing what he might ask.

He glanced back at Brynne and Samuel, but the two had their heads bent together as they spoke quietly.

"Are you just in Tombstone's employment? Or is your relationship more…"

"More what?"

"Intimate."

"Forgive me whilst I go and throw up behind a gravestone."
Her words made Devlin laugh softly. "Why is that important
anyway?"

"I don't know." He fidgeted a little. "Call it curiosity.
Perhaps concern." He reached out and took her hand.
Gwynnie supposed she should have pulled back. Devlin may
not have been a murderer after all, but he could still be arrested
at any moment. Such things could only lead to heartbreak.
Devlin bent toward her. "Another question ... are you safe
here?"

Gwynnie blinked. She could not remember anyone ever
asking her that question. It was strange to hear it now, to think
that someone would care enough to ask. "You ask me that
when you're the one who may be taken to the gallows?"

He took a small step forward. "A maid in the employment of
a lawyer in a royal palace, one who raises a dagger to a
murderer and creeps around at night... I wouldn't say she was
safe. Would you?"

"It doesn't matter," she whispered, looking down their
hands.

"It does matter."

"No, it doesn't." She looked up again. "For now, do not
think about me or why I am here. Let us think about how we
get you out of this mess."

Devlin smiled. "Rather hard not to think about you, flower."

She inhaled, stunned at his words.

"Gwynnie?" Tombstone's voice called from the darkness
near the church. "We don't have time to dally!"

Gwynnie smiled back briefly at Devlin then disentangled her
hand from his. Slowly, he let her go.

"Stay safe," he said.

"Take your own advice."

When she reached the side of the church where Tombstone was waiting for her, she couldn't help glancing back. Devlin hadn't moved. He still stood on the bank, watching the two of them.

Tombstone grunted as he walked away.

"What?" Gwynnie ran to catch up with him. "What does that grunt mean?"

"It means that falling for a convicted murderer is not a wise thing, Gwynnie."

"I don't know what you're talking about," she said, walking ahead of him in her irritation. "Though you're one to talk. Didn't you take a blackmailer for a lover once?"

"Don't remind me. Hearts aren't always as clever as heads."

CHAPTER 25

"Well? What do you make of it all?" Tombstone asked, pacing up and down Pascal's office as Gwynnie sat on a chair nearby.

Pascal had been woken from his slumber for this particular conversation. He sat at his desk with an open doublet thrown over his nightshirt. The hose he had pulled on were ill tied, forcing Gwynnie to look away when he fidgeted in his seat.

He placed down the parchment on which Tombstone had written Devlin's account.

"Well..." Pascal paused and rubbed a hand across his balding head. It glistened in the candlelight. "If this is true, then there has been a gross miscarriage of justice."

"If?" Gwynnie repeated. "You doubt what is in this testimony?"

Pascal glared at her. "Maids would do well to keep quiet," he warned her in a low tone.

"I'm no ordinary maid."

"Shadows should be even more silent," he snapped.

"Pascal," Tombstone cut in, "please, tell me what you think of this testimony."

"I'm tempted to believe it." The magistrate placed a hand over the parchment. "It certainly makes more sense than a chained man being able to overpower six soldiers."

"Then..." Gwynnie leaned forward. "We can clear his name?"

"I do not have that power." Pascal shook his head. "It is not simply a case of writing a statement to clear his name. He would either have to be given a royal pardon, or we would need to appeal against the original conviction. To do that, we need more than just his word."

Gwynnie slumped back in her chair as Tombstone rubbed his brow tiredly.

"What more do we need?" Tombstone asked Pascal. "A confession?"

"Yes." Pascal pushed the parchment across the desk. "If you could get this Henry Magner to confess to the murders, that would be enough to prove Devlin's innocence, but I imagine the chances of making a man confess to so many sins would be nigh on impossible."

Tombstone picked up the parchment, folded it neatly, and returned it to his doublet.

"Do you even know where Magner is?" Pascal asked, looking between the two of them.

"He could still be at the barracks," Tombstone suggested.

"If he's a smart man, he will have run." Gwynnie sat forward again. "We could go and find out."

"Then start there," Pascal urged, waving a hand at the two of them in dismissal.

"Major Widgeon, this is a direct order from the Magistrate for the City of London. I have the right to question you as to which men are stationed in these barracks."

"In case you have not noticed, we are rather busy here." The major didn't even turn to look at Tombstone as he strode across the soldiers' yard. Gwynnie struggled to keep up with the two men, weighed down as she was by the heavy satchel she carried over her shoulder once again.

"I understand that, Major; however, this will be much swifter if you cooperate," Tombstone said, losing his patience.

Gwynnie and Tombstone had arrived at the barracks early that morning. So far, they had been brushed off by two lieutenants and now the major as they attempted to ask questions about the whereabouts of Henry Magner.

"What is it you want?" Major Widgeon asked with exasperation. He was already flicking his fingers at a nearby soldier, urging the man to come to his side. He whispered orders in the ear of the soldier, who hastened off again. The whole time, the major barely paid attention to what Tombstone had to say.

"You have here a man by the name of Henry Magner. Where is he now?"

"Magner?" Major Widgeon was distracted. He turned away and walked into the adjoining yard, where some of the men were running drills with their swords.

"Yes, Henry Magner." Tombstone followed relentlessly at his heel. "Have you not heard of him?" Gwynnie hurried behind them, listening in.

"Magner has not been here for some time."

"What?" Tombstone caught the major's arm. "What became of Magner? Where is he now?"

Widgeon pulled his arm back so sharply, he nearly knocked Tombstone from his feet. "I don't know." He shook his head. "No one has seen him for some weeks. There, I have answered your questions, and now I must attend to my responsibilities. Good day, Brimstone."

"Tombstone!" Tombstone barked after the major, though it did little good. Widgeon was already talking with the soldiers who were leading the drills.

"Are you all right?" Gwynnie asked Tombstone, who was cursing under his breath.

"Save me from the arrogance of men in high positions. He doesn't want to answer my questions because he knows the moment he does, the peace here is destroyed." Tombstone looked away, turning his gaze on the barracks behind them. "They've left Devlin's chamber shut up since he left. I wonder if they've left Magner's too?"

"It may be locked."

"Since when did that stop you?"

Gwynnie's brows lifted. "When did you start to break the rules, Tombstone?" she asked with a smile and led the way toward the barracks. "I rather like this new side to you."

As they entered the building, a long line of soldiers marched past them. Hanging at the back was the same soldier Gwynnie had overheard the last time she was here. Urwin was as miserable now as he had been then, staring at the ground as he marched by. Gwynnie elbowed Tombstone and pointed out Urwin in the line.

Tombstone stepped in front of Urwin, blocking his path so that he could not follow the others. Urwin looked up in alarm, his eyes widening.

"Sir?" he croaked in surprise. "Did I not answer all of your questions the last time you were here?" He looked around anxiously. "I think it unwise for you and I talk again. The men are saying I'm weak, dwelling on the past." He sighed. "I'm tired of it."

"I have two very quick questions for you, then I swear I will be on my way," Tombstone promised. "What do you know of a man named Henry Magner?"

"Henry?" Urwin's brow wrinkled. "A sorrier-looking man would be hard to find. He was never the same after he heard about his brother's death in the rising in the north."

"And where is he now?"

"He left, sir."

"When?"

"Weeks ago. In fact, I don't think I've seen him since..." Urwin paused. "Since Devlin ... you know." He cleared his throat uncomfortably.

"Where did Magner sleep?"

"In the same dormitory as me, sir. Upstairs, second door on your left. It's a shared room. His bed has been unoccupied since he deserted."

"Thank you." Tombstone waved a hand in the direction of the courtyard. "You'd better catch up with the rest of your men."

Urwin nodded and hurried on.

The moment he was gone, Tombstone took the satchel off Gwynnie's shoulder and led the way up the stairs.

"You looked like you were about to crumple under its weight at any moment," he murmured.

"Don't let anyone see you helping a maid," she reminded him, but all was quiet now the men had left.

Together, they made their way up the staircase to the top floor of the barracks building. They headed straight for the door Urwin had described, pushing it open when they found it unlocked.

Creeping into the room, Tombstone dropped the satchel as Gwynnie looked around. There were six beds in all, most showing signs of having recently been slept in — all except one. It was neatly made up and was completely bare of any personal items.

Gwynnie crept toward it and spied a small coffer at the bottom of the bed. She reached for the lid, only to find it locked. Pulling out the thin rod she kept up her sleeve, she pressed it into the lock and began to move it around.

Tombstone lifted the straw mattress, looking for anything Magner may have wanted to keep secret.

The lock eventually popped back, allowing Gwynnie to lift the lid. Inside were many piles of clothes, but in the lid she discovered some letters, pressed beneath a slat to keep them in place. Gwynnie prised them free and handed them to Tombstone to read as she searched the rest of the coffer.

"*My dear brother,*" Tombstone read aloud from the first letter. "*You would no doubt laugh if you were here and had seen what they have brought us to. They think the uprising is nothing but peasants, men without tools or weapons, but they are wrong. These men are highly organised and very prepared, not to mention passionate. They outnumber us. After our ale last night, a group of us made a short trip to the camp. Though they made merry, they were confident of their success. I wish I was as confident of our success. Trained soldiers we may be, but the odds are not in our favour.*"

Gwynnie looked up at Tombstone. His face had turned pale as he flicked the page over.

"He goes on at length," he summarised. "He even talks about the orders they were given, how their major refused to give them more ammunition or more men."

"It's as Devlin said then," Gwynnie replied. "Magner's brother was ordered to his death because of the uprising."

"It would seem so." Tombstone flicked through the other letters. "They're all from Magner's brother, Lucius, but this is the last one according to the date. He didn't write again." He stuffed the letters into his doublet, swallowing uneasily.

"What was the uprising about exactly?" Gwynnie asked, rifling through Magner's clothes.

"You don't know?"

"I heard the rumours, but rumours can become distorted. We both know that."

"Some say it's because of religion. That's rubbish, in my opinion." Tombstone sighed and sat down on the bed. "There have been poor harvests in the north. There are more and more land enclosures going up all the time. The people are starving, unable to afford the increase in the price of grain and the like."

"They wanted feeding?"

"They claimed it was not an uprising against King Henry, but against the suppression of the monasteries." Tombstone pulled out the letters and flicked through them again. "If you ask me, the people jumped at the chance to fight and have their say, to try and change their fortunes."

"So, starving men were pitted against trained soldiers?"

"The king was not the only one to underestimate the power of the rebellion," Tombstone explained. "It has dragged on and on. Only now has Henry agreed to meet the leaders of the rebellion to broker peace. He and Robert Aske are in negotiation."

Gwynnie found something small and metal at the base of the coffer. Pulling out a small tin box, she chewed her lip, thinking of the poor starving man that would have killed Magner's soldier brother. Did it amount to self-defence? Or was it pure brutality on both sides?

She prised open the tin to find more letters inside. These were older, the parchment turning brown with age.

"From Magner's mother." She raised the tin for Tombstone to see himself. "The letters are old."

"Perhaps she has left this world." He lifted a letter out of the tin and turned it over, his eyes widening. "There's an address, Gwynnie, here in London." He held the letter out for her to read. "If Henry Magner was looking for somewhere to hide, why not make it his mother's house?"

"Then we are agreed." Pascal climbed down from his horse, cracking his back and reaching for the cane that Tombstone held out to him. "I shall lead this conversation. Tombstone, you will make sure he doesn't leave, and you..." The magistrate turned to face Gwynnie. "Just don't do anything."

"Don't do anything?" she repeated in surprise, pointing at the building behind them. Made of wattle and daub, the small townhouse was pressed between the two timber-frame buildings on either side of it. The house was evidently old and poorly looked after, the windows covered in cloth rather than glass, and the door standing askew in its frame. "I can be useful here. I'm the reason we know Magner's inside."

Since leaving the barracks that morning, Gwynnie had kept watch over the house of Magner's mother. Though no woman had been seen to come and go, Gwynnie had seen a figure move behind the cloth-covered windows. She had even seen a man leave and go to market, the hood of his cloak pulled up over his head. The light was fading from the afternoon sky now, and inside, the glow of a candle could be glimpsed.

"Just wait here," Tombstone pleaded, taking Gwynnie's shoulder. "Remember what you said about Devlin? There's only so much you can do against a trained soldier?"

"I remember."

"Well, we know Magner doesn't have the principles Devlin has, don't we?" Tombstone whispered as Pascal loped toward the house. "I don't want you to get hurt."

"Protective, are we? Perhaps we are friends after all, Elric."

Tombstone released her shoulder with an exasperated sigh.

"Or maybe you just don't want to deal with the paperwork if I end up dead," she suggested wryly.

Tombstone shook his head and urged her to stand with their horses. "Stay here and keep watch. Please."

She nodded reluctantly and watched as he approached the house with Pascal. The two men talked together in low voices, then Tombstone walked away, tiptoeing around the line of houses, clearly intending to approach the back door as Pascal went in through the front.

Pascal waited a few moments then raised his cane and knocked on the door. Gwynnie's eyes flicked to the window of the house. No one moved, but the candle must have been blown out, as all fell dark. Gwynnie moved to stand behind one of the horses, who was munching on a hay bale that had been left discarded on the side of the street.

When no one answered the door, Pascal reached for the handle and turned it, entering the house.

Gwynnie looked around. The street was busy with men ambling to and from the tavern, as women hurried home from their working day with baskets in their hands. Few people looked at each other now darkness had fallen, all preferring to keep their heads bowed in what little lantern light filtered out from nearby windows.

A sudden thud from inside the house made Gwynnie turn. The cloth at the window on the first floor shuddered a little, a sign of movement from within, before it fell still.

Determined to hear some of what was going on, Gwynnie crept forward, moving away from the horses and toward the downstairs window. She pressed her head close to the gap.

There were voices coming from within the house, but Pascal and Tombstone must have found the soldier upstairs, for they sounded far away.

"No. No!" a man's voice suddenly bellowed from within, so alarmingly loud that Gwynnie took a step back.

"You're under arrest, Magner." Tombstone's voice matched the soldier's in volume. Pascal was speaking now too, but Gwynnie couldn't discern his words.

"I won't tell you anything. I'm a deserter, aren't I? That's it! I deserted my post!"

"Then explain these bloodstained weapons."

Gwynnie took a step back from the window as more sounds followed from within the building. There were heavy thuds, suggesting a tussle was taking place. Someone cried out in pain, then there was a grunt as someone else was attacked.

"No!" Pascal screamed, his voice suddenly so high-pitched that those walking past in the street stopped and stared.

Footsteps rumbled upstairs, followed by another thud.

Gwynnie jumped back as she saw the cloth move in the window above her. Someone was tussling with the soldier beside the window. Then something lurched out.

"Argh!" A great cry of fear erupted as a figure crashed through the frame, taking the cloth that covered the gap down with them.

CHAPTER 26

"Pascal!" Gwynnie bellowed his name, already reaching to grab the hay bale. She tore it free from the horse who was nibbling at it, kicking it into place beneath the window.

It barely landed there before Pascal fell onto it.

Gwynnie bolted forward, reaching for Pascal. He was breathing heavily, his eyes bright and wide as he stared up at the sky. He no longer had his cane and the cloth he had torn down from the window in his fall was still clutched in one hand. Kneeling on the hay, Gwynnie checked him for injury, vaguely aware of raised voices around her.

"Someone help him!"

"He needs a physician!"

"The physician is drunk in the tavern. You think he will do much good?"

A crowd gathered around Gwynnie and Pascal as the sound of footsteps thudded from inside the house. The front door flew open, and a man burst out. When he saw the crowd, he sprinted off down the road, knocking some out of his way and causing the horses to buck and whinny in alarm.

"Neville!" Tombstone cried from within the building.

Gwynnie knelt down over Pascal again. Someone in the crowd raised a lantern high over their heads, casting enough light onto Pascal for her to see a thin line of blood across his temple. She mopped it up with the sleeve of her gown as she gingerly lifted his head to check the back. Fortunately, there seemed to be no further injury.

"Is he alive?" Tombstone cried, pushing people aside as he too emerged from the house.

"He's alive," Gwynnie assured him. "He's winded."

Pascal tried to move, but both Gwynnie and Tombstone held his shoulders still.

"Stay still. I need to check your injuries." Tombstone reached for Pascal's wrist and started measuring his pulse.

As the crowd continued to cry out for a physician, someone asked what had happened.

"Did he fall?"

"How could someone fall out of that window?"

"Did you not hear him scream? No, he was pushed."

When Pascal's eyes found Gwynnie's, she stiffened in surprise. Then his hand clasped hers with such urgency, she was startled at his strength after such a fall.

"Thank you," he muttered between heavy breaths. "You pushed the bale, didn't you?"

Uncertain what to say, Gwynnie held his hand between both of hers and just nodded.

"Thank you," he said again, then he let his hand fall away from hers as his head dropped back onto the bale.

"How's your back?" Tombstone asked desperately. "Neville, I need you to stay awake. How's your back?"

"Hurts," Pascal muttered simply. "What about Magner? Did you get him?"

"No. Forget about Magner for now."

Gwynnie peered through the crowd. Wherever Magner had gone, he had a good head start. Even if she ran after him, she doubted she would know which paths to take to find him.

"Leave him, Gwynnie," Tombstone pleaded, clearly reading her thoughts. "Help me with Pascal. We need to get him back to the palace."

Pascal opened his eyes again. For a change, when he looked at Gwynnie, it wasn't with disgust.

Gwynnie hurried around Pascal's bed, carrying a fresh bowl of water. Tombstone plumped up the pillows for Pascal as he sat back on them. The old man sighed deeply, as if all the breath was leaving his body as he leaned back. The man who had looked so powerful in his deep black clothes was now a shell of his former self. His thin hands clutched the blanket Tombstone pulled up over him, the sagging skin at his neck all the more prominent as his head tipped back.

"Well?" Pascal asked Tombstone expectantly. "You have your mother's training. How bad is it?"

"Cracked ribs." Tombstone spoke with quiet confidence as Gwynnie offered the bowl to Pascal for him to wash his hands. He did so, then dried them on the towel she held out. "You may have damaged your spine too. Your legs seem … reluctant to move."

"My legs are always reluctant to move, Elric. That's what comes with old age."

Tombstone did not respond.

Gwynnie set the bowl and towel down on the side as the silence stretched, broken only by the crackling of the fire and Pascal's laboured breathing. Changing the subject, she asked, "What happened in that room?"

"We came up different staircases. We found Magner on the first floor," Tombstone replied. "I accused him of the murder and he started yelling, saying that we couldn't take him away."

"Did he confess?"

"Not exactly," said Pascal, almost wheezing.

"Rest," Tombstone said softly, placing a hand on Pascal's shoulder. Once again, Gwynnie had the distinct impression that their relationship was much deeper than that of an employer and lawyer.

"It wasn't enough of a confession, Tombstone. You know that." Pascal struggled to get the words out.

"I know." Tombstone released his shoulder. "Gwynnie, without a written confession we can't clear Devlin's name. And without knowing where Magner is now…" He trailed off as Gwynnie felt tears prick her eyes.

She turned away, busying herself with throwing out the old water and adding more logs to the fire. How could it be that after all of this, even after Magner had thrown Pascal out of a window, it wouldn't be enough to clear Devlin's name?

"He attacked us both," Tombstone continued. "I was stunned by the cane he tore off Pascal, then he pushed Pascal out of the window."

"She saved my life." Pascal's voice made Gwynnie pause by the fire. He tried to lift himself off the pillows to look at her, but Tombstone urged him down again. "Why?" His voice was strained. "Why do it?"

"You ask me that?" Gwynnie struggled with the lump in her throat as she threw another log onto the fire, watching it spit and catch light. "You may think me no better than cat turd beneath your shoe, Pascal —"

"Gwynnie," Tombstone hissed, but she ignored him.

"But I'm no killer. I'm no cold and heartless creature." Gwynnie walked to the door. "I'll leave you to your rest."

She was on the spiral staircase outside when Tombstone caught up with her. He carried a candle with him, casting a welcome glow over the stairs.

"He was trying to show he was grateful. You may have saved his life, Gwynnie."

"Yes, yes." She waved a dismissive hand at him. "Because who would think anyone as insignificant as a maid would try to save another's life?"

"Gwynnie." Tombstone caught her arm and stopped her from walking on. "I know you're upset, and I'm sorry we weren't able to get Magner's confession. If I knew where else to look for him, I'd be looking for him now, but I don't."

"I know." Gwynnie folded her arms, staring up at him in the candlelight. "So? Are you going to tell me or not?"

"Tell you what?"

"How are you and Pascal related? Is it so inconceivable to think I could be trusted with such a secret?"

"Gwynnie, you know that's not what I think."

"Then why continue to keep this secret?"

"Because it's not my secret to tell!" His voice had risen. "I made a vow not to tell anyone. For the sake of a friend, I will hold onto that vow. I will not break it for you."

Gwynnie took a small step back. "I suppose we aren't friends then, are we?" she said quietly. "Because you don't trust me after all."

Tombstone's shoulders slumped. Whatever he was going to say, he must have changed his mind, for he closed his mouth firmly.

"So much for friendship," Gwynnie muttered and walked away. To her relief, Tombstone didn't try to follow her.

As Gwynnie stepped out into the tiltyard, she knew she should go straight to her chamber and go to bed. Instead of heading to the servants' quarters, however, she turned left and cut through the orchard and garden, heading through the palace grounds toward the churchyard. In the distance, she heard the owls hooting in the yew trees, even the distant laughter of yeomen who must have been playing games to keep themselves awake. She kept on walking until she stumbled down the bank toward the curtain wall.

As she had now come to expect, the pikes were leaning against the wall, the dice game discarded on the stool. She looked about, searching for Devlin, but he was nowhere to be seen.

Pursing her lips, she whistled the same two notes that Brynne had used previously. Devlin's head soon appeared above the crenellations as he climbed out of his hiding place.

"Flower? You all right?" he asked, leaning forward over the stone wall.

Gwynnie didn't answer. Instead, she moved toward the tree that he always used to clamber down. She tucked the long skirt of her woollen gown into her belt and began to climb. She was not a natural climber and struggled, her boots slipping on the dark knots of the bark more than once. As she reached the branch that brushed the wall, she came to a halt, uncertain how to cross the distance.

"Use that branch." Devlin pointed to another branch above her head. "Hold onto it and walk along this one." She nodded, following his instructions, coming as close to the wall as she possibly could, though there was still a gap between her and the wall.

Devlin moved to stand up on one of the crenellations and extended a hand toward her.

"I've got you," he promised, his voice deep.

Gwynnie reached out to take his hand, her small fingers caught in his large palm, and jumped across onto the stone wall. He caught her with ease, then helped her down onto the wooden boards on which he walked.

"What has happened, Gwynnie?" he asked, bending toward her. Her eyes pricked with tears again when she thought of the man before her and how she could not clear his name, though no words would come.

When the first tear slipped down her cheek, it was as if a wall broke. The tears flooded out of her, and she gasped as she covered her mouth with her hand.

Devlin wrapped his arms around her as she fell into his chest, embracing her tightly.

Gwynnie couldn't remember being hugged by anyone other than her mother, but this hug was entirely different. It was strange to feel so safe in a man's arms, one whom she barely knew at all. As she cried, he made no effort to pull away. He just held her, his head resting on her own.

"Bad day, eh?" he said after a moment. She managed to laugh through her tears, though she kept her head firmly against his doublet.

"Something like that."

"Tell me something, Gwynnie," he whispered, leaning back so that she was forced to lift her head to look at him, though he didn't release her. "Why do you work for that lawyer?"

"Because we made a deal," she said in a rush. "He saved me from the noose, and he agreed not to go looking for my mother."

"Your mother?"

"He would hang her if he could. Any man of the law would." She bit her lip, trying to stem the flow of tears. "She has blood on her hands." Devlin cupped Gwynnie's cheek, using his thumb to wipe away the tears under her eye. "If I work for him, then he won't go looking for her. I thought ... I thought we were friends."

"Some friendship when one holds the other's life in their hands." Devlin said, shaking his head. "You don't have to stay here forever, Gwynnie. You don't have to be in his employment."

"For now, I do. I have no choice." She looked up at him. His blue eyes looked silver in the moonlight. "I'm sorry."

"What for?"

"Henry Magner escaped us tonight. We weren't able to stop him."

Devlin smiled rather sadly.

"Why are you smiling?" she asked in disbelief, her tears threatening to fall again.

"Because you tried. That is a kindness I didn't think I was worthy of anymore."

She stepped forward into his arms again, more tears coming as he held her tight.

CHAPTER 27

"Gwynnie?" a voice murmured through the darkness. "Aye, flower, I'd like to stay like this too, but we cannot."

Gwynnie opened her eyes. She was sitting on the battlements, her head resting on Devlin's shoulder.

"Oh." She yawned as she sat up and stretched. "We slept like this all night?"

"We did." Devlin nodded, seeming in no hurry to stand. "I was hardly going to send you back to your chamber, was I?" She smiled up at him, seeing that he looked almost as tired as she felt, with shadows under his eyes.

"I am sorry," she murmured again. Last night, after he had held her for some time, she had told him what had happened with Magner and how he had disappeared into the streets of London.

"Don't be sorry," he said now, shaking his head. "You did all you could. I suppose if they do find me, there's not much difference between being arrested for one death and being arrested for seven, is there? They still think I killed that man in the queen's chamber, don't they?"

Gwynnie frowned. In her effort to clear Devlin's name of the six soldiers' murders, she had almost forgotten about the death of Jasper Ashdown and Cromwell's conviction that Devlin was responsible.

"Maybe there is something we can do about that." She stood up and peered over the crenellations, wondering how she was going to get back down.

"What do you have in mind?" he asked, moving to stand beside her. When she struggled to reach the tree, he wrapped an arm around her waist.

"What are you doing?"

"Helping you." He practically lifted her off the wall and onto the branch. She clambered across it, scurrying down the tree as Devlin followed, jumping and swinging from one branch to another. As they both landed on their feet on the earth, she frowned and folded her arms. "That glare is an odd way to thank me, flower."

"I didn't need your help."

"I don't imagine you need anyone's help." He bent toward her with a smile. "Indulge me. I quite like being useful to you." He hovered there for a moment then moved away, leaving Gwynnie strangely breathless as he walked to his place by the gate. He pulled on a yeoman's cloak that had been hanging from a hook in the wall, then lifted the pike. In an instant, he was a yeoman guard once again.

"What are you planning to do about Jasper Ashdown?" he asked as Gwynnie combed her fingers through her hair, trying to tuck it back up into her white coif.

"I plan to find out how he ended up in Donsen Tower in the first place. I know it's easy enough to get through a locked door, but the question is, how did Ashdown know?"

"And how would you know that?" Devlin called after her as she walked back up the bank.

"I'll tell you another time." She looked back at him, watching as he waved goodbye. She waved back, then hurried to her task.

"Come on, Ricard, you must have seen something," Gwynnie pleaded with the yeomen manning the door to Donsen Tower.

"You and another were keeping guard here that night. Did you honestly not see Jasper Ashdown at all?"

"I saw him," Ricard said. "But if you want to know more..." He waved his fingers in her direction.

"You want paying?" she spluttered.

"Not exactly." He pointed at the cob poking out of her apron that she had pilfered from the kitchens. "The Advent fast is a hard time for us all."

"Very well." Gwynnie lifted the cob and split it into two, handing him half. "Now, what did you see that night?"

"I saw Ashdown approach Donsen Tower. I thought he was going the long way to his own chambers." Ricard pointed to the topmost floor of the palace building as he chewed on his bread. "He didn't pause to talk to anyone, not even his brother as he walked past him."

"His brother? Which one?"

"The elder of the two," Ricard replied, "Owen Ashdown. He tried to stop his brother here —" he pointed to a spot in the cobbled courtyard — "but Jasper Ashdown walked around him, ignoring his pleas." Gwynnie recalled that Devlin had described another with Jasper, trying to get his attention. It seemed that Ricard and Devlin had seen the same thing.

"What pleas? What did Owen say?"

"He said that Jasper had to listen to him. That he had already risked enough."

"I see." Gwynnie fidgeted with the bread in her grasp, thinking about what Tombstone had said of the gambling place listed on Ashdown's known haunts. "Maybe he had lost the family too much money already."

"They weren't talking about money, Gwynnie." Ricard spoke around a mouthful of bread. "If you ask me, they were talking about a woman."

"What makes you think that?"

"For one thing, Owen said, 'She is not worth the risk.'"

"Oh." Gwynnie spoke in a low voice. "Ricard, do you think Jasper Ashdown was going to see one of the queen's ladies that night? That one of them was his mistress?"

"It's possible, isn't it?" Ricard shrugged. "Lady Rutland is a firm favourite with many of the men, isn't she, with her fine looks? When I heard what had happened, I assumed that was why Ashdown was in those rooms."

"How did he end up dead then?"

"I don't know." Ricard shook his head.

"Thank you, Ricard."

"No, thank you, Gwynnie." Ricard waved the last chunk of bread in the air. "Believe me, this makes a big difference." As he turned back to his post by the door of Donsen Tower, Gwynnie hesitated.

"Ricard, do you remember what Ashdown was wearing that night?"

"Are you going to tell me why you are asking so many questions?"

"Curiosity." Gwynnie waved his concern away easily. "I was one of the people who found the queen that night. It upsets me to think what she went through."

"Very well." Ricard swallowed the last of his bread. "He wore fine clothes. He had a hat and a cloak, and he was carrying a knife."

"What sort of knife?" Gwynnie asked sharply.

"One of those ornate daggers the aristocracy like to keep at their hips. Probably useless in a fight."

Gwynnie thanked him and headed into Donsen Tower, thinking about what she had seen that night in the queen's chamber. "There was no knife," she whispered aloud, recalling the scene — not at Ashdown's hip, nor on the bed or on the floor, but she had to be sure.

She climbed the stairs up to Queen Jane's rooms and hovered outside the door, planting her ear against the wood. There was no sound, nothing to suggest that either the queen or any of her ladies were inside.

It was common knowledge in the palace that Queen Jane had been moved out of her usual rooms on the day of the murder, but it had not lasted long. Tombstone had said it was on Cromwell's insistence that the queen returned to these rooms. They didn't want to draw the king's attention to what was happening with the queen, while the imperative peace talks were taking place.

Gwynnie glanced back over her shoulder. There were no yeomen guards nearby, nor any of the queen's ladies-in-waiting. Slipping the rod out of her sleeve, she picked the lock of the chamber, then stepped inside.

The room was empty. This outer chamber contained a table with gifts that had been sent to Queen Jane to lift her spirits. There were even signs of what the queen had recently been through, with numerous crucifixes laid out and bundles of herbs to ward off evil spirits.

Gwynnie tiptoed toward the queen's most private chamber, sweeping aside the heavy curtain that separated the two rooms.

She glanced around then stepped forward and bent down, searching under the bed for any sign of the knife Ricard had described. She reached under coffers and behind cabinets, but there was no sign of the weapon. It was just possible that the knife Ricard had seen Ashdown wearing was the very one that had been turned on him in a fight.

Gwynnie moved toward the window and opened it wide. The bloodstains she had seen had long since been cleaned away, leaving behind only pristine glass. Gwynnie leaned out.

Queen Jane's chamber overlooked the riverbank and the Thames. Fortunately, all was quiet, with no one to witness Gwynnie pulling herself out through the window. She was small and just about managed it, though it struck her that it was a remarkably tight fit, even for her. The killer would have had to fold themselves up very small in order to have made it out of the room this way.

As Gwynnie stepped out onto the rooftop, a gust of wind rippled off the water. She sat down hurriedly, gripping the slate tiles beneath her as she looked around the rooftop. She could just about make it across to the next rooftop if she needed to. Determined to follow the path the killer had taken, she moved slowly forward on her hands and knees until something caught her eye.

Wedged deep in the gutter was something silver and ornate. Gwynnie reached for it, her fingers clutching the engraved pearl-white handle. She pulled it free with some difficulty, finding that the blade had pierced the metal gutter. She held it up in the air, watching the early morning sunlight bounce off the metal. If it had once been bloodstained, that blood had been washed away by all the rainwater in the gutter, but she had little doubt that this was the blade that had killed Jasper Ashdown.

Gwynnie turned and looked back at the window behind her. Either someone had placed the blade here when they had made their escape across the rooftops, or they had reached out of the window and plunged the knife into the gutter, before retreating back inside.

"It wasn't planned," Gwynnie said to herself as she tucked the blade into a pocket in her apron. "They turned his weapon on him."

"This doesn't seem like a wise idea," said Devlin when Gwynnie had explained her plan.

"You already go about the palace disguised as a yeoman. Why not stand somewhere else for a while?" Gwynnie gestured to Devlin's uniform as he followed her up the staircase.

"Aye, fair enough. Where are we going?"

"I need you to stand guard outside a room whilst I search it." They walked along a corridor, heading to the Ashdowns' rooms.

"Search it? Why, Gwynnie?" Devlin hissed.

Two well-dressed gentlemen appeared at the far end of the corridor. Gwynnie cleared her throat and Devlin jumped into place, holding onto his pike as he stood against the wall. Gwynnie busied herself, taking out a cloth from her apron and dusting the frame of a nearby painting. They remained silent as the two men passed by. The moment they were out of earshot, they turned to face one another again.

"Why are you searching someone's room?" Devlin asked impatiently.

"I'm trying to prove your innocence."

"And what if you get caught?"

"Calm down, it's not the first time I've searched a room." Gwynnie pushed past him and continued down the corridor.

"Exactly how often are you searching rooms? Quite a grand habit, is it?"

"More often than I'd like to admit." Gwynnie halted outside a chamber door. She had visited the Ashdowns' shared sitting room previously with Tombstone, but she had not yet been to

Jasper Ashdown's bedchamber. She knew at once that this was the right one, for some people of the court had left winter flowers by the door, in memory of Jasper Ashdown. There were white cyclamens and milky-coloured hellebores, their heads all drooping. "Just keep guard," she pleaded with Devlin.

He turned and stood beside the door, the pike beside him, though he shook his head.

Gwynnie dropped the rod down her sleeve and plunged it into the lock, all too aware of Devlin watching her.

"You're supposed to be keeping a lookout."

"There's currently something more interesting to watch." He nodded as the lock clicked back. "You've done that before."

"Perhaps. Let me know if someone comes and don't let anyone in." She opened the door and stepped inside.

She wouldn't have long, for the Earl of York and his sons were at breakfast. She wanted to complete this search as quickly as possible and get out before they returned.

Jasper Ashdown's chamber extended before her. It was messy, the bedding ruffled as if he had just left it. Gwynnie walked past the open coffers, the clothes spilling out, and made her way toward a writing bureau tucked into the corner of the room.

She searched through the drawers, looking for any sign of a woman's handwriting or a woman's name in the letters and papers, Lady Rutland's name in particular, since Ricard had thought her the most likely candidate to be Jasper's lover. Yet her name was nowhere to be seen.

Tucked away at the bottom of a drawer was a note written by Jasper's brother Owen. Gwynnie scanned the parchment, her eyes catching the odd phrase here and there.

Listen to reason...

This is a relationship that cannot continue. It's too dangerous...

This is not about our father or the earldom. It's about your own life…
Do you want to lose your head for the sake of sharing her bed?

Gwynnie folded up the letter and slipped it into her pocket, hoping that Tombstone could read the slanted writing better than she could. It was plain from the letter that Owen had discovered whatever affair Jasper had been having, and that he was determined to stop his brother from continuing with such a relationship.

"Why would he lose his head for it, though?" Gwynnie whispered. She thought of Lady Rutland. She was indeed a married woman. Gwynnie knew nothing of Lady Rutland's husband, and could only assume that he had to be a violent and vengeful man.

As Gwynnie turned to leave the room, she spied a jewellery box beside one of the coffers.

"Gwynnie," Devlin suddenly hissed from the doorway. "There are footsteps coming this way. Time to go."

"I'm nearly finished." She reached for the jewellery box and lifted the lid. Inside were pendants, and the now familiar crest of the two eagle heads bent together emblazoned on family rings. Distracted, Gwynnie stared at the jewellery. Had she come across such valuable items when she was a cutpurse, she would have taken the lot. They could have helped her and Emlyn to escape a life of crime for good. She ran her fingers over the rings, tempted to take one.

"Gwynnie!" Devlin's voice came again, more urgently.

"I'm coming." Her fingers closed around a pendant; there were no eagles on this one, but another bird entirely, rising out of a tower. She tucked the pendant into the palm of her hand, wrapping the chain around her wrist, and hastened toward the door.

The moment she stepped out, Devlin took her shoulder and marched her away down the corridor.

"Go quickly," he urged, "before we are seen."

At the end of the corridor they darted toward a small spiral staircase, aware of voices in the passageway behind them.

It was the Earl of York and his sons. The earl was expressing his wish to return home, while his sons reminded him that if they didn't want to be associated with the rebels, they had to stay at the palace for Christmas.

"A poor tribute to your brother," the earl hissed. "Celebrating at Christmas when he is…" He broke off.

As a door shut behind him, Gwynnie halted in the middle of the spiral staircase. Devlin peered over her shoulder as she held up the pendant for him to see.

"Do you know what this is?" Gwynnie asked him, pointing out the heraldry.

"It's a bird. A tower. And some roses. Are you expecting me to know the jewels?"

"They're rubies." She brushed her fingers lightly over the ruby roses. "And the bird is a phoenix."

"How do you know that?"

"Because I have seen it before. I've seen it emblazoned on tapestries at King Henry's wedding. I've seen it in a stained-glass window in the palace, beside the Tudor rose of our own king. And I've seen it adorning a royal gable hood."

"Wait." Devlin took the pendant from her to look at it more closely. "Are you telling me that Jasper Ashdown had a token from…?" He trailed off.

Gwynnie nodded. "From Queen Jane."

CHAPTER 28

"Hurry, get inside!" Gwynnie urged Devlin into Tombstone's office. She had just picked the lock, and Devlin was looking at her with a curious smile. "What?"

"You pick locks the way others breathe."

When they heard footsteps in the corridor, he glanced around and then hurried into the room, with Gwynnie following. She leaned against the door, planting her good ear to the wood to listen as Devlin discarded his pike. Seeing a roaring fire, he hurried toward it, dropping to his knees and stretching out his hands.

"It feels so good to be beside a warm fire again."

Gwynnie saw the relief in his face as he held his palms close to the flames, then shifted her attention back to the door as she heard voices outside.

"See that Pascal is well taken care of," Tombstone was ordering someone. "His wife will be arriving soon."

"Shall I bring her to see you?"

"No." Tombstone's reply was fast. "Take her straight to him. She'll want to see him."

"Yes, sir," the other voice said.

Gwynnie stepped away from the door just as Tombstone thrust his key into the lock. Evidently finding it already unlocked, she heard him curse as he swung the door open.

"I'm going to stop locking this door," he said with a sigh, before he noticed Devlin by the fire. "What in God's name —" He kicked the door shut behind him. "Gwynnie, you brought him here? What if he's seen by Cromwell? I won't be able to stop his arrest then."

"We had to come and see you." Gwynnie held up the pendant, but Tombstone barely looked at it in his indignation.

"We had a deal, Gwynnie. No more thieving."

"Ah, that explains a lot." Devlin smiled. He was now stretching out on the rug in front of the fire, stuffing one of Tombstone's cushions under his head. "Raised a thief, flower?"

Gwynnie felt heat rise to her face. Oddly, it wasn't something she wanted to admit to. Her face burned with embarrassment as Tombstone walked past her toward his desk.

"Please, make yourself at home," Tombstone grunted at Devlin.

"Thank you," Devlin replied with no hint of irony.

Gwynnie followed Tombstone. "Look again at what this is."

"What is it?" Tombstone took the necklace but still barely looked at it. "Where have you been all morning? I couldn't find you in the kitchens or the laundry."

"First, I went to Donsen Tower and found this." Gwynnie reached into her apron and pulled out the knife she had taken from the gutter. She threw it down onto the desk. Both Tombstone and Devlin's heads jerked toward it. "Someone had hidden it in the gutter outside Queen Jane's chamber. If you ask me, they could have reached out and put it there without having to scramble across the rooftops. Ricard, one of the guards," she added hastily at Devlin's look of confusion, "saw Jasper Ashdown on the day of his death. He said Jasper was arguing with his brother Owen. He overheard Owen say 'she is not worth the risk' and was trying to stop him from going into Donsen Tower. Jasper also carried *that* —" she pointed at the blade — "in his belt."

Tombstone finally lifted the pendant closer to his face. "It can't be," he whispered. "Where did you get this?"

"From Jasper Ashdown's chamber. It bears the emblem of the Seymour family — the phoenix rising from the tower. Now, why would Jasper Ashdown have that?"

Tombstone slowly lowered the necklace, looking slightly pale.

"There's this too." Gwynnie pulled out the letter she had taken from Jasper's room and handed it over. "Owen is trying to persuade his brother to give up on a woman, that she's not worth Jasper risking his neck."

"Oh, my God." Tombstone stumbled back into his chair. "The last man who slept with a queen…"

"Who *supposedly* slept with a queen," Gwynnie reminded him. "Every man accused of sleeping with Queen Anne, even her own brother, lost their heads at the Tower. What if Owen was trying to save his brother from the same fate?"

"That would mean —" Tombstone swallowed hard — "Queen Jane took a lover."

Gwynnie nodded slowly. It was hard to imagine the meek woman she had so often seen at the king's side this last year doing anything to disobey him or break her wedding vows, but Gwynnie didn't know her well. She only knew her mild manners. She also knew the way that Queen Jane had screamed with fear when Ashdown's body was discovered on her bed.

"Someone could have murdered Jasper Ashdown to keep Queen Jane's secret, or to punish her for having a lover in the first place," Tombstone said slowly, holding the chain up so that the pendant swung back and forth.

"She found him, didn't she?" Devlin said. "Sounds like a cruel form of punishment, to kill your wife's lover and have her find him."

"King Henry isn't behind this." Tombstone shook his head. "He would have his wife publicly humiliated and charged. That doesn't mean that someone else hasn't taken vengeance on his behalf."

"So?" Gwynnie asked, reaching for the carafe of wine Tombstone kept on his desk. She poured out two glasses and handed one to Devlin, who downed half the glass in one go. "What do we do now?"

"Oh please, drink all of my wine, why don't you?" Tombstone waved a hand impatiently at them.

"Why, thank you." Gwynnie topped up both of their glasses.

"Gwynnie!"

"I'll pour you a glass too." She smiled broadly as she handed him the glass, then she asked again, "What do we do now, Tombstone?"

"We keep this secret," Tombstone said. He stood and moved to the buffet cabinet, pulling out the medicine box and tucking the pendant inside. "And we discover who else was in Queen Jane's chamber that day."

"This is a risk," Devlin whispered as they walked into Donsen Tower.

"Just stand outside Queen Jane's bedchamber and keep watch," said Tombstone as Gwynnie followed them. "People see what they want to; Gwynnie has demonstrated that many times. Listen to what the ladies say as they walk by, and report anything of interest that you hear. Just don't talk to anyone."

Devlin nodded and made his way up the stairs. He was halfway up when he turned back and looked at Gwynnie. She smiled encouragingly at him, but before she could see if he smiled back, Tombstone took her arm and dragged her away.

"You two need to stop this," he warned.

"Stop what?"

"You know very well what I'm talking about." He eyed her carefully as they walked on. "Now, let's go and see Owen Ashdown and question him about the night his brother was murdered."

Gwynnie glanced back at the staircase up which Devlin had disappeared before she raced to catch up with Tombstone. They entered the corridor of the Ashdowns' chambers, where one door had been left open. Gwynnie peered inside to see Owen drinking alone at a table.

"Master Ashdown? May I speak with you?" Tombstone called into the room.

Owen released a drunken burp. He must have gestured for Tombstone to enter, for he went into the room, leaving Gwynnie to peer around the doorframe and watch the two of them together.

"Drink?" Owen asked, offering the carafe.

"No, thank you." Tombstone shook his head as he took the seat opposite him.

"I've been drinking all day," Owen muttered miserably. "I told myself I'd toast my brother's memory." He topped up his glass. "Then I found myself wishing to forget all the memories he's left me with." The carafe slipped, but Tombstone caught it before the wine could spill everywhere. "Do you have any brothers, sir?"

"Not exactly, no."

"Then you are fortunate. It's a strange bond." He sighed. "We're bound to love our brothers, but they can test that love to its limits. The truth is, I'm not sure I loved him anymore at all. Oh, I tried to protect him. Tried to take care of him." Owen's northern accent was stronger in his drunken state. "Little good it did ... the selfish bastard." He lifted the glass to his lips and took a heavy gulp. "Have you ever known a man who does everything for his own gain? His own ... *enjoyment?*"

"I have." Tombstone nodded slowly. "The fact that your brother frequented brothel houses and taverns suggests to me he was such a man."

"He was." Owen nodded languidly as he placed the glass down on the table in front of him. "You have come to ask me more about him, haven't you?"

"Yes." Tombstone leaned forward. "I wish to know which woman you were discouraging him from seeing when he was heading to Donsen Tower."

Owen blanched. His hand shook as he raised the glass to his lips once more.

"Then say no more," Tombstone continued. "If it is who I think it is, then you have my word — her name will never cross my lips."

"Th-thank you." Owen stammered. "Jasper was a fool. He didn't once think of how his life was at risk, how we were *all* at risk by association." He leaned forward. "How many men were sent to the Tower last time? How many men were executed on the orders of the king last spring?"

"I know." Tombstone raised a hand soothingly. "Now, did you follow your brother into Donsen Tower?"

"What? No!" Owen cried. "I wouldn't have taken the risk of being discovered there. Wait, you think that I...?" He clutched a hand to his chest. "I did not kill my brother." His hand fell to the table. "I tried to stop him from going in. We scuffled, but he went anyway. I stood outside and waited for Jasper to come out of the tower, but I did not go in there."

Gwynnie watched Owen Ashdown's face intently. The pain and grief were obvious, but so was the fear. Even in his drunkenness, he was terrified of who would discover the reason his brother had been in the queen's chamber.

"How often did he visit her chamber?" Tombstone asked.

"I don't know." Owen toyed with his glass, staring down into the depths. "Often enough. I caught the two of them looking at one another across rooms. People can't hide it very well, can they? When they feel something."

Gwynnie shifted her weight between her feet, thinking of the way Tombstone had just dragged her away from Devlin.

"What was amazing was that no one else seemed to notice. Only me."

"Maybe someone else did notice," Tombstone suggested. "As you waited for your brother to come out of the tower, did you see anyone else? Did any other enter the tower?"

"No other man entered." Owen raised his gaze from the glass. "Lady Rutland returned first, then the queen and her ladies followed. I saw a maid go up, then the shouting began."

Gwynnie flinched when she realised Owen had seen her go to the chambers. He had clearly kept a vigilant watch.

"So Lady Rutland entered the chambers first?"

"Yes, she did."

"And no man entered?"

"None," Owen confirmed. "I'm beginning to wonder if my brother was not slain by a man at all, but by a spirit." He raised his glass to his lips again.

"Thank you." Tombstone stood. He extended his sympathies, but Owen didn't seem to be listening.

She hurried down the corridor, thinking hard about what she had just heard. When Tombstone caught up with her, he was walking fast.

"Did you hear that?"

"Every word," she assured him. "Tombstone, if no man killed Jasper Ashdown —"

"And no spirit did either," Tombstone added. "I do not believe spirits walk this earth to kill men."

"Then maybe a woman did it."

Tombstone nodded. "The question is, which woman? Lady Rutland entered the chambers first, but did she go as far as the queen's bedchamber? It wouldn't have taken long to kill a man and pull back the bed curtain to hide him, would it?"

Gwynnie raced to keep up with Tombstone as they returned to Donsen Tower, climbing the staircase they had sent Devlin up. As they reached the top, they found Devlin with his hat pulled low, standing by the door to the queen's chambers.

"You two look as if you have seen a ghost," he whispered, pushing the brim of his hat up a little.

"Has anyone come by?" Tombstone asked.

"Only Queen Jane and her ladies — they're inside." Devlin pointed the pike at the door. "But they said something interesting."

"Yes?"

"One of the ladies had a leather binder in her hand. She told the queen she had taken it, that now all was safe, and no one would discover what was inside." Devlin shook his head. "They didn't even look at me as they walked past."

251

"Few people look at those standing in the shadows." Gwynnie moved beside him as she looked at the queen's chamber door.

"The queen insisted they had to get rid of it if they were to keep their secret safe," Devlin went on. "It sounded as if they intended to burn it."

Tombstone turned to look at the chamber door too. "Gwynnie?"

"Yes?"

"Would you mind taking up your thieving ways again for a short while?"

"I daresay I'll be able to put up with such a burden."

CHAPTER 29

"Are you ready?" Gwynnie asked, nudging Devlin up the stairs of Donsen Tower.

"Are you sure this will work?"

"It worked once before. I don't see why it wouldn't work again."

He turned to stare at her. "Exactly how many times have you had a need to cause a distraction to steal something?"

"You may not want to know the answer to that question," Tombstone muttered as he hurried up the stairs after them. "I've told the guards to leave the base of the tower for now. They've gone. That should give us a short while to act."

"Then take up your places." Gwynnie tore off Tombstone's cloak and threw it over her shoulders so that it swamped her body. Tugging the hood over her head, she made her way toward Queen Jane's chamber door. She glanced back at Devlin and Tombstone and nodded.

The two men stood at the top of the stairs, beside a suit of armour. Gwynnie and Emlyn had once pushed that suit over to cause a distraction. It would certainly bring the ladies out of the chamber, but she wasn't certain it would make them dally long enough.

"Ever thrown yourself down a set of stairs before?" Devlin asked Tombstone, standing behind him as he took hold of the suit.

"No." Tombstone gazed at the staircase apprehensively. "I just hope I get through this without breaking my neck."

"Good luck." Devlin nodded and pushed the suit over with his pike.

The armour tipped forward, clattering loudly as it struck the landing. Tombstone shouted and then hurried down the steps, stamping as loudly as he could. His shouts continued at such length that Gwynnie had to stop herself from calling after him that he didn't have to sound so ridiculous.

Tombstone threw himself to the ground at the base of the staircase just as doors began to fly open, thudding against the walls. Devlin discarded his pike and jumped down the stairs, with those who had hurried through the open doors following in his wake.

The door closest to Gwynnie opened wide.

Lady Rutland stepped out first, with Margery Lyster and Lady Monteagle at her shoulder. Behind them was Queen Jane.

Peering out from beneath her hood, Gwynnie focused on the queen. She was not the woman she had once been. Since she had lost her child, she had grown paler, her hair was somewhat thinner and her once round cheeks had become rather hollow.

"What has happened?" Lady Rutland demanded.

"A man has fallen," Devlin called from the bottom of the staircase. It sounded to Gwynnie's ear as if he had tried to flatten his Irish accent as much as possible. "He's severely injured."

"How did he fall?" Queen Jane stepped past her ladies and strode toward the stairs.

"Your Majesty, please —" Lady Rutland tried to take her arm to stop her, but the queen shrugged her off.

"I will not shatter into pieces yet. There is a man down there. Come." Jane stepped out onto the staircase, with her ladies following closely.

"Where are all the guards?" Lady Rutland called as she made her way down. "You there, go and fetch more. We do not yet know if this man tripped or was pushed."

Gwynnie waited until they had disappeared onto the staircase, then reached for the door they had left ajar, slipping inside.

As before, the scent of the herbs hit her suddenly. There were bundles of lavender and dried columbines, making the air quite sickly. Gwynnie searched the table of gifts that had been left for the queen, but found no leather binder.

She hastened into the queen's private chamber. The queen had placed an ornate cross on the mantelpiece. It was very elaborate, the struts of the cross bedecked with a myriad of jewels. Gwynnie barely let herself acknowledge the emeralds and sapphires before she moved toward the coffers. Pulling open the lids, she searched through them, trying her best not to disturb the fine clothing, the coifs and gable hoods, or the silken skirts. She kicked over a loose farthingale left at the side of the room and had to hurry to right it again.

She had moved back into the first chamber when she heard footsteps in the corridor.

"Ah!" Tombstone cried out in pain.

"Do not try to move him." Lady Rutland's voice matched Tombstone's in volume. "We must be careful. One wrong move and the man could be immobilised. Your Highness, you can leave this with us."

Though Gwynnie could not hear her answer, she supposed Jane must have refused, because all fell quiet again.

Gwynnie turned on the spot helplessly, looking for a clue as to where the binding might have been hidden. Her gaze shot to the fire. It was a small fire, the embers barely burning at all — a stark contrast to the queen's chamber, where the fire had been roaring madly.

"Burn ... they said they needed to burn it." Gwynnie repeated the words as she darted back into the queen's private chamber.

The fire screen had been pulled in front of the stone hearth. Gwynnie gingerly took the edge of the screen, trying not to burn herself as she saw that there was something nestled in the fireplace, resting on the logs.

A folio bound in leather and held together with a piece of string was currently burning to cinders.

Gwynnie grabbed the poker from the hearthstone and jabbed at the leather binding. At first, she couldn't move it from the logs, but the more she prodded at it, the more it wobbled. Finally, it tipped off the wood and onto the stone. She shrugged off Tombstone's cloak and threw it onto the binding, starving the flames and putting out the fire.

The stench of smoke and burning leather filled her lungs. She coughed a little, doing her best to breathe as she stood, folding the cloak around the folio. Kicking the fire screen back into place, she hurried out of the queen's rooms.

At the top of the stairs, she halted. People were now returning to their rooms, shaking their heads and muttering.

Lady Monteagle and Margery Lyster had their heads bent together.

"Poor man. He must have tripped on the armour." Lady Monteagle pointed to the top of the stairs. "I hope he wakes again."

Gwynnie looked around for a place to hide what she had taken. Seeing the shattered pieces of armour lying across the floor, she picked up a few of the plates, pretending to tidy them up. She held them on top of the cloak-wrapped folio, then walked down the stairs.

Coming the other way was Queen Jane and Lady Rutland, walking hand in hand.

"The physician will take good care of him," Jane whispered to her friend. "When I was young, my mother used to talk about haunted buildings, places where the demons walk. They cause death and injury, wherever they roam." She paused a few steps away from Gwynnie, looking at the ceiling. "I'm beginning to suspect this tower could be one such place."

"Come, Your Highness, no more of that." Lady Rutland ushered her up the stairs. "Such superstition doesn't help us now."

Gwynnie reached the bottom of the stairs and walked out into the courtyard. Tombstone was lying on a stone bench, with Devlin standing beside him.

Gwynnie looked around. Seeing that everyone who had helped move Tombstone to this spot had left, she nudged his shoulder.

"You're safe to wake up now."

Tombstone's eyes shot open.

"I honestly didn't believe that would work," Devlin murmured in amazement as Tombstone sat up.

"Well? Did it work?" Tombstone stood up.

"I have it." Gwynnie pointed to the bundle in her arms. "It may be burned beyond recognition by now, but I have it."

"Then come quickly, before anyone sees me walking away from here."

As Tombstone's door closed behind them, Gwynnie dropped the bundle onto the rug. Armoured plates rolled away as Devlin bent down beside her. Together, they unwound the cloak from the folio.

"You destroyed my cloak," Tombstone said pointedly.

"We're talking about murder here," Gwynnie reminded him. "Does your cloak really matter that much when we're trying to save Devlin's neck?" She glanced at Devlin, who smiled.

"If I make it out of this alive, I'll buy you a new cloak someday." Devlin held out the half-burnt cloak to Tombstone, who took it with a huff.

Carefully, Gwynnie reached out and opened the folio, tearing what was left of the blackened string free, so they could peer inside.

"Letters," Devlin said with interest as they rifled through them. Most were burnt beyond legibility. "Wait, look at this." He held up one that was only half burnt. "It's addressed to Jasper Ashdown."

Tombstone dropped his cloak and took the letter from Devlin, while Gwynnie turned the folio over. Across the back, the initials JA were just about visible where they had been etched into the leather.

"Is it possible that someone else searched Jasper's chamber before you did, Gwynnie?" Tombstone asked.

"I unlocked the door myself." She grimaced, remembering how quickly she had departed from the room. "I didn't lock it once I left."

"Devlin, you said that Lady Rutland had this folio in her hands. Perhaps she searched Jasper Ashdown's room after you did, Gwynnie?" Tombstone gestured down at the file. "She might have taken it after you opened the door."

"You think these letters are from the queen?" Gwynnie asked, reaching for more of the letters. She couldn't read the handwriting, but Devlin managed to decipher some of what had survived the fire. He held up one letter and read aloud:

"You must stop this. You cannot think that by persisting in this affair, it will do either one of us any good. What passed between us was a

mistake that must never be repeated. It's been signed by Jane."
Devlin passed the letter to Tombstone before picking up
another. *"Do not mistake me,"* he read. *"I may be smaller than you, I
may be meeker in character, but I have a strength in me you know not. I
will not share my predecessor's fate because you threaten to reveal what
passed between us that night. If you reveal our secret, it will be as good as
murder."*

Gwynnie picked up another scrap. Most of the letter had
been destroyed, but she could make out one line all too clearly.

*"I am prepared to do anything to save my own life. Truly, I would shed
your blood before I would see my own spilt."* Gwynnie dropped the
letter as if she had been burned by it. Devlin picked it up, then
passed it to Tombstone.

"You don't think —" Devlin began, but Gwynnie was
already nodding.

"What if the queen wasn't shouting that day because she had
discovered Jasper's body?" Gwynnie stared at the burnt leather
in front of her and the scraps of letters. "What if she went into
her bedchamber and found Jasper hiding there, wanting to
speak to her? When he threatened to reveal their secret, she
stabbed him with his own knife. Perhaps she was screaming at
the horror of what she had done. She could have stuffed the
knife into the gutter, desperate to be rid of it, then cowered
away as the full weight of what had happened hit her."

Gwynnie closed her eyes, remembering Jane's bloodcurdling
screams.

An unpleasant memory returned from when she had
searched for Jasper Ashdown's pulse. "He was still warm. I
thought how strange it was… He hadn't had time to turn
cold."

Tombstone jerked forward sharply. Clearly his mind was
working as fast as hers was.

"Ashdown's injuries would have meant blood, Gwynnie. Was there blood on the queen's gown? Think."

"No," she answered swiftly, but she shook her head a moment later. "But her cloak was bundled up into a small ball. Lady Monteagle took it out of the room. If there was blood on it, we wouldn't have seen it."

Devlin stood and took the letter back from Tombstone. "This is why I am hunted in this palace?" Devlin asked wildly. "I will go to the gallows. And why? Because a woman took a lover? And she killed him to keep that secret?"

"It's not that simple." Tombstone held a hand out toward him, trying to take the letter back, but Devlin jerked it out of reach.

"It is exactly that simple."

"This is our queen," Tombstone hissed at him. "Wife to King Henry. He has already killed one wife, possibly two. What else was Queen Jane supposed to do?"

"And what is supposed to happen to me? Should I swing from the gallows to save Queen Jane's life?"

"I didn't ask you to do that." Tombstone tried to take the letter again, but Devlin was backing up, moving away from the two of them.

"Devlin, what are you doing?" Gwynnie asked, moving to her feet.

"I want to know why. I need to hear it from her lips." He stuffed the letter into his doublet and sprinted out of the room, kicking the door shut behind him.

"What are you doing? Devlin!" Gwynnie cried, running after him. She flung herself at the door, but it rattled in its frame, refusing to move.

Tombstone tried the handle too, but to no avail. "The pike," he muttered. "He's barred us inside. Probably jammed it through the handle and into the frame. Gwynnie, what will he do to the queen?"

"He's no killer." Gwynnie rounded on him.

"He's a soldier. A murderer he may not be, but a killer? He's certainly that!" Tombstone barked at her.

Gwynnie backed away from the door, her breathing quickening. Looking at the window, she saw another way out. She pushed it open and clambered out.

"What are you doing?"

"It's not the first time I've escaped your chamber this way. Come," she said, dropping down to the ground. She could slide through the gap easily, but Tombstone could not. He slipped and nearly fell flat on his face. The only thing that kept him from planting his jaw in the earth was Gwynnie catching his arm and dragging him up.

She took off at a sprint, with Tombstone struggling to keep up behind her. When they reached the tiltyard gate, she waved a hand at the guard, begging to be let inside.

"No one is allowed in." The guard shook his head. "Cromwell's orders. The councillors' meeting has just —"

"I work for Cromwell, damn it, man!" Tombstone bellowed, appearing behind Gwynnie. "Your queen's life could be in danger. Now let us in."

The guard dropped his pike in panic at Tombstone's voice. He unlocked the gate, swinging it wide so they could both run inside. They took off across the courtyard, with Gwynnie outsprinting Tombstone, holding her skirt high.

When they reached the inner courtyard outside Donsen Tower, Gwynnie skidded to a halt. A crowd had gathered.

"What is this?" Gwynnie turned her head back and forth.

"Look." Tombstone pointed at those in the middle of the crowd. Cromwell and King Henry were leading the way, with a myriad of lords following. They were waving at the crowd as people clapped around them. Behind them followed the Duke of Norfolk. His hand gripped Robert Aske's shoulder very tightly. Though Aske smiled, there was something tense about his demeanour. "They've reached a deal. The rebellion must have come to an end."

Gwynnie strained to look through the clapping hands and gable-hooded heads of the crowd, but there were too many for her to see clearly. "Where is he?" she hissed.

"I can't see him." Tombstone turned and half-clambered up the wall beside them. No one else seemed to notice; their focus was too much on the smiling king and the men who followed him. People were calling for drinks, pleading for the fast to end early so they could celebrate properly.

"There!" Tombstone pointed across the crowd.

Gwynnie's stomach lurched. "Where?"

"I don't see him, but I see the queen. She's heading toward the church."

Gwynnie took off across the courtyard, but she didn't get far. She kept bumping into people, for they did not see her coming, too busy cheering for the king. Tombstone made even slower progress, for he wasn't small enough to slip through the gaps that Gwynnie could find.

At the other end of the courtyard, she stumbled through the archway and out onto the estate, sprinting toward the church. Far ahead, Gwynnie glimpsed the queen's gable hood. Jane stepped into the church, Lady Rutland at her side.

Gwynnie reached the church, threw open the door and stumbled inside. She was breathing heavily as she hastened down the aisle. At the front, Jane was kneeling before the altar, praying. Lady Rutland sat in a nearby pew.

"Your Majesty," Gwynnie cried, rushing forward.

"Do not disturb the queen at prayer." Lady Rutland twisted around in her pew, her eyes wide when she saw that it was Gwynnie who had spoken.

"We must disturb her." Tombstone's voice sounded behind Gwynnie as he too hurried into the church. "There is another coming here. He is coming to find the queen, and we do not know what he will do. We must leave before he gets here."

"You're too late." Devlin's voice echoed across the church.

CHAPTER 30

Gwynnie cursed when she saw Devlin standing in the doorway to the vestry. It was the same way he had made his entrance into this church before. If she had thought about it, she could have cut him off there, rather than following the queen in.

Queen Jane stood, her hands gripping a glittering gold chain. Her eyes were wide as she looked at Devlin.

"Is it... Oh!" She backed up fast. Lady Rutland scrambled to her feet and took hold of Jane's arm, pulling her as far away from Devlin as possible.

Gwynnie couldn't move. The Devlin she had come to know was altered as he walked forward. He was abruptly the soldier, marching, his eyes narrowed at the queen.

"Why am I being blamed for a murder that you committed?" He raised his finger and pointed at Jane.

"I —"

"How dare you!" Lady Rutland thundered, cutting off the queen before she could say any more. "Do you know who you are speaking to? You!" She waved a hand at Tombstone. "Why have you not seized him yet?"

Tombstone took a step forward. Devlin jerked his head around. A warning in his eyes told Tombstone not to come any closer.

"He'd beat you in a fight. You know that," Gwynnie hissed at Tombstone. Rather reluctantly, Tombstone took a small step back, so he was just behind Gwynnie's shoulder.

Gwynnie tried to catch Devlin's eye, but he appeared to be doing his best to avoid looking at her. Those blue eyes darted right past her, returning to the queen, who cowered on the other side of the altar with Lady Rutland.

"I didn't kill that man." Devlin reached inside his doublet. He pulled out the burnt letters they had taken from Ashdown's folio and threw them on the floor. "Yet *you* threatened to spill his blood."

"Enough!" Lady Rutland screeched.

Jane raised a pale hand to cover her lips, just as Lady Rutland pushed herself in front of the queen, shielding her.

"Whatever you think is in those letters, you are mistaken." Yet Lady Rutland's eyes darted toward the burnt cinders. "I doubt a man such as you can even read."

"Maybe I'm not the heathen you think I am," said Devlin, his Irish accent strong and deep. "I've been taught to read. I know whose name is at the bottom of those letters. I know you just tried to burn them all so that they would never be found—"

"No!" Jane cried, but Lady Rutland once more tried to silence her, waving her hands frantically at the queen.

Lady Rutland's eyes turned on Tombstone. "You have made a remarkable recovery, sirrah." She wrinkled her nose in distaste. "What is in those letters means nothing."

"Nothing?" Devlin's voice was so loud that the altar plate rang with its echoes. "Her crime will see me at the gallows —" He thrust an accusatory finger toward the queen. "I want answers." He moved forward.

"You will come no closer!" Lady Rutland screeched, throwing her arms out wide in front of the queen. It didn't stop Devlin, who took another step.

Gwynnie moved at the same time, sprinting across and placing herself in front of Devlin, her hands planted in the centre of his chest.

"Get out of my way, Gwynnie." His voice was hollow as he stared over her head at the queen.

"I won't let you hurt her."

"Flower…" His voice broke into a momentary whisper. "I'm not that kind of man," he hissed for her ears only as he smoothly took her arm and put her aside. She gripped his elbow, trying to drag him back.

"I would die before I let you hurt her!" Lady Rutland was screaming again.

"All I want is to know what happened!" Devlin bellowed. Lady Rutland's strong spine bent a little as she backed up further. Jane was now sandwiched between her friend and the stone wall, her gable hood slipping, the gold chain in her grasp shaking.

"The truth?" Jane's voice was tiny in comparison. "You already detest me for your suspicions. What good can the truth do?"

Gwynnie tried to throw herself in front of Devlin again, but he stepped around her. Reaching beneath his doublet, he pulled out the string of rosary beads he carried everywhere with him. He held them high so that the cross swung from side to side, and Jane's lips parted as she slowly raised her glittering chain.

Gwynnie saw that it was a string of rosary beads.

"Let him judge you," Devlin urged, his voice dangerous. "Not me."

Queen Jane's voice hitched. A sudden wail escaped her.

"Your Highness." Lady Rutland grabbed hold of Jane as she slid down the stone wall. Her white and pink embroidered skirt fell about her, the beautifully made material stark against the stone floor. "Please —"

"He is right — I'll be judged for this. God has seen it. God knows what I did…"

"Please, you know you had no choice."

"What happened?" Devlin held the queen's gaze. "Tell me that. If I am to go to the gallows for your crime, Your Highness, I need to know why."

It was the first time he had addressed Jane by her title. It seemed to upset her all the more, for she screwed her eyes up tight and shook her head frantically.

"Your Highness, please —" Lady Rutland tried to pull her to her feet, but Jane suddenly pushed her off. Though she was much smaller than the lady beside her, she somehow managed it at once, in a kerfuffle of skirts. Jane halted on her knees as Lady Rutland sat awkwardly, her farthingale jutting out at an angle as she stared at the queen.

"You wish to know?" Jane's voice shook and her eyes filled with tears.

"It's a place for confessions, isn't it?" Devlin nodded at the altar beside them.

"Yes. Yes, it is." Jane spoke quickly. She tried to stand, then fell back against the stone wall. Lady Rutland reached out to help her, but she was not the first to reach the queen. Devlin took the queen's arm and steadied her.

Slowly, carefully, Devlin steered Jane back toward the altar. She seemed both in awe and terrified as she stared up at Devlin. He lowered her to the steps. She sat, her skirts tucked up beneath her, as the first tears started to fall.

Devlin knelt beside her, waiting for her to begin.

"It was never supposed to happen," she mumbled. She lifted her chin, not in a regal manner, but as a supplicant, up toward the roof of the church. "It was a weakness. A weakness induced by too much wine and sadness. I haven't had many choices in my life. You know that, as I do. When the king chose me…" She broke off briefly, her breath hitching as she closed her eyes tightly. "I saw two queens die, then Henry made me his third. The ladies in the palace aren't the only ones who whisper, wondering how long I will last. I wonder the same thing."

Jane's hands tightened around the golden rosary beads. "Jasper was kind and charming, at first. Then one night, we…" She trailed off.

Devlin looked away, as did Gwynnie. She had no wish to hear about what the queen and Jasper Ashdown had done.

"I thought it was over, that the mistake wouldn't come back to haunt me. Then it did." She lifted her head, now staring vacantly down the aisle as tears ran down her cheeks. "I was with child."

Gwynnie raised a hand to cover her mouth. The child Queen Jane had been carrying was not the king's child after all, but Jasper Ashdown's.

"I made the mistake of telling him." Her voice became high, the fear palpable as she leaned forward off the steps toward Devlin. "He threatened me. He said he was in debt. I had to pay him, or he would tell Henry that the next child to be born in this palace was actually a bastard child."

"Your Highness," Lady Rutland began, trying to comfort her, but the queen turned her head away in shame, her lips pressed tightly together as she fought back her tears.

"I couldn't pay him. Every shilling I own belongs to Henry. Everything that is ever spent comes from his coffers. He would know. How could I give Ashdown what he wanted? The threats became worse… He grew vengeful." She lifted her head to the ceiling once again. "When I found him in my chamber that day, waiting for me on the bed, he said…" She swallowed, clearly struggling to bring herself to say the words. "He said, 'Maybe he'll have you killed, as he did with the last one.'"

Lady Rutland made a pained sound, then staggered toward the nearest pew and sat down heavily.

"It was my life or his. We fought. It started out as a whispered argument — my ladies were in the chamber next door. I was so frightened they would hear." The words came thick and fast now. "I had to stop him. I grabbed hold of him." Jane reached for the air in front of her. "He threw me off, saying he would tell my ladies. I moved in his way, and he backed toward the bed. It was *there*..." Jane lowered her right hand a little, staring at empty space. "The knife at his belt. He didn't even cry out as the blade went in. Why didn't he cry out?"

She stared at Devlin, who slowly shook his head.

"There was blood everywhere. I rid myself of the knife and tore off my cloak. Then I realised..." Her voice trembled. "I realised exactly what I had done." Jane's shoulders slumped as the tears came again. She lifted the sleeve of her gown and used the fine material to wipe her eyes.

"How did I become a part of this tale?" Devlin asked quietly.

"Lady Rutland saw you."

Lady Rutland shifted on the pew. "I saw you creeping through the yard that day as I moved the cloak to my chamber. After we led the queen out of her chamber, I took the cloak from Lady Monteagle. When I saw the blood, I realised what had happened." She glared at Devlin. "I had seen the ballad sheet of your likeness that morning, being circulated among the other ladies-in-waiting. It seemed too perfect. After all, you were a man already sentenced to death for murder. Since you broke into the palace the same day a man was found dead, they would naturally assume it was you."

A memory shot across Gwynnie's mind: a woman standing in the shadows in the graveyard on the night of the storm.

"What happened to the cloak?" Gwynnie asked Lady Rutland.

"I buried it in the graveyard."

Gwynnie took a deep beath. She had near enough witnessed Lady Rutland's subterfuge to protect her queen, and yet Gwynnie had been too distracted with chasing Devlin to take notice.

"Does the king know anything of this?" Tombstone spoke for the first time.

"No." The queen flinched, apparently having forgotten he was in the church at all. "He doesn't even know I was with child. God has taken that child now. He saw fit to punish me, didn't he? A life for a life."

Devlin shook his head. "The innocent sometimes have to fight, Your Highness. A threat can make us capable of so much more than we thought possible."

His words made Gwynnie stare down at the palms of her hands. For a moment she thought she could see blood, but then she blinked and it was gone.

"None will hear of this tale from me." Devlin's voice was clear. "You have my word. I will carry your secret to my grave."

Jane leaned forward and her lips parted, but no words came out.

"Devlin," Gwynnie said, stepping forward, "people will still think that you are the murderer."

"Then let them think it, Gwynnie." He looked up at her, meeting her eye for the first time since they had entered that church. "I won't be the reason a queen goes to the chopping block."

Before Gwynnie could argue with him, Lady Rutland spoke suddenly.

"Do you hear that? Someone is coming."

The sound of footsteps outside the church was unmistakable. It was accompanied by a deep male voice.

"Where is she?"

"I believe she came in here, Your Majesty," another voice replied.

The formal address made them all act fast.

Gwynnie jumped away from the altar as Devlin offered his hand to Jane and pulled her to her feet. Tombstone jerked on the back of Devlin's doublet, tugging him to the side of the church as Gwynnie picked up the burnt letters.

She led the way to the vestry, flinging the door open so that she, Devlin and Tombstone could hide inside, just as Queen Jane tried to dry the last of her tears. Beside her, Lady Rutland stood, looking ruffled as she attempted to straighten her gown.

The door of the church opened, just as Gwynnie pulled the vestry door toward her. She left it open a crack so she could peer out.

King Henry had entered the church and, unusually, he was smiling.

"My darling wife," he called out to Jane with a laugh. "We have done it. Ha! Indeed, we have found peace at last!" He held his arms out wide as he marched down the aisle. Gwynnie could just make out the shadows of men hovering in the doorway, waiting for his return. One shadow she judged to be Cromwell, for he was deathly still as he watched the king and queen together.

Henry halted at Jane's side and bowed his head, saying a quick prayer to God.

Jane turned to look at her husband. The fact she had been crying was obvious. Her cheeks were blotchy and red, and her sleeves were damp with her tears, but Henry didn't seem to notice.

"Come, we are to celebrate, and Robert Aske is to be our honoured guest for the Yuletide celebrations." Henry offered Jane his arm. "Join us for our feast."

Gwynnie saw the look of relief on Jane's face. This was the first time in over a month that she had been asked to join her husband for dinner. Whether or not the rumours that the king was bored with his wife were true, it seemed he wasn't going to get rid of her just yet.

Hurriedly, Jane took his hand.

CHAPTER 31

"I don't understand," said Brynne, echoing Gwynnie's thoughts.

She stood by the fire in the kitchen, the flames from the grate the only light left in the room this late at night. Close by, Samuel sat deep in thought with his hands pressed together, as Brynne stood restlessly, shifting her weight between her feet. Gwynnie leaned on the stone hearth as Tombstone stood at her shoulder.

"It was my decision, Ma," said Devlin, as Brynne moved toward him. She clutched his folded arms as she shook her head.

"You are willing to take the blame for a murder you didn't commit?" Her voice shook. "Why? Why would you do such a thing, Connal?"

Devlin unfolded his arms and took his mother's hands. "There is no way to prove I didn't kill those six soldiers. The man who did it has escaped. I'll always be thought guilty of his crime."

"I have sent word to all the officials at the docks," Tombstone cut in quickly. "If Henry Magner makes himself known —"

"And you think he would use his own name if he boarded a ship?" Devlin's words made Tombstone fidget from side to side.

Gwynnie stared at Devlin. He had clearly made up his mind to stop fighting the false allegations levelled against him.

"You can't prove I didn't do it without Magner." Devlin patted his mother's hand, though he spoke to Tombstone. "If

I'm discovered, I'll be hanged at Tyburn. Queen Jane and her lady were right — what difference does it make if I am hanged for one more death?"

"Connal!" Brynne wailed.

"Calm yourself, Ma," he said in a softer tone, turning his focus on her. "I didn't say I would make it easy for them to hang me."

"Do you know what you are doing, lad?" It was the first time Samuel had spoken since Tombstone had explained what had happened in the church. Despite his earlier coolness toward Devlin, there was pain in his eyes as he sat taller on his stool beside the fire. "You'll always be thought of as the man who tried to kill the queen."

"Will it save her life? To let people think that?" Devlin looked between them all as Tombstone nodded.

"It would," Tombstone whispered. "She can't be executed for murder then."

"Good. Then my mind is made up." Devlin patted his mother's hand again. "Ma, I had to sit chained to a chair and watch six good men die. I took an oath as a soldier to protect them, and I couldn't do it." His voice trembled as Brynne held a hand to her mouth. "If I can save one life now, then aye, I will."

He reached into his doublet, pulling out the burnt scraps that Gwynnie had gathered from the church floor before they left. He looked at Tombstone, waiting for confirmation as he held them out to the flames.

"Do it," Tombstone said.

Devlin dropped the letters into the fire. What little hadn't already been singed turned black and crumpled into ash in seconds. Gwynnie flinched at the sight of it, knowing that with the disappearance of those letters, all evidence of who had really turned that knife on Jasper Ashdown was gone for good.

"They'll hang you," she whispered in fear. "If they ever find you, you'll be hanged at Tyburn."

"Then I best make sure they do not find me, flower."

She jerked her head up, realising what he meant. "You're going to run?"

"It's my best bet now, isn't it?" He glanced at Tombstone, who stepped forward.

"It is." Tombstone bowed all of a sudden. "It seems I owe you an apology, Devlin."

"You thought me the devil, aye?" Devlin smiled for the first time.

"Maybe a little." Tombstone matched his smile. "You have my respect for this."

"It only takes something small, then, like saving a woman's life to earn your respect." Gwynnie's wry tone made Devlin laugh, but Tombstone did not. His grey eyes narrowed at her rather curiously.

"I'll help get you out of here, Devlin," Tombstone said with sudden fervour.

"I don't have enough to get him on a ship, not yet." Brynne glanced at Samuel. "I've been saving up."

"I'll pay for it." Tombstone nodded at her, a sign for her not to worry. He turned to Devlin. "I can have you aboard a ship in the next couple of days. You wish to go back to Ireland?"

"Aye. I do." His words made Gwynnie hang her head. It was strange to think that she may never see Devlin again, for a sea would separate them. "It will be far easier to disappear there."

"Then I'll make the arrangements." Tombstone's voice was matter-of-fact as Brynne's breathing hitched.

"I cannot believe it has come to this," she whispered as Samuel patted her hand soothingly.

Gwynnie lifted her chin, aware that Devlin was now looking at her with the same curious gaze as Tombstone. She tried not to look back at him, in case he glimpsed the weakness that made her gut feel like writhing snakes.

"If this is to work, we should leave a trail elsewhere." Gwynnie addressed her comments to Tombstone. "Tell Cromwell that we have found evidence Devlin has already left the palace and has headed north. Say he's joined forces with the rebellion, if you must. Anything to misdirect him and his men."

"It is a good thought," Tombstone said. "We know Cromwell was not afraid to be a part of the death of one queen. We don't want to give him reason to hurt another."

Silence fell upon them all. Gwynnie realised that they had done all the talking they needed to. They had their plan. Queen Jane's secret would forever remain between them, never spoken of again, and Devlin would have to flee if he was to survive.

After a moment, Samuel stood and moved toward Devlin.

"I am sorry to say it, lad," Samuel sighed as he held out his hand, "but I think it unlikely you will ever see your mother again. If anyone knew you were her son —"

"Samuel!" Brynne squeaked.

"He's right, Ma," Devlin said, taking Samuel's hand. "I will not put you in danger. It will have to be goodbye between us." The two men shook hands. It was a mark of respect and friendship.

Brynne moved forward, throwing herself into her son's arms. Devlin was almost knocked over by the sheer force of her embrace, then he held her tight.

Gwynnie swallowed a sudden lump in her throat, ignoring Tombstone's eyes on her.

"This isn't goodbye just yet," Tombstone assured Devlin. "I'll get your passage to Ireland sorted, then you can say goodbye. In the meantime, I suggest you return to your hiding place. No one has found you there yet."

Devlin nodded. He turned to face Gwynnie, apparently about to say something when Tombstone spoke again.

"You should go now." He spoke sharply. "We don't wish to run the risk of anyone seeing you here."

"As you wish." Devlin hugged his mother one last time and shared a nod with Samuel. Lifting a guard's felt bonnet onto his head, he turned to leave the room. In the doorway, he glanced back at Gwynnie, making her stomach lurch, then he was gone.

"It is a good plan, Gwynnie."

She did not reply as she looked down at the map of Greenwich Palace on Tombstone's desk. She had dragged up a stool and sat leaning over the parchment as Tombstone drank rather a lot of claret beside her. She had no taste for wine tonight, though, and just continued to stare at the parchment in the candlelight.

"I can get Devlin on a ship out of London tomorrow night. He won't need to go as far as Southampton. It will take him straight to Dublin."

Gwynnie nodded numbly, pushing away the quill with which they had made marks on the map.

"I'll make my report to Cromwell and Pascal when you get him out of the palace. At that time of the evening, most of the guards will be watching the great hall. It is their duty to watch the king and queen, especially on Christmas Eve."

She nodded yet again.

"Are you going to say anything, Gwynnie? Usually, I can't get you to be quiet. That tongue of yours always finds something to say."

"I don't have much to say." She turned her head back to the parchment.

Tombstone was right; it was a good plan. She would help Devlin out of the palace while everyone was distracted by the feast to mark the beginning of the Christmas celebrations and the bringing of peace in the north. Despite knowing this was all to save Devlin's life, she felt sick, her sadness so great that the mere thought of food or drink made her mouth taste of bile.

If all went to plan, she would never see Devlin again.

She sniffed, fighting back her tears. When a hand took her shoulder, she jumped and looked up. It was Tombstone, trying to get her attention. His grey eyes were soft.

"Just make time to say goodbye," he said gently.

"I don't know what —"

"No more pretence." His voice deepened. "I know what it's like to care for someone and then lose them. The biggest regret of my life is not telling them just how important they were before they were gone."

Gwynnie chewed her lip, uncertain whether Tombstone referred to the mother he had evidently lost or a past lover. Either way, the memory seemed to cause him pain.

"Say goodbye to him, Gwynnie."

"If I say goodbye to him, do you promise to stop teasing me about him?"

"I never made that promise." He smiled a little as he sat back, releasing her shoulder. "Do it all the same. For your own peace of mind." He drew the map forward across the desk.

"Tomorrow morning, I'll get the ticket for Devlin. We'll meet here at noon, so you can give it to him, then get him out in the evening. No matter what it takes, get him out, Gwynnie, when the feast begins."

She nodded, sniffing again. Tombstone reached into the sleeve of his doublet and pulled out his handkerchief, offering it to her, but she shook her head. The tears that did escape, she dried on the sleeve of her gown.

Tombstone sighed as he tucked the handkerchief away again. "Go to him." He waved at her. "Please, Gwynnie."

She walked away, not sure she could bear this conversation for any longer regardless.

Closing the door behind her, Gwynnie left the lawyers' chambers and stepped out into the tiltyard. It was a cold December night, making her lungs ache as she breathed in the chilly air. On the gate of the tower in the tiltyard stood two guards, but they were so busy playing their game of dice that they either didn't notice her passing or didn't care to ask where a maid was going at this time of night.

Woodenly, she walked through the garden and the orchard, heading toward the church, her gaze fixed on the spire that was silhouetted against the white moon. She pulled her cloak tighter around her body, remembering that Devlin had given it to her, not wanting to see her so cold.

As she reached the graveyard, the dew made the ground slippery. The wetness reached up the hem of her cloak as she stumbled down the bank, looking up at the curtain wall where she knew Devlin would be hiding.

As before, she whistled the same notes that Brynne had made. At first, no one appeared. Gwynnie's stomach knotted at the thought that maybe Devlin had already escaped, without saying goodbye.

Clearing her throat, she whistled again. This time, a shadow appeared at the top of the crenellations, leaning toward her. It was Devlin.

She didn't hesitate to climb the tree. She slipped more than once, struggling to see where she was putting her hands in the darkness. Grabbing onto the top branch, she walked along another, inching closer to the curtain wall. Devlin reached out, taking hold of her waist and lifting her onto the stonework.

As she stepped down to his level, his arms came up around her. She fell into his chest, hugging him tight, not sure what to say now she was beside him. She couldn't tell him the truth, that deep down she didn't want him to go. It didn't matter that she had known him for so brief a time, for she knew she would miss his smile, miss his humour. She would miss the fact that he had noticed her, when so few others did. He had recognised that she was something more than just a maid.

"Our last night, flower," he whispered in her ear. Her hands tightened around his waist, and he chuckled softly. "Bet you'll be glad to be rid of me."

"Rid of you?" she said, leaning back a little to look into his face.

"Well, I've caused a little trouble, haven't I?"

"Oh, it's been so peaceful since you arrived." Her dry tone made him chuckle again. He bent toward her, resting his forehead against hers.

Gwynnie found herself longing for something she had not wanted in a long time. She had only had one kiss in her life, from the man who had once asked her to marry him, though she had turned him down. She couldn't remember indulging in such thoughts since, until now.

But Devlin didn't move any closer toward her, despite her hands tightening on his arms. He just kept their foreheads together, his eyes tightly closed.

"Sleep beside me again?" he asked, his voice so low she had to strain to hear it. He lifted his head a little, allowing her to nod.

The moment had passed as he moved to slide down the wall, sitting on the boards beneath them. Trying not to think about what that kiss could have been like, Gwynnie moved to sit beside him. His arm came up around her as she nestled herself into his shoulder, his cloak wrapped around them both.

Despite the cold, Gwynnie had no wish to be anywhere else. She closed her eyes and thought only of Devlin and the fact she would never know this embrace again.

CHAPTER 32

"It's time," Gwynnie called back into the storeroom. She peered out at the corridor, which was now emptying as the staff hastened toward the great hall to serve the Christmas Eve feast. Great shouts pierced the air, cooks demanding the boar's head to be stuffed with more holly, as great roosters that had already been cooked were being pressed back into their skins.

"Not yet," Brynne pleaded. "Just a minute more."

"We have to let him go," Samuel said.

Gwynnie glanced back to see Brynne and Devlin hugging. It reminded her of the night that she and Emlyn had said goodbye. Even though they had known it was the right thing to do, it hadn't made it any easier.

"Look after her," Devlin pleaded over his mother's shoulder, appealing to Samuel, who nodded hurriedly.

"With my life," he vowed.

Devlin released his mother. Brynne was clearly doing her best not to cry again. It was a wonder to Gwynnie that the poor woman had any tears left.

"We need to go," Gwynnie urged. "Everyone is busy with their tasks now. They will not be paying attention to us." As she spoke, someone dropped a trencher of quails in the corridor.

A great furore erupted.

"Foolish lad."

"Pick them up!"

"You can't serve quails that have been on the floor to the king."

All the competing voices gave them the perfect opportunity. Gwynnie waved a hand at Devlin.

"Goodbye, Ma." Devlin kissed his mother on the forehead and turned to follow Gwynnie, pulling the yeoman's bonnet low over his brow.

"Goodbye, my boy." Brynne's voice broke.

Gwynnie saw Brynne bury her head in Samuel's shoulder as she pushed open the door to the corridor. They walked past a small group of boys now desperately picking up the quails as the cooks continued to argue over what was best to do with them.

"Serve them up," one cook barked. "The king won't know."

Devlin kept his head low as he walked closely behind Gwynnie. No one turned to look their way as they left the corridor and moved out into the courtyard.

"Tombstone?" Devlin asked Gwynnie, falling into step beside her.

"He has asked for a meeting with Cromwell and Pascal tonight. Pascal knows you didn't kill those six soldiers, but Tombstone hasn't told him about Jasper Ashdown." She shared an uneasy look with him as they crossed the courtyard. A long line of staff carrying flagons and pewter jugs of wine and mead filed into the great hall. "Tombstone thinks it best that as few people as possible know about *her*."

Devlin nodded in agreement.

"Tombstone is laying a false trail, saying we have talked to a cart driver who took you north of the river, heading to a coaching inn that's known to take paying customers to the Midlands." Gwynnie turned sharply under Donsen Tower. Devlin turned to follow, looking about in surprise at their direction.

"Where are we going?" he asked, hurrying to catch up with her.

"The quickest way to St Katherine Docks isn't by road." She came to a halt at the end of the dockyard that stretched out across the Thames.

Darkness was already falling, casting streaks of dark purple across the muddy Thames. A wherryman sat in his boat, counting out the coins that Tombstone had paid him to be there at this time.

"He has his instructions." Gwynnie nodded at the wherryman as Devlin halted at her side. "He is to take you to the docks. From there, there will be a ship leaving in an hour. It will take you straight to Dublin." She reached into the pocket of her apron and pulled out a yellowish paper Tombstone had given her that afternoon. "Here is proof of payment for your passage."

Devlin took it from her, their fingers brushing before he tucked it into his doublet. They both stared at the wherryman for a moment, neither one of them speaking.

Devlin cleared his throat, shifting his weight between his feet. He reached into his doublet and pulled out the handkerchief she had spied in his hiding place in the yeomen's barracks, bearing his initials, then handed it to her.

"What's this?" Gwynnie asked.

"So you don't forget me."

"Oh yes." She made her voice as sarcastic as possible. "I would have forgotten you within a couple of days otherwise."

He laughed softly. "Who are you, Gwynnie? You're not just a maid." He smiled sadly. "You're much more than that."

"You must have an inkling." She looked down, her hands fidgeting together. She hadn't felt anything like shame before about her past. It was the way she had been raised, the way that she and Emlyn had survived. "You are a man who believes in honour and doing what is right, Devlin."

"Connal." His correction made them both smile.

"You must see that I am not quite the same." She shrugged helplessly.

"Oh, you do what's right, again and again." He moved toward her. Gwynnie's breathing grew faster as he reached for her hand. "You're a thief."

"I am." Her voice was small. "But I work for Tombstone. He pays me, and being at his beck and call, I survive."

"We all have to do what we must to survive." He entwined their fingers together. "Well, flower, I wish I didn't have to say goodbye to you." He smiled fully as she met his gaze. "I would have liked to know you better."

"And I you."

"In another life, eh?"

"Yes. In another life." Her voice had become strained.

He lifted her hand between them. For a moment, she thought he was going to kiss it, but then he pulled her forward, and bent down toward her. He brushed his lips against her own in the softest of kisses. It was all too brief for Gwynnie's liking, the rush of excitement filling her momentarily, and then it was over as he pulled back. The broad smile on his face mirrored her own.

"Aye, in another life, flower." He released her hand, turning to step out onto the docks.

Gwynnie watched him go, holding onto that feeling of his fingers brushing her own as he moved toward the wherryman. Without asking any questions, the wherryman beckoned him aboard and began to row, turning the tiny boat out into the middle of the river.

Gwynnie wasn't sure how long she stood there, staring at Connal, just as he stared at her. The boat drifted away, and she remained there, even after she couldn't see it anymore.

She knew she should return inside. The other maids would need some help now the Christmas celebrations had begun, but she couldn't move her feet. Instead, she slid down, sitting on the damp dock in her woollen gown, with her skirts gathered around her. She stared at the water, feeling a strange rush of excitement and emptiness all at once.

At the sound of footsteps behind her, Gwynnie reached into her apron and pulled out the handkerchief Connal had given her, raising it to her cheeks and drying the tears she found there.

"Our meeting is done," Tombstone said with a sigh, sitting down beside her and looking out across the river. "Cromwell didn't question it. Pascal looked doubtful, but he soon accepted my explanation."

"How is Pascal?" Gwynnie asked, thinking of the moment Pascal had been thrown from the window by Magner.

"He's recovering. He walks at an odd angle, but I think he will be fine. I've asked him to spend a few more days resting in bed. I think he listened to me."

"He does listen to you. He may be your superior, but he values your thoughts. I'm glad he's recovering."

"As am I." Tombstone smiled sadly. "He keeps talking of you, you know."

"Me? Why?" Gwynnie looked at him in surprise.

"I don't think he thought you capable of saving his life. It's rather hard for him to swallow his pride and accept you may have a good heart after all."

"Oh, I'm blushing," she replied drily.

"He's gone?" Tombstone nodded at the dock.

"He's gone." Gwynnie looked out across the water. "I'm wondering if it made any difference."

"What do you mean?" Tombstone asked sharply.

"Devlin will always be thought of as a killer now. We couldn't save him from that fate." She shook her head.

"Gwynnie, we helped save an innocent man from being hanged. Of course it made a difference. You have given him back his life. It may not be a completely free life, but at least he is still breathing."

"Yes, he is." She sought comfort from this thought. Devlin might now have a shadow over him wherever he went, a fear that someone would recognise him, but he was alive.

"Saying goodbye is never easy."

"I seem to keep saying goodbye to the people that matter." Gwynnie's voice was hoarse as she thought of Emlyn and now Devlin.

"It's the way of the world." Tombstone sighed. "Some have good fortune in this life. Others…"

"Bad?" Gwynnie finished the sentence for him as he nodded slowly.

"We can't all have a life of love, Gwynnie. You and I both know that."

Gwynnie knew how hard Tombstone worked to keep his relationships a secret. Since Pascal had discovered that secret, he was even more careful. "You could have love —"

"No, I could not," Tombstone cut in. "I can have passing likings, but what would the world say if I tried to keep a man for longer? What would Pascal say?"

"You place great stock in his opinion."

"I do." He spoke without hesitation. "We don't all have the freedom to choose who we give our hearts to." He looked down the Thames, to where the wherryman and Devlin had not long disappeared. "I am only sorry that you don't have that freedom either."

Gwynnie screwed up her hands in her apron, trying not to think of the pain she felt, knowing that she would never see Devlin again. When Tombstone nudged her with his elbow, she released her hand, and he took it. They sat there, side by side, as another tear rolled down her cheek.

"The queen is safe," Tombstone whispered as Gwynnie moved around him, collecting the empty flagons of wine in the great hall. "That's what matters, isn't it?"

Gwynnie peered up at the mummers performing their masque of St George and the Dragon for the court's pleasure. Between all the elaborate silken masks and swathes of golden cloth, she glimpsed Queen Jane, seated beside the king. Henry was in his element, laughing raucously and making comments to his guests about how good the masque was this year. When he took the queen's hand, she beamed, though her skin was still pale and her gaze was restless.

"She's safe," Gwynnie agreed. "For now, at least." She wasn't sure how long Jane's safety would last. Devlin may have ensured she would not lose her life yet, but one thing Gwynnie had learned in Greenwich Palace was that Henry's moods could change as quickly as a burning candle could be blown out. "I would pray for her safety to last, but there doesn't seem to be much point in it."

Tombstone raised a finger to his lips, urging her to be quiet. When the other lawyers and clerks around him stood to join in with the dancing, Gwynnie took the seat beside him.

Her gaze moved from Jane to another at the table. Lady Mary sat primly, not looking anywhere near as happy as her father as she watched the king and queen together. Gwynnie stared at the lady, wondering for how long she would be welcome at the palace.

"I asked Cromwell again in our meeting," Tombstone said as he took a sugared pastry from the trencher on the table. He tore it in two and surreptitiously handed her the other half. She smiled her thanks.

"Asked him what?"

"If Fitzroy is truly dead." Tombstone shook his head. "Curiously, Cromwell said Lady Mary had asked him the same thing."

Gwynnie jerked her head back around to Lady Mary. She had worn black tonight, perhaps as a sign of mourning for her half-brother, though she also wore many glittering jewels, in an ostentatious display of wealth.

"She doesn't believe it either," Gwynnie replied with interest.

"It seems not." Tombstone ate his pastry. "Cromwell also insisted that I should stop asking the question." His grey eyes narrowed. "If you ask me, Gwynnie, that means Fitzroy is very much alive."

Gwynnie discarded the last of the pastry, no longer hungry. The king had killed one queen to obscure the fact that his son was a murderer. Apparently, he was now prepared to perpetuate the rumour that his son was lost just to keep him safe.

"He'd do anything for his boy, wouldn't he?" Gwynnie asked, not needing to say the king's name for Tombstone to nod in agreement.

"I think Fitzroy may just turn up here again one day. He'll have a different name, and he may look a little different, but I fear the king will welcome him back."

Gwynnie wondered what Fitzroy would do to her, if indeed he did ever come back to the palace.

"Well, I made a promise to you, didn't I?" Tombstone's voice broke into her thoughts. "I promised that if you helped me find Devlin, I would give you everything I had on the Shadow Cutpurses."

Gwynnie sat up so swiftly that she nearly fell backwards off the bench.

"Do you want to see it? Now?"

"No, in a year's time will do. In Jesu's name —"

"Gwynnie!"

"Of course I want to see it now!"

"You and your cursing tongue," Tombstone reprimanded her, though he chuckled as he stood. "Come, then. You'll have what you want."

Gwynnie raced to stand and follow him out of the room. As they fell into step beside one another in the courtyard, Gwynnie's heart thudded with anticipation.

"I didn't think you'd show me," she whispered to him. "I thought you'd find another reason to keep all those papers from me."

"I made you a promise." Tombstone spoke determinedly as they turned into the tiltyard. "I keep my promises."

They reached Tombstone's office and Gwynnie stood beside his desk, practically bouncing on her toes.

Before finding the papers, he lit three candles, taking so long that she fidgeted all the more.

"Please, take all the time you need," she muttered.

"You are so patient."

"Oh, believe me, I am," she said as he chuckled.

Stepping toward the shelves that Gwynnie had searched only a short time ago, Tombstone pressed his palm against the wall. A plank of wood swung back, and she cursed.

"You have a hidey-hole," she observed.

"It proves useful when you have a thief in your office nearly every day."

Gwynnie folded her arms. "What else are you hiding in there?"

"Nothing." Yet there was clearly more in this secret cupboard, from which he pulled a leather chest with a padlock. He placed it down on the desk and unlocked it with a key he took from the buffet cabinet, then lifted the lid, turning it toward her.

There were many yellowing papers inside the chest, some so old that Gwynnie was reminded of the ballad sheet which had revealed that the Shadow Cutpurses had been around for much longer than she'd thought.

"Take your time, Shadow," Tombstone urged, stepping back from the desk. "I shall be at the Christmas Eve feast." He moved toward the door, smiling, though she saw some tension in his grey eyes as they flicked toward the chest.

"You're worried about something."

"It doesn't matter. I hope you find what you're searching for." Then he was gone.

Alone in the room, Gwynnie delved into the chest and pulled out a whole myriad of ballad sheets.

One paper bore a song about the Shadow Cutpurses, making them out to be nothing but spirits that walked at night, with springs in their heels, allowing them to jump from rooftop to rooftop like cats. Another paper depicted the Shadow Cutpurses as men from the underworld, who had risen to steal from the living.

Gwynnie's hand shook as she lifted a handwritten parchment. At the bottom, it bore the name and title of a nightwatchman in London. Her eyes flickered over the testimony he had written:

The men came in the middle of the night. I could see them on the rooftops. It didn't matter how much I shouted at them or called for them to come down, they were brazen. One broke an attic window as the other threatened to throw roof tiles at me. They left again across the roofs, clutching jewels to their chests.

Gwynnie pushed the paper away. Emlyn had never been particularly good at clambering across rooftops. She was so tall and long of limb, that such tasks had always been Gwynnie's responsibility if needed.

The top of the page was also dated. It read 1518.

Gwynnie put the page down and reached for more papers. Again and again, she read testimonies and ballad sheets that were dated either before she was born, or when she had been very young, far too young for these tales to be about her. The figures in these stories didn't even sound like Emlyn. One thing was certain: whoever saw these two thieves were convinced they were men.

"What if they *were* men?" Gwynnie mumbled.

At the bottom of the chest was a rolled-up scroll. She untied the string and unravelled the parchment, struggling to make the paper lie flat enough for her to read it.

In scribbled handwriting, the parchment recorded a huge-scale theft that had taken place on the king's ship when it was moored in Southampton. Not only were jewels taken, but great sums of money too, which had been stored in sacks. It had been a great secret that these jewels were kept there at all.

In the early hours of the morning, two men were seen running away from the scene, carrying these sacks. It was presumed they were the Shadow Cutpurses as they had fled across the rooftops, as was their pattern, to avoid capture.

Another line of text had been added at the bottom of the page, in a different hand to the rest and in different ink too. To Gwynnie's mind, it looked as if the text had been added much later, perhaps even years later: *The money and jewels taken that night have never been found.*

Gwynnie put down the scroll. She let it naturally curl up again then reached for the final ballad sheet, which had been tucked into the lid of the chest.

This sheet talked of how the Shadow Cutpurses hadn't been seen for years, how London had thought it was free of their thefts at last, until strangely, jewels had started disappearing again. The two thieves had been glimpsed in the night. The year of the ballad sheet read 1522. She baulked, for it was the year that she and Emlyn had started thieving. Gwynnie had been just thirteen at the time.

"What does it all mean?" she said aloud.

There was a sound behind her. Gwynnie grabbed a candle and spun around, straining to see into the shadows of the office, but there was nothing there. Slowly, she placed the candle back down again and turned to the papers, thinking through all that she had discovered.

It was confirmation that the Shadow Cutpurses had indeed existed before she and her mother had taken the name. They had performed a large-scale theft, and the jewels had never been seen again. After they had disappeared, she and Emlyn had started thieving. Gwynnie wasn't even certain how the name had become attached to her and her mother, unless the idea of two people stealing jewellery was enough to forge the connection.

"If only I could ask you what this all meant, Ma," she whispered into the air, thinking of Emlyn and wondering if she was still in Bristol.

There was another sound behind Gwynnie. She jerked to her feet so fast that she knocked one of the candles off the desk. It was snuffed out instantly.

In the corner of the room stood a tall shadow.

"Good evening, miting."

HISTORICAL NOTES

This book is designed to entertain. Though elements of the book are inspired by true events, please note that this book is a work of fiction. I have taken facts and used them to inspire a story meant for entertainment. I truly hope you have enjoyed the creative aspects of this story.

The Pilgrimage of Grace took place at the end of 1536, incited by the Lincolnshire Riots. As well as ill feeling about the monasteries being closed, there were grievances over religion, poor harvests and high taxes. Difficult living conditions led to the uprising and sadly many hangings. Though peace was found in December 1536, it was only temporary, as unrest broke out again in the winter of 1537. Though Robert Aske returned to the north to help quell the riots, he was executed for treason in July 1537.

Crucial to this story, as with the others in this series, are the lives of Henry VIII's queens. It is sometimes speculated that Queen Jane did suffer a miscarriage in the winter of 1536, though no firm evidence has been found to support this. There was also a rumour that Queen Catherine of Aragon may have been poisoned due to a 'black heart' discovered in her autopsy. According to Alison Weir, modern science suggests that the black growth found in her heart may have actually been a cancerous tumour. There is no other evidence that Queen Catherine was poisoned. These tales have been used in this novel to create intrigue and a good story.

Key to the novels in this series are the chosen settings. Greenwich Palace, though it no longer exists, was indeed a beloved palace of Henry VIII, and we know that he and Queen Jane spent the Christmas of 1536 there.

I hope you have enjoyed the historical references in this tale.

A NOTE TO THE READER

Dear Reader,

Thank you for taking the time to read *The Body in the Chamber*. I truly hope that you have enjoyed reading it as much as I have enjoyed writing it. Gwynnie will be back in a new adventure soon.

Reviews by readers these days are integral to a book's success, so if you enjoyed this tale, I would be very grateful if you could spare a minute to post a review on **Amazon** and **Goodreads**. I love hearing from readers, and you can talk with me through **my website** or **on Twitter** and follow my author page **on Facebook**. If you are enjoying this series so far, I recommend giving the *Kit Scarlett* series a go — a complete adventure available to buy now.

I hope we'll meet again in the next adventure.

Adele Jordan

Sapere Books is an exciting new publisher of brilliant fiction and popular history.

To find out more about our latest releases and our monthly bargain books visit our website:
saperebooks.com

www.ingramcontent.com/pod-product-compliance
Lightning Source LLC
Chambersburg PA
CBHW060854250626
47159CB00008B/2736